W9-BLH-919

HE WHO WAITS

❖

Also by John R. Riggs

HE WHO WAITS

John R. Riggs

❖

A GARTH RYLAND MYSTERY

BARRICADE BOOKS, INC.

NEW YORK

Published by Barricade Books, Inc.
150 Fifth Avenue
New York, NY 10011

Printed in the United States of America.

Book design and page layout by CompuDesign

Library of Congress Cataloging-in-Publication Data

Riggs, John R., 1945–
    He who waits / by John R. Riggs.
        p. cm. —(A Garth Ryland mystery)
    ISBN 1-56980-096-0
    1. Ryland, Garth (Fictitious character)-Fiction.
    2. Journalists-Wisconsin- Fiction. I. Title.
      II. Series: Riggs, John R., 1945–
    Garth Ryland mystery.
    PS3568. I372H4   1997
    813'.54—dc20   96-42559
                          CIP

First Printing

For Aunt Helen and Uncle Ray
and always to Carole

All things come round to him who will but wait.

Henry W. Longfellow

CHAPTER 1

The fire siren rang. Oakalla, Wisconsin, is one of the few towns left in America where the fire siren still rings at noon—every noon, including Sundays and holidays. A long shrill blast that carries well out into the surrounding countryside of pine woods and maple groves, dairy farms and corn and alfalfa fields, Oakalla's fire siren at high noon literally can raise the hair on your head, even if you are expecting it. But when it rings at night, especially between midnight and dawn, it raises a lump in your throat. For you never know whose house or barn might be burning down, whose life might be about to go up in smoke.

I sat up in bed, dropped one foot over the edge, and prayed that it was a false alarm. I am Garth Ryland, owner and editor of the *Oakalla Reporter*, a small weekly newspaper, and the author of a weekly column that continues to grow in syndication every year. Though technically not a volunteer fireman, I try to make it to every fire because I want to be there if help is needed. If not, I can stay out of the way with the best of them.

The fire siren continued to ring. When the hall light went on, I knew that it was going to be a short night.

"You going to get up or not?" Ruth asked from the hall.

Ruth Krammes has been my housekeeper ever since I left Milwaukee and moved to Oakalla over a decade ago. A tall, broad-shouldered, big-boned Swede in her seventies, who suffers neither fads nor fools, she believes firmly in the principle that everyone is guilty until proven innocent, and that I am prone to be more guilty than most. Still, here we are together after all of these years. And while we don't necessarily trust each other to tell the truth, which we've both shaded on occasion, we do trust each other to be ourselves. There is something comforting in that—and lasting.

I groaned as my feet hit the floor. The temperature outside was bumping zero when I had stumbled up the stairs to bed.

"Do I have a choice?" I asked in answer to Ruth's summons.

"Not from where I'm standing."

I went out into the hall where Ruth stood in her ancient pink flowered robe once traded by a French Voyageur for a beaver pelt shortly before the fall of Quebec. Ruth's hair is a pale blond with streaks of grey, and she almost always wears it up, along with an imperious frown that makes you want to hang your head, put your hands in your pockets, and mumble.

"You don't think it's a false alarm?" I said.

"Look south out the spare bedroom and tell me what you think."

"Crap," I said, then went back into my own bedroom to put some clothes on.

Outside, it was one of those still, pinch-your-nose January nights that makes you pay for every breath. About eight inches of snow, four of it freshly fallen, were on the ground. The moon, starting its last quarter, was just high, white, and bright enough to lace the street with tree shadows. I walked briskly with my head down and my gloved hands in my coat pockets. I wasn't cold. But I was shaking nevertheless.

What I had seen from the south window of the spare bedroom was the long red light of a fire truck, as it swept Home Street and Jackson Street in turn. The truck was parked in the yard of what was known around Oakalla as the Old Baldwin Place, even though no Baldwins had owned it for at least five years now. Diana, the last surviving Baldwin, lived near Santa Fe, New Mexico, where she made her living as a landscape painter, and secondarily, as an art teacher. I had once loved her with all of my heart. She had once loved me with all of hers. We now sometimes exchanged Christmas cards, if either thought of it in time.

White brick and set well off the street with pines and cedars in its front yard and apple trees, a grape arbor, and a garden out back, the Old Baldwin Place was strong and sure without appearing massive. Its wide windows seemed to catch every ray of sunlight and gave the inside of the house an open, airy look, even in the dead of winter. And where it sat, where it had always sat from the beginning, which was at the heart of Oakalla as the town grew up around it, the Old Baldwin Place was the house to own, if you wanted people to notice you.

But when I reached the Old Baldwin Place, I saw no fire burning as I had feared, only a small knot of firemen gathered around something in the yard. Hushed, seemingly

spellbound by what was before them, they appeared reluctant to leave each other's company, like ghost-filled boys
around a dying campfire. Easing my way up to them, I saw
the reason why. Someone had burned a cross there.

"What do you make of it, Garth?" Danny Palmer
asked a few minutes later, as I stood beside him in the yard.

Danny Palmer, wearing his fireman's garb—yellow
boots and helmet and stiff black rubber coat—and I stood
in a mushy patch of snow, looking down at the partially
burned wooden cross. A thirty-something family man with
a ready smile and boundless energy, Danny Palmer was
Oakalla's volunteer fire chief, the owner of the Marathon
Service Station, and now that doctor-surgeon Abby
Airhart had left town for Henry Ford Hospital in Detroit,
the person that Oakalla could least afford to do without.

"I don't know what to make of it, Danny," I said. In
truth, I had been so relieved to discover that the fire was
in the yard instead of the house that I hadn't given either
the cross or its implications much thought.

Danny glanced up at the house, where the new sheriff
of Adams County, Wayne Jacoby, was about to enter the
front door. "Maybe Dudley Do-Right will tell us something
when he comes out."

I thought that I heard a sneer in Danny's voice, which
wasn't at all like him.

"You don't like our new sheriff?" I asked. I hadn't
made up my mind yet, but despite some reservations, was
still willing to give him the benefit of the doubt.

"No," Danny said with atypical bluntness. "I don't like
him."

"You have a reason?"

Danny's look was as harsh as the blackened cross. "Do
I need one?"

We watched the remaining volunteer firemen roll up

their single hose and climb in the fire truck, as they prepared to head back to the City Building, where Oakalla's
three fire trucks were housed.

"Who called in the fire, do you know?" I asked Danny.

Danny nodded toward the pay phone next to the Five
and Dime where a lone figure sat huddled under the street
light with his arms folded and his head bowed. "I think he
did."

"Then maybe we should talk to him."

Danny's gaze returned to the house. His eyes seemed
to smolder with the afterglow of the fire. "You go ahead,
Garth. It's time I was heading home."

But as I watched him get in his new Dodge Ram pickup and drive away, he didn't head for home, which was on
Fair Haven Road two houses north of the Marathon. He
headed south in the direction of the City Building, though
I couldn't be sure that he stopped there.

I walked across Home Street and discovered that it
was Stevey La Fountaine who sat on the curb under the
streetlight. I couldn't decide whether he was numb from
the cold, numb from shock, drunk, or all of the above, but
he had a look of total stupor, as if his mind had already
shut down, and his body was only moments away from the
same fate. He didn't even look up as my shadow fell over
him.

"Stevey?" I said.

No response.

He wore only a long green Army coat over his jeans
and sweatshirt. His head was bare. His long, thin, black hair
hung stiff at his shoulders and offered him little protection
from the cold. As I tried to nudge him to life, I noticed a
hole in the toe of his tennis shoe.

"Stevey?" I repeated. "Hadn't you better get up and
get moving?"

He looked up at me, but I saw no recognition in his

eyes. We weren't fast friends, but over the past two weeks we had shared some late night beers together at the Corner Bar and Grill, as I "celebrated" being alone again.

"What was that?"

Normally his keen brown eyes would have had no trouble focusing on me, even when three sheets to the wind, which he usually was by this hour. Like a lot of the regulars at the Corner Bar and Grill, Stevey La Fountaine could drink most of the rest of us under the table without even trying.

"Here. Let me help you up," I said. "We can talk as we walk."

He let me pull him to his feet and steady him, as he rocked back and forth from one foot to the other, as if trying to get the feeling back in his toes. All the while he stared at the melted patch of snow where the cross lay. Then, before I could stop him, he jerked away from me and ran across the street into the yard.

"What the hell are you doing?" I asked when I finally caught up to him.

He bent down, and with surprising strength shouldered the cross. "Taking this home."

"You can't. It's evidence."

"Of what?" he said, starting toward Home Street with the cross still on his shoulder.

I looked around for help, but didn't see any. "The fire," I said, catching up to him again.

He hit a patch of deep snow, stumbled under the weight of the cross, which was about ten feet tall and six feet wide, and nearly went down.

"Here," I said, for no good reason that I could think of, "let me help you with that."

So together Stevey La Fountaine and I took off along Home Street toward the north end of town with the cross between us. My only hope was that Ruth wasn't still looking out the window.

Fifteen minutes later we arrived at his house, which was on the east side of Fair Haven Road, a block south of the city limits sign. I could feel neither my fingers nor my toes, and my back had a crick in it that went all the way down my right hip, but I had plowed along behind Stevey without stopping, as if, like him, I had all of the energy in the world. Never the first one to say uncle, I often regretted that decision.

"Thanks, Garth," Stevey said, as he shrugged the cross from his shoulder. "I don't think I could have made it without you."

"You couldn't prove it by me."

I let my end of the cross drop down into the powdery snow. Within seconds, it was all but buried.

As I stood waiting for an explanation, I saw that Stevey's eyes had come back to life again. And there was a spring in his step as he turned and headed for his front porch.

"What do you plan on doing with the cross?" I asked, trying to slow him down.

He stopped with his back to me. "Leave it where it is for now. It's come home at last."

"Do you mind explaining that?"

"If you would understand it."

He was up the steps and in his front door before I could stop him.

"Don't ask" were my first words to Ruth as I stomped in the back door, trying to knock the snow from my boots. "What time is it, anyway?"

Still in her housecoat, Ruth sat at the kitchen table. She had fixed a fresh pot of coffee and set my bottle of Old Crow on the counter with my shot glass beside it. She must've read my mind.

"What's the matter with your watch?" she asked.

"It doesn't glow in the dark."

"It was three AM the last time I looked," she said. She glanced up at the kitchen clock. "Which was fifteen minutes ago."

I put my gloves in the pocket of my coat, stuffed my stocking cap down its sleeve, then hung my coat in the hall closet, which was under the stairs between the living room and the kitchen. Then I took off my hiking boots and stood on the register in the kitchen in the hope of thawing out my toes.

"You buy a good pair of boots, that wouldn't happen," Ruth said.

"Those are a good pair of boots. They're just not designed for eight inches of snow."

"And how long have you lived in Wisconsin?"

"Call me an optimist."

She took a sip of her coffee. "Other words come to mind."

When I could feel my toes again, I poured a shot of Old Crow into my coffee mug, then added coffee, half-and-half, and sugar. I am not one of those people who likes his coffee black, or who would care to learn to drink it that way. Neither was Ruth, so at least we could agree on something.

"So where have you been?" she asked as I sat down across from her at the table. "The fire was out an hour ago."

I knew better than to ask how she knew. Ruth, her cohorts in town, and her many relatives scattered about the state were the original Internet.

I blew on my coffee to cool it and could smell the bourbon on its breath. "I was helping Stevey La Fountaine carry a cross to his house."

Her brows rose ever so slightly, the way they did whenever something piqued her interest. "I'm listening."

"There's not much more to it than that."

"I'd still like to hear it."

So I spent the next few minutes telling her what had happened. When I finished, she looked thoughtful, and not that eager to tell me how stupid I'd been, which I was expecting.

She said, "Somebody burned a cross in Senator Springer's yard, and later, before you could stop him, Stevey La Fountaine picked up the cross and started carrying it home. At which point, you decided to help him. Is that about it?"

"That's about it," I said, remembering something else.

"What did you leave out?"

"Just before Stevey and I parted ways, he said, 'It's come home at last.'"

In the silence that followed, I could almost hear her think. "Meaning the cross?"

"That's what I took him to mean."

She sighed. There seemed great reluctance in it, to have to open this particular can of worms.

"What am I missing, Ruth?"

"Gilbert La Fountaine."

"Stevey's father?"

"Yes."

"What about him?" I asked.

"You didn't know that he was black? Or an octoroon, if you want to get technical."

"No. I didn't know. But I don't recall ever meeting the man."

As I remembered from his obituary, Gilbert La Fountaine had owned and operated a body shop behind his house for the most of his life until his death about five years ago. A misanthrope, according to my best sources, he was known to pinch a penny even harder than I, and while he was generally acknowledged as the best body man in the area, he died with few friends, and even fewer mourners.

"You'd have remembered him if you'd met him," Ruth said.

"Why? Was he as bad as people say?"

She gave me a strange look, then began to blush as only Ruth could. "What are you talking about, Garth?"

"I hear he was a real ogre—to his family and everybody else."

"Not when I knew him." But that's all that she would say.

"Which was when?"

She got up from the table to pour herself another cup of coffee. "What's the point, Garth? The man's dead."

"You said that I would have remembered him if I'd ever met him. I want to know why."

Ruth took her time getting back to the table. Either her hip was bothering her again or something was weighing heavily on her mind.

"Can't this wait until morning?" she said.

"I've got a full docket tomorrow." When she didn't say anything, I tried to help her out. "So what was he—tall, dark, and handsome, a Clark Gable type? He must've been tall. All of his kids are."

"Gil was no more than five-seven at the most. All of their height came from Merle's side of the family."

"Merle?"

"Merle La Fountaine. Gil's wife, the one who used to clerk at the Five and Dime. She's now at the Lutheran Home."

"With Alzheimer's?" I thought I remembered her now.

"Yes. Alzheimer's." Ruth continued, "Gil was a handsome man, that's true, but he wasn't any darker than say you are in the summertime. And while he did have a very thin mustache, he in no way resembled Clark Gable, who always seemed kind of lazy to me. Gil was a bundle of energy. You could almost hear the air crackle when he walked."

"And when did it start being Gil?"

"When I brought in our '51 Chevrolet to have him pound out the dent in the right front fender."

"Your dent or Karl's?" Karl was Ruth's late husband, who had died from lung cancer the year before I moved to Oakalla.

"Mine. I cut the corner too short coming in one snowy night and hit the gatepost." Ruth gave me the evil eye, which told me that she knew what my game was. "What else do you want to know? Did I sleep with him? That's my business. Wasn't I too old for him? I didn't think so at the time. Am I sorry for anything that did or didn't happen? No. Any more questions?"

I took a sip of my coffee and made a face. Cold coffee and bourbon was not my favorite drink.

"Just one question," I said. "Whatever happened to him? The Gilbert La Fountaine you describe is not the same Gilbert La Fountaine who had twenty people show up at his funeral. Not unless he made love to so many women that he had the whole town mad at him."

"How do I know what happened to him, Garth?" she said, not wanting to talk about it. "I have enough trouble figuring out my own bad days."

"But do you agree that he changed over time?"

"As we all do. What's your point?"

"My point is that somebody burned a cross on Senator Springer's lawn tonight, and Stevey La Fountaine, who most likely called in the fire, carried it home."

"What has that to do with either one of us?"

"I don't know about you, but if it has to do with Oakalla, it has to do with me. We've been over this before,

Ruth."

She didn't agree. "Garth, there's no point in going looking for trouble. We have a sheriff now. Let him handle it."

"I am. His end of it. I just want to know why someone would burn a cross in Oakalla, of all places, and someone else would feel the need to carry it home?"

"Then you'll have to ask someone else besides me." She rose from the table and dumped her coffee in the sink. "Or at least ask me at a civilized hour, because right now I'm going to bed."

"Suit yourself," I said, feeling let down.

"It *can* wait, Garth. So don't be holding any pity parties. And if you're missing Abby so badly, why not give her a call."

"We already talked once tonight. It didn't help."

"Then make arrangements to go see her."

"I can't, Ruth. Not in the foreseeable future. I have too much to do as it is now."

"Then take Daisy for a walk. You know she's standing at the basement door."

Daisy was an English setter and my present to Doctor William Airhart after his old setter, Belle, died. Daisy had fallen to Abby when Doc died and now to me until Abby came back from Detroit——if Abby came back from Detroit, which was the crux of my problem. She insisted that she was coming back once she finished her residency in pathology. Pessimist that I often was, I had my doubts.

"Daisy, are you there?" I said to test Ruth's theory.

Daisy's bark assured me that she was.

"Maybe tomorrow we'll take a walk," I said to no one in particular.

Ruth shrugged, then started up the stairs for bed. Daisy whined hopefully a couple times, then gave up and padded down the basement steps for (presumably) her wooden box bed beside the furnace. I remained at the kitchen table to finish my cold bourbon and coffee.

It was a short while later when I heard the snow crunch outside the kitchen window an instant before I heard Daisy's bark of alarm, as she came racing up the basement steps, wanting out. I went to the window to see what I might see. Seeing nothing but my own reflection, I let Daisy out of the basement and then outside, which is where she wanted to go. There, she made a quick circle of the back fence, barking all of the while.

Soon she was joined by a couple other dogs in the far north end of town. I couldn't tell if they were barking at her or at something else closer to home. What I could tell, however, by the footprints that I found there, was that someone had been standing under my kitchen window, looking in. His footprints came in from the west and left to the east. I lost them in the alley that ran behind my house.

I stood there in the alley long enough to get cold. Then I put Daisy back in the basement and went to bed.

CHAPTER 2

"I want your badge," Sheriff Wayne Jacoby said to me.

The morning had started innocuously enough. Unable to sleep, I had risen earlier than usual, showered and dressed, put on a pot of coffee for Ruth, ate a bowl of cereal, drank a glass of orange juice, and walked to work in the dark. Once there, I had begun to lay out that week's edition of the *Oakalla Reporter*, which would go to press sometime after midnight on Thursday and be at the post office ready to mail out before six AM Friday.

Monday I had spent gathering the news from all of my sources and checking with my advertisers to see what they wanted to change, if anything, before Wednesday's deadline. Today was Tuesday. Normally I liked Tuesday because it was usually the quietest day of the week, and I could putter along, sorting my thoughts as I went. However, I could tell by the angry look on his face, the way that he had strode uninvited into my office as if he owned the place, that Sheriff Wayne Jacoby was about the change all that.

"Why?" I said.

The badge he was referring to was the special deputy badge that Rupert Roberts had given me years ago when he was still sheriff. He had given it to me for his own reasons when we were well into a fifth of Wild Turkey on a night as cold as the last few had been. For a long time I had carried it as a joke, never intending to use it, until that one fall when Nellie Brainard and a 1936 Cadillac came into my life. Since then, particularly since Rupert had left office, it had taken on a life of its own. I now carried it proudly because Rupert was the one who had given it to me. And I carried it by necessity, because all of those who had followed in his footsteps had found his shoes too big to fill, putting Oakalla at risk.

"You know why. You questioned Stevey La Fountaine without my permission," Sheriff Wayne Jacoby said.

"I did no such thing." Only because he never gave me the chance.

"He says differently."

I leaned back in my chair to study him. Wayne Jacoby, I knew, was the only son of Wilson and Amelia Jacoby, longtime Oakalla residents, who now lived in Atlanta, Georgia. A former Army Ranger who had fought in the Gulf War, after leaving the Army he had joined the Dane County Sheriff's Department, where he had served as a deputy the past couple years.

When the County Council had advertised for someone to fill the post vacated by Harold Clark, who had resigned to become a computer jock for the Madison Police Force, Wayne Jacoby had applied for the job and beaten out several other applicants in getting it. In the County Council's collective eye, he had a lot of things going for him, not the least of which were his service record and the fact that he was a native son. His age, twenty-eight, and his size, at five-eight and a hundred sixty pounds, were not in his favor, but were things that the County Council could overlook if he got results. His being single with no love interest in sight got mixed reviews from the council. The men viewed it as a plus. The women had their reservations. Given their druthers, they would have preferred someone older and more rounded. All agreed, however, that his starched shirts, close-cropped hair, neatly trimmed black mustache, and combat-fit body were quite an improvement over what we'd had in the recent past.

But, I now noted, no one had mentioned his dark brown eyes, overflowing with pride and ambition. Or the muscle in his jaw that jumped every time that he clamped down tight.

"Well, I guess that makes one of us a liar," I said in reference to Stevey La Fountaine.

"I guess it does," he said, still believing that I was the one.

He waited. I waited. This early in what might prove a long fight, neither one of us wanted to throw the first punch.

"You can't have the badge," I said at last. "It's a gift from Rupert Roberts, and that says it all. What I will do, however, is promise not to flash it ever again until you say so. Is that fair?"

He had to think it over. The fact that he did bothered me more than it should have.

"I guess that's fair enough," he said, not giving much ground. "It's nothing personal, but I can't have every amateur in town trying to do my job for me. That, I believe, was the mistake that my predecessor made."

"Among others," I said, not wanting to have to debate or defend Clarkie. I'd fought enough of those battles in the past.

"So that's the end of it?" he said, assuming that it was.

"The end of what?"

"Your investigation into the cross-burning."

"I didn't know I was investigating the cross-burning. But if I decide to, I won't be asking your permission."

His jaw began to twitch. I could hear his molars grind. "But you just said . . ."

"I said I wouldn't flash my badge ever again until you asked me to. And I won't. But that has nothing to do with my readers' right to know what goes on in this town, or my right to ask." I leaned forward and began to shuffle the papers on my desk. "Was that all?"

His tight-lipped expression was more one of shock than of anger, as he backed up a step, unsure of what to do or say next. But he recovered quickly.

"Just don't get in my way. I'm not asking either," he said.

We left it at that. He went on his way. I got up to fix myself a cup of instant coffee.

The kettle on my hot plate had just begun to sing when I saw a black Mercedes pass by on Gas Line Road, then turn south on Berry Street toward me and the long low concrete block building that housed the *Oakalla Reporter*. I hoped the car would go on by. When it didn't, I waited for the knock that was sure to come.

"Coffee?" I asked State Senator Jonathan Springer, when I opened my office door to let him in.

"No thanks. I've had three cups already this morning."

I fixed myself a cup of coffee while he surveyed my office walls. He was bound to be disappointed by what he found there, which was essentially nothing beyond my first edition of the *Oakalla Reporter* and a couple of other things from my past that reminded me of who I was, or at least who I had been. On my desk were some books by Robert Frost, Kurt Vonnegut, John D. MacDonald, Mark Twain, Ayn Rand, and Thorton W. Burgess that he might have found interesting, if he had gotten that far.

"Have a seat," I said, offering him one of the two straight-back wooden chairs along my east office wall.

He shook his head. "Can't. I'm running late the way it is."

"The legislature?"

"A meeting. I'm chairman of the finance committee."

I nodded. I knew that. I also knew that Jonathan Springer would likely be his party's nominee for governor this year, now that the race was wide open. And if he did run, I would likely vote for him.

"I can't stand and drink coffee at the same time," I said, returning to sit at my desk. "I'm not that well coordinated."

"Be my guest," he said. "It's your office." A fact, I noted, that Sheriff Wayne Jacoby had never acknowledged.

But for a man already late for a meeting, he seemed in no apparent hurry, as he ambled to my north window to look outside, then turned to the east wall to scan the front page of my first *Oakalla Reporter*. A deliberate, thoughtful man, known more for his cautious reasoning than his fiery rhetoric, Jonathan Springer looked more like the English professor that he once was than he did a politician. Tall, fair, and solidly built, with wispy white-blond hair and solemn grey-blue eyes, he had taught at Winona State University for several years until he could no longer stand the way that the state government was run and decided to try to change things. Though still fit for a man in his mid-fifties, he in his long camel's hair coat, wine shirt, and wingtips in no way resembled the whippet that

I saw pitch for the Louisville Cardinals my senior year in high school. A rising star destined for the Big Dance, he'd had his career ended in much the same way as Herb Score. Only this line drive shattered his kneecap, instead of his cheekbone.

"You know why I'm here, I suppose," he finally said.

"No. But I can guess."

He sighed heavily, the way that Ruth had earlier that morning, as if reluctant to broach the subject for fear of where it might lead. "I hate to ask favors. I used to be a man who didn't believe in them."

"I've heard politics can do that to you," I said.

"Or life."

"What's your favor?" I said, trying to make it easier for him.

"Last night's incident. The less said, the better."

"The better for whom?"

He had his answer ready. "Me, you, Oakalla. I figure we're all in this together."

"Go on. I'm listening."

He shrugged. He hadn't prepared a speech, which, for me, was in his favor. "I don't know. Obviously, I don't want anything that might detract from my candidacy for governor. By the same token, you don't want anything that might put Oakalla in a bad light. Neither do I for that matter, since I now live here, and hope to retire here when I'm through with politics. If we invite the jackals in, it might be hard to get them out again."

"National media types, you mean?"

"Yes. That's what I mean." His eyes narrowed in concentration as he prepared to deliver the next pitch. Despite the years gone by, he knew right where the strike zone was. "I've read enough of your writing to know that you probably care more about Oakalla than you do anything else in life, outside of those you love. Some men go out into the world to save it, or themselves. You've stayed home, so that you might do both."

"If you know me that well, then you know what you're asking."

"I'm not asking you to overlook anything where I'm concerned. Just to tread lightly, that's all. Until you can see your way clear."

I studied him to see if there was an implied threat in his words. Seeing none, I said, "Did you and Sheriff Jacoby have this same conversation very early this morning?"

"We did."

"And what did he say?"

Jonathan Springer frowned. He seemed genuinely puzzled by Wayne Jacoby. "Sheriff Jacoby is still a young man with a lot to learn."

"No, in other words."

"In other words."

"You didn't threaten him, did you?"

"No. I tried to bribe him, which was probably worse."

"Much worse," I agreed. "What did you try to bribe him with?"

"Power. Which I thought was the right button to push. Evidently I was wrong."

Recalling what little I knew about Wayne Jacoby, I would have chosen the power button, too. He seemed to relish being in charge.

"What kind of power?" I asked.

"I hinted that once I was governor, I might need someone of his obvious diligence to oversee my personal safely."

"Don't the state police take care of that?"

"I was grasping at straws," he said, obviously embarrassed, as the color rose in his face. "My God, man, it was two AM and somebody had just burned a cross in my yard. What would you have done under the circumstances?"

He intended it as a rhetorical question, but I felt the need to try to answer it. "First, I would have asked if there is a reason why someone would *want* to burn a cross in my yard. Is there, Senator Springer?"

He pulled up the sleeve of his camel's hair coat to look at his Rolex. "That question will have to wait for another time. But thanks for asking."

"I'll do what I can," I said as he was leaving. "About keeping the jackals at bay."

"Then I'll owe you."

"No. Because I'm not doing it for you. I'm doing it for Oakalla. But then that's what you counted on, isn't it?"

He smiled. There was a lot to read into it, but nothing for certain. "I'm not often wrong about people," he said.

"And when you are?"

His look was ironic. "I'm usually the last to know."

I watched as he got back into his black Mercedes and drove south on Berry Street on his way to Madison Road. Here was a man who intrigued me, someone with whom (if the gods permitted) I might like to be friends. I'd known only a handful of such men in my life, fewer than I would have liked to have known. So when fate threw one my way, perhaps I would be forgiven for not wanting to put the gift under a microscope.

CHAPTER 3

At six that evening, I found myself sitting in the Corner Bar and Grill with a draft of Leinenkugel's in one hand and a cheeseburger with fried onions in the other. Ruth was playing bid euchre with some of her cronies at Liddy Bennett's house, so I had to fend for myself. Either I could stay home alone, warm up some week-old chili and feel sorry for myself, or I could go to the Corner Bar and Grill, sit in what had become Abby's and my booth, and feel sorry for myself. I chose the Corner Bar and Grill because, in theory anyway, it should be harder to feel sorry for myself with people around.

As I glanced around the barroom, I saw a half-dozen of the regulars seated at the bar, a couple others playing darts, and another pounding quarters into the juke box, as if it were a slot machine. Just what I needed, I thought

when the first record started to play. Ten rounds of country music to chase the blues away.

When Hiram, the bartender, came over to check on
me, I said, "What time did Stevey La Fountaine leave here
last night? Do you remember?"

"About five minutes before the fire alarm went off,"
Hiram said, as he wiped some crumbs from my table into
his hand.

"So there's no way that he could've burned that cross
in Senator Springer's yard?"

"None that I can see."

"What kind of shape was he in when he left here?"

"The usual. Too drunk to drive, but okay to walk. I
never know when to cut him off because I haven't learned
yet what his saturation point is." Hiram glanced at the
Hamms clock above the bar, which featured my favorite
bear. "He'll be here within the hour, if he's keeping his regular schedule. You might ask him these questions."

"I might at that."

I thought our conversation was over and that Hiram
would then move on back to the bar. Instead, he put both
hands on my table as he leaned in toward me. "Bad business, Garth. That cross-burning is bad business. No good
can come of it."

"Is that the talk of the town, too?"

"Most people don't even want to talk about it. They're
embarrassed, I think, that something like that could happen
here. Not only here, but right in the heart of town, not
over a block from the City Building. Then, of course, there
are those who blame Senator Springer for bringing the
trouble down on us."

"Those of the opposing party?"

"Straight down the ticket."

Between bites on my cheeseburger, I asked, "Did anyone offer an opinion about where the cross might have

come from?"

Hiram glanced at the bar to see who might be listening in. Satisfied that no one was, he said, "Most folks, at least those without an axe to grind, don't think it was aimed so much at the Senator as the one who found the cross."

"Stevey La Fountaine, you mean?" I said, not seeing the logic.

He nodded. "Ever since he came back to town, there's been a regular war going on between him and his family." He double-checked the bar again, then bent down even closer to me. "Then there's all that talk about him being a little light on his feet."

"That's news to me."

"It was to me too. But that's what the word is." This time, he glanced all around the bar before he said, "Gerald Marshall swears that it was our new sheriff who told him."

"What's the La Fountaine family war about?" I said, not liking the direction we were headed.

"His mother for one thing. For months Stevey's brother, Hubert, has been wanting to put her in the Lutheran Home. Their sister, Ellen, has been fighting just as hard to keep her out. Talk is, Stevey came back to break the tie."

That satisfied at least one nagging question of mine. Why had Stevey La Fountaine, a supposedly successful painter, left Madison and come back to Oakalla, where the demand for artists of any type was right below that for turnips? But knowing Oakalla and its people, I also guessed that there might be more to it than that.

"Why would Hubert La Fountaine be so intent on putting his mother in the Lutheran Home and Ellen La Fountaine be so intent on keeping her out?" I said. "I thought that Ellen was the one living with her until Stevey came back and took over the house?"

"It's the money, Garth," Hiram whispered.

"What money?"

Hiram never got the chance to answer that question. Someone at the bar raised an empty glass, and he was off and running.

I finished my cheeseburger, nursed my beer to its last drop, watched three games of darts, listened to Reba, Mary, Trisha, and Kathy tear my heart out, and was about to leave for my office when Stevey La Fountaine walked into the bar and sat down at my table. Wearing last night's clothes, including his long green Army coat, last night's stiff black hair and knotted black tennis shoes with a hole in one toe, and the scent of sweat and smoke, he looked and smelled much as I imagined Walt Whitman did in his day. After all, anyone who would sing praises to his armpit probably didn't carry either a bar of soap or a box of HandiWipes in his pocket.

As Hiram came over to take Stevey's order, he gave me a questioning look. I shrugged as if to say that I didn't know what was going on either.

Stevey ordered Canadian Club on the rocks, and another draft of Leinenkugel's for me. His eyes were red and tense, as if he needed sleep.

"Sorry about last night," Stevey said after Hiram had left. "I don't know what got into me."

"It's not last night that bothers me. It's what you said this morning."

"This morning?"

"When you sicced Sheriff Jacoby on me."

Stevey smiled apologetically. "Oh, that. I didn't think he'd take it personally."

"He did."

Hiram brought our drinks and Stevey had half of his down before I even bent my elbow. Then he seemed to relax, though his hand never strayed too far from his glass.

"Well, then I'm sorry about that, too," he said. "I thought maybe he'd back off if I told him that you'd already questioned me."

"Back off from what?"

Stevey finished the rest of his Canadian Club in one swallow and waved Hiram over to our booth again. "Make it a double this time, Hiram," he said. Then turning to me, "What was your question?"

"You said you sicced Sheriff Jacoby on me in order to get him to back off. My question is, back off from what?"

Now that the booze was working its magic, Stevey's face took on the guileless look of a practiced liar. "That's easy. He thinks I'm the one who burned the cross in Senator Springer's yard."

"Did you?"

"How could I have?" he said as Hiram approached. "Ask Hiram here. I was no more out the door when the fire siren began to ring."

"I thought you were the one who called in the fire?" I said.

Hiram hurriedly set down Stevey's drink and left before he got caught in the middle of something.

"Says who?"

"Danny Palmer."

"Well, he's wrong. I followed the truck to the fire, not the other way around."

I let it ride for a moment. If I wanted to call him on it, I'd have to bring Hiram into the discussion, and there were a lot of reasons not to do that.

"Let's get back to Sheriff Jacoby," I said. "Why do you think he's so intent on blaming the cross-burning on you?"

"I have no idea, Garth. Maybe he just doesn't like long hairs."

"Or gays?" I said, testing the waters.

"That's always a possibility," he said with the utmost aplomb, leaving me sorry that I'd asked.

"Has he been back to see you since?"

"No. But he promised he would be."

"I wonder what angle he's working?" I meant to say to myself.

"I told you. He doesn't like my type, whatever you want to take that to mean. I'll tell you something else, Garth," he said as he rose from the table, taking his drink with him. "If something ever happens to me, don't trust Sheriff Wayne Jacoby to work too hard at finding out why. I'm counting on you for that."

"You hardly know me, Stevey."

"I know you well enough." Grim though the subject was, he allowed himself the luxury of a small smile. "I mean who else in this town would help me carry a half-burned cross home at three o'clock in the morning?"

"You might be surprised."

His smile, not very substantial to begin with, had already been put away. "I don't think so."

Stevey went to sit at the end of the bar, where he usually sat, two stools removed from the regulars' inner circle. No longer in the mood to work, I finished my Leinenkugel's and started home.

The day had gone from early morning clear to cloudy, and back to clear again now that the sun had set. That was the trouble with January. It never did what I expected it to. I could stand a cold, cloudy, cheerless day, without either sunrise or sunset, morning or afternoon, if I thought I had a Chinaman's chance of doing better on the morrow. So when the clouds parted and the stars came out, I naturally assumed that tomorrow would be better. In Florida, it would be. I'd even place bets on Texas and California. But not Wisconsin. At least not in January. No. Red sky at night was no more a sailor's delight than a sharp stick in the eye. Red sky in the morning, though, he'd better take warning. He'd better batten down the hatches, find himself a bottle of good bourbon and a good book to read. And a good friend to share his close quarters, until the storm was over.

At home, I tried to call Abby and got her answering machine. Normally I would have said, "Hi, Babe, I love you. Call me when you can." Tonight I hung up before she even finished her spiel.

With nothing better to do, I let Daisy out of the basement, built myself a fire in the fireplace, my first of the new year, and sat on the floor in front of it, drinking Old Crow and ginger ale. Staring into it, watching its flames dance and its colors run, thinking those thoughts reserved for such times. Feeling its heat caress me, draw me ever closer, until I sat with the screen open, my hands just above the coals.

The phone rang. Thinking that it might be Abby, I nearly tripped over Daisy in my eagerness to answer it.

"Hello," I said.

"Is this Garth Ryland?" Whoever it was, she sounded other worldly.

"Yes. Who is this?"

"Ellen La Fountaine. There's been a shooting."

"Where? Who's been shot?"

"My brother Stevey." Panic in her voice now. She was near the breaking point.

"Is he still alive?"

"I don't think so."

"Have you called Sheriff Jacoby?"

"I tried, but I can't get him to answer."

"Have you called Operation Lifeline?"

"No. I didn't see the point. *Please.* Why won't *you* help me?"

"Where are you now?" I tried to sound calm and

reassuring, even though I felt anything but.

"At home."

"Your house there beside the Marathon?"

"No. My *real* home. Where Stevey's been living."

"I'm on my way. In the meantime, keep trying to call Sheriff Jacoby. It's important he be there."

"All I keep getting is his damn machine."

"Then leave a message."

She didn't answer.

"Ellen, did you hear me?"

"Yes . . . Dear God! Oh, dear God!"

I grabbed my coat and was out the door before I realized that I hadn't set the screen back in front of the fire or put Daisy back in the basement. But Ruth should be home soon. She'd figure it all out.

The night was much as the one before had been. Clear, bright, and bitterly cold, it clamped down on me after the first few steps and wouldn't let go. No one else was out and about as I walked down my alley toward the north end of town. I could hear my footfalls crunch the hard crusted snow, feel the solitude seep into my bones.

Stevey La Fountaine lay sprawled partway up his front porch steps. Coated with snow and ice, the steps were smeared with red almost all the way to the top, indicating that Stevey had managed to get that far, then slid back down again. His right cheek rested on one step, his right hand rested on the step above, his right knee rested on the step below, while the rest of him seemed suspended (as he would remain that way in my mind) for all time. I touched my hand to his face and felt myself recoil. Already it was marble hard.

With no help for Stevey, I went on up the front steps and into the house where Ellen La Fountaine sat in the dining room with a blank look on her face and the phone's receiver in her lap. Beep, beep, beep, the phone went.

Ellen seemed not to notice as I lifted the receiver from her lap and called Ben Bryan, the county coroner, who up until Christmas had been grooming Abby for the job. When Ben answered, I told him what had happened and asked him to try to get hold of Wayne Jacoby before he made his way here.

"This would have to happen now," he said in reference to Abby's recent departure. As deputy coroner and a budding pathologist, she had been only too happy to shoulder most of Ben's work load.

"Murphy's Law," I said.

"Somebody's anyway," he said before he hung up.

Ellen La Fountaine still hadn't moved so much as an eyebrow to acknowledge my presence there. I glanced around the dining room. Except for a small walnut dropleaf table and some padded pink- flowered walnut chairs, upon one of which Ellen La Fountaine was sitting, the dining room was mostly dusty hardwood floor and empty space, its white plaster walls bare of everything but an oval, black-framed print of Jesus praying in the Garden with a halo around his head and a cobweb draped across his shoulder.

Then I glanced at Ellen La Fountaine, who with her short red hair and sallow skin, bony arms, hollow cheeks, sunken eyes, and long pea-green polyester dress that buttoned up the front and looked like new, looked like the Ghost of Christmas Past. I had heard that she wasn't well, that never too strong to begin with, she had been in failing health ever since her father died. I saw nothing to dispute that claim.

"Ellen, it's Garth Ryland. You called me, remember?" I was afraid to touch her, for fear that she might break apart in my hands.

"Garth," she said, "how nice of you to come."

I left her staring straight ahead into the shadowy parlor

and went in search of the nearest bedroom, which was in the back of the house off from the kitchen. There, I pulled the checkered quilt off the bed, carried it into the dining room, and wrapped it around her. She showed life for the first time, as she closed her eyes and nuzzled it with her cheek.

"Mother and Daddy's quilt," she said.

"Yes," I agreed, hoping that it was the right thing to do.

"Mother wouldn't approve." Then she smiled. "Too bad."

A Queen Anne chair with a red rose embroidered in the seat stood over the register in the parlor. I carried it into the dining room and sat down on it.

"Mother's chair," Ellen La Fountaine said. Then she giggled. "She bought it after Daddy died."

"Why then?"

"Because he would never let her before."

"Nice man, your father."

"Oh yes," she said in all seriousness.

"I never knew him."

"Too bad for you. He was a wonderful man." Then she glanced fearfully about the house, as if afraid someone might overhear. "But not my mother. She was *mean*," she said with force.

"In what way?"

"In every way. To all of us—Hubert, Stevey, and me. Stevey was her little darling there for a while, but then something happened, and suddenly she couldn't stand the sight of him. She never did like Hubert or me, but in the end, I think she hated Stevey."

"In the end?"

"Before he left to go to school."

"What school was that?"

"The Stanton School of Art in Madison. It's very expensive from what I hear, but Stevey went there just the same."

"On scholarship?" I said, thinking that was the only way that he could afford it.

"Oh no. Daddy paid his way through—up until Stevey dropped out. Which is more than he ever did for Hubert or me."

"Why not?" I said, more to keep her talking than anything else.

"I wanted to be a teacher. But Daddy said that wasn't worth going to school for. He didn't understand, of course, that I couldn't be a teacher without going on to school."

"And Hubert?"

From all reports, Hubert La Fountaine was a self-made man, who had done very well working for the Adams County REMC. Starting out as a lineman, he had over the years gradually worked his way up to office manager, which, unless there was a merger, was as high as he could go without becoming president.

"Hubert wanted to be a doctor. But Daddy said he would be wasting his time. And Daddy was right, don't you know. It would've been a waste of Hubert's time."

"What did your mother have to say about all of this?" I said, wondering when Ben Bryan was going to come and rescue me.

"Oh, she was quite in agreement with Daddy in just about everything. Except for sending Stevey off to school." Her eyes became huge in her shrunken face. They were all I could see of her. "If it was up to her, she said, he could go into the Army and she'd pray for a war."

"Her exact words?"

"Yes." She seemed surprised that I would doubt her. "That's exactly what she said."

I heard at least two cars pull up outside. Thankfully, my time with Ellen La Fountaine was growing short. But I hated to pass up this opportunity.

"While we're on the subject of Stevey," I said, "do you know of anyone who might hate him enough to want to kill him?"

"Mother," she said without hesitation.

"Your mother's in the Lutheran Home." With Alzheimer's disease, I could've added.

Her look became angry, defiant, as if I'd pulled a switch and turned her into someone else. "Mother's not as sick as she lets on. She knows who and where she is most days."

"Still . . ." I said.

"Still nothing!" she shouted. "She didn't lift a finger when Stevey and Hubert kicked me out of my own house."

"And you didn't hate Stevey and Hubert for that?"

A change came over her again, as she smiled coyly, then pulled the quilt tighter around her and nuzzled it once more. "Why should I? I got it back, didn't I?"

"And Hubert won't object?"

Her smile deepened. It looked crude and garish, like something from a minstrel show. "Let him. It's one on one now."

The front door flew open and Sheriff Wayne Jacoby stepped inside with his gun drawn, bringing the cold with him. He bristled when he saw me sitting there, but to his credit, didn't shoot me. Instead, he said as he holstered his gun, "I'll take over now."

I rose, only too glad to let him. "Will you brief me later?" I said.

"About what?"

"About what went on here. My readers might want to know."

"I thought that's what you were doing." Whatever the case, he didn't look happy about it.

"No. In fact, Ellen and I were just talking about her family, how nice a man her father was."

"I'll bet."

I looked to Ellen for support, but found none. Still smiling, smugly it now seemed, she gazed up at me with eyes as blank as the wall behind her. Had I known her better, I would have sworn that she had just taken me for a ride.

"I'd suggest that you leave now," Wayne Jacoby said.

"But you *will* fill me in?"

"When I get time."

"My deadline's Thursday midnight."

"I don't give a damn about your deadline!" he yelled. "Now get out of here."

Outside, Ben Bryan and I watched them load Stevey La Fountaine's body into the Operation Lifeline ambulance. A small serious man with a love of antique cars, although he had just lately owned his first one, Ben Bryan was a former mortician, who looked like he ought to be wearing suspenders, a brown bowler, and singing first tenor in a barbershop quartet. And while we didn't talk about it, I could tell that he missed Abby almost as much as I did.

"Young Sheriff Jacoby seems on edge tonight," Ben said, as the ambulance drove away, headed for the east end of town and Ben's morgue.

"I noticed that, too."

"You know why?" His look seemed to indicate that I might.

"No. Unless he's having a bad hair day."

"I think it might be more than that," he said, as we started walking toward his tan Oldsmobile Eighty-eight. "You need a ride anywhere?" Ben asked.

"Home, if you don't mind."

"I don't mind."

The Oldsmobile hadn't been there for over fifteen minutes, but already frost had started to form again on the windows. I shivered as I climbed inside and closed the door.

"Cold?" Ben said.

"Not until now."

"Well, there'll be heat shortly," he said as he started the engine.

As Ben predicted, we had heat shortly, and lots of it. By the time we reached my house, I was almost toasty. I lingered with my hand on the door handle. I hated to go back out into the cold.

"Am I keeping you from something?" Ben said.

I smiled. It was something that Doc Airhart might have said when he was alive. How I missed him—him and Rupert Roberts both. With Doc dead and Rupert gone to Texas, I felt like the last of the Mohicans.

"If I'm not overstepping my bounds, I was wondering about Stevey La Fountaine?" I said.

"What about him? Aside from the fact that somebody put several bullets in his back."

"Several?"

"Five at least, by my count."

"It sounds like someone wanted to make sure he was dead."

Ben glanced up through his windshield at the sky full of stars. He said, "It sounds like someone with a grudge. Any one of those shots probably would have killed him."

"A crime of passion?"

"Maybe." He turned to look at me. "Then again, maybe not."

"Will you call me when you have something?" I said.

"If it's off the record. I don't want Dudley Do-Right on my case any more than he already is."

"It will be," I promised. "He's on my case, too."

"Pity," Ben said as he put the Oldsmobile in gear. "By the way, what do you hear from that girlfriend of yours?"

"She's settled into her new apartment. She seems to be enjoying her work."

"She say yet when she's coming home?"

Home? I liked the sound of it. "Not yet."

"Well, you be sure to let me know when she does."

"You'll be the first," I said, as I stepped out into the cold.

CHAPTER 4

When Daisy met me at the front door with her ball, I knew that either Ruth was still up or she wasn't home from playing cards yet. Then I noticed that the screen was back in front of the fireplace.

Figuring that Daisy could use a good run, I led her to the back door, took the nearly bald tennis ball from her mouth, and gave it a toss out into the snow. She was on it in a flash, but not before I'd closed the back door on her.

"You ought to be ashamed of yourself," Ruth said from her seat at the kitchen table. "It must be five below zero out there."

I poured myself a cup of coffee and glanced at the thermometer that hung outside the kitchen window. "Actually, it's seven below. But she can build an igloo if she gets cold."

"Why didn't you just roll her ball down the basement steps?"

"Because I didn't think of it."

Ruth sighed as she rose from the table and walked to the back door, where she let Daisy back into the house, took the ball from her, and dropped it down into the basement. As Daisy tore after it, Ruth shut the basement door.

"Now she'll paw and whine at the door," I said.

Ruth stopped to refill her coffee cup. "Better than having her cold."

"She's got a fur coat, damn it," I said.

"That's not the point." She sat back down at the table and reached for the half-and-half. "How bad was it?"

"Then you've heard?"

"No. But I figured with the house empty and Daisy upstairs and the screen away from the fireplace, you must have left here in a hurry. Then I heard the Operation Lifeline ambulance go north on Fair Haven Road."

"Somebody shot Stevey La Fountaine tonight," I said. "But he was dead by the time I got there."

Ruth sat back in her chair and didn't say anything. If I read her right, her look was one of disapproval.

"What?" I said. "What did I do wrong?"

"Nothing," she said. Which meant that I had.

"Come on, Ruth, give."

She debated with herself for a moment, then said, "I thought you told me more than once that when we had a new sheriff, you'd be only too happy to step back and let him do his job. Well, we've had a new sheriff for two months now, and that doesn't seem to be the case."

"That's only because Ellen La Fountaine called me when she couldn't get hold of him. She sounded hysterical, Ruth. What was I to do, tell her to take a number?"

She studied me to see if I was lying or not. But though

we knew each other well, it wasn't always possible to tell.

"Be that as it may, I'll bet you didn't let it end there."

"Only because I had no other choice. Or thought so at the time."

"I'm listening."

"Ellen La Fountaine. I think she did a number on me."

"It wouldn't be the first time, if she did. She's managed to live off of her father and then her mother for all of her life without lifting her hand once to work outside the home. But that's beside the point."

"What is the point, then?"

"The point is, I'd like to see you mind your own business for once."

"Damn it, Ruth. I minded my own business. And now Stevey La Fountaine is dead. So if you want to blame anyone, blame yourself for not telling me all you knew about the La Fountaine family when I asked you to."

"To what end?"

"Maybe to save Stevey La Fountaine's life."

She folded her arms and just sat there.

"Forgive me, Ruth. I shouldn't have said that."

"You keep playing with fire, you're bound to get burned."

"Meaning me?"

"Who else have we been talking about?" she said.

"I've gotten burned already, remember? By a twenty-two long rifle slug in the back. Not to mention some other close calls."

"Which is reason enough to quit while you're ahead . . ."

"I'm sorry, Ruth. It's just the way I am."

She shook her head, wanting neither apology nor explanation. She'd said her piece and now was done. It was time to move on.

"Okay, what I really want to know about the La Fountaine family is why the house is so important to each of them, Ellen and Hubert in particular? It almost seems that Hubert moved Stevey in, in order to move Ellen out."

"He did. At least that's the way I heard it. Hubert wanted to put their mother in the Lutheran Home, but Ellen wouldn't hear of it, so Hubert brought Stevey home to break the deadlock."

"Why? Just because they hate each other?"

"That's part of it. Ellen and Hubert have always been thorns in each other's side. But the rest of it is that there's supposed to be a small fortune hidden somewhere on the property, and they both want it for themselves."

"Whose small fortune?"

"Gilbert La Fountaine's. He didn't believe in banks, and dealt mostly in cash as far as he was able, so supposedly he socked away a lot of it . . . in his body shop, most believe."

"You among them?"

She shrugged as if she had her doubts. "I knew Gil La Fountaine as a young man, Garth. He didn't trust banks then, but he was a far cry from the miser that he supposedly became. So while I have to admit it's possible, I don't want to."

"What kind of young man was he?"

"I thought we covered that already."

"Only as far as we went."

"Gil was in the Korean War. I doubt I told you that. A Marine, I think, one of the survivors of Pork Chop Hill." She paused, as her eyes momentarily clouded over. "Anyway, he came here to Oakalla shortly after the war and got a job working as a mechanic for Marvin Heckel, who owned the Standard Station where the Marathon is now. Merle Heckel, who was still in high school at the time, took a shine to Gil, as did about every other young woman in town, and before long she was pregnant. With Hubert La Fountaine, it turned out to be."

Ruth took a sip of her coffee. I took a sip of mine. Both hands on the kitchen clock were pointing straight up.

"Gil had two choices, the way he told it to me. He could either marry Merle Heckel, or be tarred and feathered and run out of town on a rail. The fact that someone had found out that he was one eighth black didn't help matters any, particularly when all of the young men in town started counting noses to see how many of their girlfriends and sisters had been with him. He thought about making a break for it in the night, but where would he go? he asked himself. He had no family to speak of, and in the short time that he had been here, Oakalla had become home to him."

"Where was he from originally?"

"Louisiana, I think. The bayou country. Anyway, somewhere down South, because he said to me that he would rather wrestle an alligator any day than cross a Heckel."

"Did that include his wife, Merle?"

"Her in particular."

"So she's as mean as Ellen La Fountaine says?" In my dealings with Merle La Fountaine, she seemed soured on life, but not necessarily mean.

Ruth's look was noncommittal. "Who's to say, Garth? If I'd had kids like hers, I might have turned out like she did."

"Then she is mean?"

"I said, who's to say? You have to remember, Garth, that neither one of us has walked in her shoes. Gil La Fountaine's either. It couldn't have been easy being the only black man in Oakalla—and not a real one at that. In some ways that might have been easier on him and his family both."

I took another look at the clock and waited for her to explain.

"He never knew, you see, which leg he was standing on, and who, if anyone, might decide to pull the rug out from under him. Neither did his kids. They all looked white. Still do. But they all knew they had black blood in them. Their mother made sure of that."

"And now one of them is dead."

"So you tell me."

"Is there any chance that Merle La Fountaine is responsible?"

"I don't see how. Considering where she is, and why she's there."

"Ellen La Fountaine says Merle's not as sick as she appears."

"That's because Ellen got to stay in the house as long as Merle was there. Not only stay in the house, but to live off of Merle's Social Security and Gil's pension, such as it was. Think of it another way, Garth. Why, if she were in her right mind, would Merle La Fountaine let her children shuffle her off to the Lutheran Home, when, by hanging tough, she could get at least half of whatever money is there?"

I didn't have an answer for her, but I did have a question. "It's been at least five years since Gilbert La Fountaine died. Why hasn't she claimed the money by now?"

"Maybe she doesn't want to share it."

"My point exactly."

"And maybe she hasn't found it either. His shop's been padlocked since the day Gil died, the way he always kept it when he wasn't inside."

"Then why leave it that way? Why not open it up to see what's in there?"

"You'll have to ask her," Ruth said.

"I might just do that."

"And see how far you'll get."

"Wouldn't you want to have what's there, Ruth?"

"Not if I didn't want to share it with anyone. I'd wait until the middle of the night, then try to sneak out of town with it. I wouldn't move out of my own house and take the chance that one of them might beat me to it in my absence. Which Hubert surely would have, if Stevey hadn't died."

"Run that by me again."

"Rumor has it that the place is now up for sale. Or will be if Ellen and Hubert ever settle their differences."

"How likely is that?"

"More likely than it might seem. With Stevey out of the picture, neither one of them can win now, unless of course something happens to the other one."

I yawned, wishing that I'd gotten to bed hours ago, wishing that Stevey La Fountaine hadn't had the bad luck to get himself shot. "Who would want to buy the place anyway?" I said. "Even if Ellen would agree to sell, which I doubt."

"You might be surprised, Garth. Besides, they don't have to sell the house to get their asking price. Just the body shop. As is, of course, with the padlock still on it."

"Who in town would be so gullible to buy into that?" I said. "When there might not be any money at all?"

"Wilmer Wiemer for one. The Adams County Historical Society for another."

That surprised me because Wilmer Wiemer didn't drill many dry holes. But with Wilmer, you never knew what side of the street he was working. "Leaving Wilmer out of it," I said, "what would the Historical Society want with it?"

"They need someplace to work out of where they can

store all of their records. Leonard Frye's willing to put up
most of the money, if the Historical Society will come up
with the rest."

Leonard Frye had recently retired from his job as
Adams County's agricultural agent. Though liked and well-
respected, he wasn't necessarily known for his benevo-
lence, even to the Historical Society, of which he was a
charter member.

"That's generous of Leonard," I said.

"That's what I thought."

"So what's his angle?"

"The same as everybody else's, I figure. He thinks the
money's there."

"But he's willing to back it up with his own hard-earned
cash. So what does he know that we don't? I know," I said
before Ruth could. "I'll have to ask him that."

I rose from the table, set my coffee cup on the sink,
and started for the stairs, and bed.

"By the way," Ruth said, "Abby called."

I stopped, half afraid to ask. "What did she want?"

"What else? To talk to you."

I continued on to the stairs.

"Aren't you going to call her back?"

"No."

"Why not?"

"Because I'm not at my best right now."

"I don't think she expects you to always be at your
best."

"You know what I mean."

"No. I don't think I do. Are you saying that you're
afraid to call her now?"

"Yes."

"Afraid of what?"

"Afraid of getting her God-damn machine again. I

don't want to talk to it, I want to talk to her. And I don't want to have to wonder why it's on."

"You're afraid of losing her, is that it?"

"Yes. I think over time it's bound to happen—with her there and me here."

"Just don't make it happen" was her parting advice to me.

CHAPTER 5

I set my alarm for five and was up and gone long before daylight. Some high clouds had already started to move in, remaking the moon into a fuzzy cue ball and promising another cold, sunless day. What the clouds also accomplished, however, was to raise the temperature a few degrees to almost bearable. It was zero when I left home. Not balmy, but better than the fifteen below that I was expecting.

The cross still lay half buried in the snow where Stevey La Fountaine and I had dropped it. Its continued presence there bothered me almost as much as Stevey's murder. If he was the lawman that he was pretending to be, then why hadn't Wayne Jacoby made more of an effort to find out where it had come from?

From there, I walked back to the squat brown tile

building that had served as Gilbert La Fountaine's body shop. Ruth was right about the place being locked up. But she had neglected to tell me that it was a fortress. A large brass padlock about the size of my hand secured the corrugated steel sliding door that covered most of the front of the building, and the block-glass windows on either side of the building were clustered in small metal frames, so even if you did manage to break one out, which someone had, you couldn't crawl inside. Staring into the body shop through that one small hole, I saw nothing but blackness inside.

I returned to where the cross lay and stood over it for several seconds before deciding to pick it up. I hated the thought of its hard, blackened trunk resting on my shoulder. Also, the last man who had carried it was now dead. That wasn't the least of my concerns.

After stopping momentarily to check for traffic, I took off south down Fair Haven Road as fast as I could walk. A half block later, I veered to my right and rolled the cross from my shoulder in front of Edgar Shoemaker's welding shop.

Edgar was inside. I could tell by the thick column of wood smoke rising from his chimney. The ground outside of his shop was littered with metal carcasses of some of Edgar's failures, many of which were already dead on arrival, and some of the things that he hadn't gotten to yet. In the snow, it was hard to tell what was what—which was junk and which merely looked like junk.

I went into the shop where Edgar was bent over the stove, trying to light his cigar. Cold, with the dense smell of oil and grease, the shop was nearly as cluttered as the ground outside. And with only a single sixty-watt bulb burning, it was dim as a cave.

"You need some lights in here," I said.

Startled, Edgar nearly hit his head on the stove as he

swung around to look at me. "Don't you ever knock?" he said, recognizing my voice.

A widower, who was blind in one eye and partially blind in the other, with a bad heart and only one lung, Edgar was testimony to the triumph of the human spirit. The way his luck had gone, he should have given up on life years ago.

He walked over to the south wall where his welder lay and flipped a switch, flooding the place with the light from two two-hundred watt bulbs. "How's that?"

"I stand corrected."

"I guess you do." He turned the lights off. "There's coffee in that thermos over there, if you want some."

His dented grey metal thermos stood behind me just inside the door, along with Edgar's sack lunch—a sandwich, a dill pickle, and probably an apple, instead of a Twinkie, now that he was trying to eat healthier.

"Thanks, but I'll get some up at the Corner," I said, meaning the Corner Bar and Grill.

Edgar puffed on his cigar, finally getting it to go. "What's the matter, Ruth quit fixing breakfast?"

"We had a late night. She's sleeping in this morning." In truth, I was avoiding her, so that I wouldn't have to tell her what I was up to.

"The shooting, you mean."

"How did you know about it?"

"Picked it up on my scanner. Dudley Do-Right calling Operation Lifeline." Edgar's laugh was at his own expense. "Talk about the blind leading the blind."

"Maybe in time Sheriff Jacoby will prove his worth," I said without much conviction.

"That's what you said about Clarkie. And I guess he did—more or less." Edgar picked up his thermos and poured himself half a lid full of coffee. Then he carried the coffee over to the stove where he stood warming his hands.

I joined him there. "Is this business or pleasure?" he said.

"Business, I'm afraid. There's something outside that I want you to take a look at."

"Why not bring it in here so I can look at it in the warm?"

I nodded. It made sense to me.

Edgar held the door open as I carried the cross inside. Searching for a space big enough to hold it, I finally laid it down alongside some old water pipes.

"Where did you get that?" he said, keeping his distance.

"Senator Springer's front yard. Somebody burned it there night before last."

"Yeah, I heard that. You carry it all the way from there?"

"Stevey La Fountaine and I did."

"I see. And now he's . . .?"

"Dead. That's what the shooting was about."

"So now you want to know where the cross might have come from?"

"In a nutshell."

"To what end, Garth?" Edgar had laid his cigar down and was holding his coffee in both hands, so that he could blow on it to cool it.

"Stevey must have had a reason for wanting to take that cross home with him. I don't think he was just being a good citizen. So if we find out where it came from, we might also find out who shot Stevey."

"It could have come from anywhere, Garth," Edgar said, deliberately keeping some distance between him and the cross.

"Nothing ventured, nothing gained," I said.

"You mind if I drink my coffee first?"

"Just give me a call when you know something. I should be at my office by nine."

"You keeping banker's hours now?"

"I've got some stops to make first." I was at the door when I said, "Gilbert La Fountaine."

"What about him?"

"You ever do any work for him or he for you?"

"Hardly ever. In the beginning maybe, when he was just starting out on his own and didn't have everything he needed yet."

"Do you think he squirreled away all his money somewhere?"

"I wouldn't want to bet either way." His smile spoke volumes. "But it would be easy enough done, if you put your mind to it."

"And your next-door neighbor to the south, Leonard Frye? Any particular reason why he might be interested in the La Fountaine property?"

Edgar raised his brown leather cap to scratch his head, then reached under his welding apron to scratch his chest. "It's the wood heat," he said. "Dries my skin right out."

I waited for him to finish scratching.

"Leonard Frye, you say?" Edgar shook his head. "He and Gilbert used to be next door neighbors. But that was several years ago."

"Call me when you learn something?"

Edgar picked up his cigar, which by then had gone out. "If I learn something."

Since Leonard Frye lived just across the street and since there appeared to be a light on inside the house, I decided to save myself some steps later. His was a two-story yellow frame house, whose brown brick front porch had been enclosed in glass and used by Leonard as his county agent's office before he retired.

Normally a friendly, easygoing man with a medium-to-tall, spare build and a growing pink bald spot in the center of his head, Leonard Frye, in the years that I had known him, had seen his light brown hair turn nearly white and his bushy white sideburns creep down his cheek until they reached his chin. His face was round, as were his eyes, and he had the contented look of someone who, by learning early on his limits, had never tried to outreach them.

Today, however, he seemed almost surly when he answered the front door in his pajamas and slippers. "I thought you were the paperboy," he said, holding open the door, but not inviting me in. "Telling me he'd thrown the paper on the roof again."

"If you'd rather, I could come back another time."

"No. Step on in," he said. "We'll have to talk out here, though. Martha's still asleep."

Martha Frye, Leonard's wife, was the third cog in the cozy wheel of the Historical Society behind Leonard and then Beulah Peters, who either ran or tried to run every organization in Oakalla. A plump, white-haired, pink-skinned, pleasant woman, Martha Frye looked after Leonard with the same diligence that he looked after her.

"I won't keep you," I said. "You might have heard that Stevey La Fountaine was killed last night?"

"I heard," he said.

"Since you are a former neighbor, I wondered if you knew anyone who might have a long-standing grudge against Stevey?"

"Shouldn't Sheriff Jacoby be the one asking that question?" he said.

"He should be," I agreed. "But he's not."

"I sure don't want any of this going in that newspaper of yours," he said.

"It won't, Leonard. I can promise you that."

He walked over and closed the door from his office into the house, which in effect left us without heat. "You didn't hear this from me," he said, "but if you're asking who had a long-standing grudge against Stevey, I say it was that crazy sister of his."

"But not his brother?"

Leonard shook his head no. "Hubert always seemed above it all. But those other two, they fought like cats and dogs. Sneaky mean, both of them were."

"What about Merle La Fountaine? Ellen claims that she was the mean one."

"Merle was more a victim of circumstances than anything else. Married to a black man in an all-white town, she could hardly expect people to overlook that. Not that very many deliberately snubbed her, but then hardly anyone came calling either. Which left her only her family to take up the slack, which proved pretty slim pickings, especially after her dad died. He was the only one of the whole bunch of them, including her mother, who put much stock in Merle. She was his favorite—at least up until she married Gil La Fountaine."

"She and her kids never got along?"

"Not so that I could see. But I can't say that anyone in the family ever got along. It seemed doomed from the start."

The temperature was dropping fast in there. Leonard had started to shuffle from one foot to another in an effort to keep warm.

"Thanks, Leonard," I said. "What about the rumor that the La Fountaine place might come up for sale soon, and that the Historical Society might be interested in buying it?"

"Talk's all it is, Garth." Already Leonard was reaching for the inside door. "You know how to let yourself out."

CHAPTER 6

I ate breakfast at the Corner Bar and Grill—coffee, orange juice, two eggs over medium, hash browns, and a slice of whole wheat toast. It was cozy in there, warmed by the smell of bacon and donuts, and freshly baked pies cooling on the counter, and by the morning ebb and flow of several conversations going on at once. So when the time came to go back outside into the cold again, I had to talk myself from my stool at the counter all the way out the door.

I'd debated long and hard about my next stop, but in the end I decided that I'd just have to risk it. You couldn't get to the bottom of the well without starting at the top.

Allison Springer, Jonathan Springer's wife, was the one who answered my knock at their front door. Dressed in navy heels, a light-blue blouse, and a navy wool suit, she appeared to be on her way somewhere.

"Is Senator Springer in?" I asked.

"No. I don't expect him until late tomorrow evening."

"Then would you mind answering a couple questions?"

"In regard to what?"

"The cross-burning in your yard the other night."

"Are you here in an official capacity, Mr. Ryland, isn't it?"

"No." I wanted to lie, but had given Wayne Jacoby my word.

"Then come on in."

She stepped back out of the way, so that I could go on inside. As I did, I caught a whiff of her perfume. I didn't know what it was, but it smelled expensive—and seductive, though I tried not to think about that.

I followed her into the small dining room, which Diana had used as her studio and whose east bay window looked out on Home Street and the west side of the Five and Dime. Had there been sunlight, it soon would have been streaming in the bay window. But the day outside was as grey as yesterday's fire.

"Would you like coffee?" she said.

"I don't want to impose."

"It's no imposition."

"Yes. Then I'd like coffee."

While she went into the kitchen after the coffee, I had the chance to glance around the dining room, my first in several years. An oak table for two stood in the middle of it and was covered with a lace runner on which stood a cut glass vase that held a sprig of baby's breath and a single pink rose. Above the table was a small brass hanging lamp with an amber shade, attached to a dome white plaster ceiling that stretched to nine feet above the oak parquet floor. Little did I realize then, when Diana had this covered with bed sheets and canvasses, what all was here. Or at least, what all might be here. But in those younger, more innocent days, her presence alone was more than enough to fill my eyes.

"Please sit down," Allison Springer said as she came back into the dining room, carrying my coffee in a bone china cup.

She set the cup down on the table, then, after I had taken the chair in front of it, sat down across from me. I took a sip of my coffee and tried not to make a face. As good as it was, and I judged it to be excellent, it would have tasted a whole lot better with at least some sugar in it.

"Is something wrong with the coffee?"" she said. "Jonathan and I like ours a bit on the strong side."

"No. It's fine," I lied.

"You couldn't prove it by me." Then she smiled in understanding. "I'm sorry. How rude of me. I'll bet you're one of those infidels who take cream and sugar with their coffee."

I returned her smile. "Guilty as charged."

A moment later she returned from the kitchen with a sterling silver creamer and a matching sugar bowl. The sugar spoon was also sterling, as was the teaspoon I used to stir my coffee.

"Thank you," I said.

"You're welcome."

As she sat back down across from me, I tried to decide on the real Allison Springer, but had no luck. Now in her mid-to-late forties with pale blue eyes, full red lips, peaches-and-cream skin, and a sea of blond hair, she seemed to enjoy her role as mistress of the mansion and yet in some subtle way disdain it. I couldn't decide if she would be happier wearing boots, jeans, and ten-gallon hat and riding a quarter horse, or in purple and a powdered wig, saying "Let them eat cake."

"Was there something else, Mr. Ryland?"

I shook my head no. "The coffee's excellent, by the way."

"Good. I'm glad."

Was she really glad? In my heart of hearts, I doubted that. But more than one had said that I was a cynic.

"You said you had some questions for me," she said.

"Actually, they were for Senator Springer, but perhaps you can answer them."

We were interrupted by what seemed to be a man's voice coming from the back of the house. Allison Springer blushed at the sound of it. Like Ruth, she was a natural.

"My scanner," she hurriedly explained. "Old habits die hard, I guess."

"You were once a cop?" Somehow I couldn't see her in that role.

"An ambulance chaser. That's how I first met Jonathan. I won a damage suit against him. He figured anybody that dangerous ought to be taken off the street, so he fired his old lawyer and hired me. One thing led to another . . ." We were interrupted again by the squawk of her scanner. "And we were married six months later."

"Do you still practice law?"

"I did up until Jonathan decided to run for governor. There's not time now. Not and do all of the things expected out of a candidate's wife."

Her voice, I noted, had suddenly gone dead. "You don't like politics, Mrs. Springer?"

"I *hate* politics, Mr. Ryland. But don't quote me on that. And it's Allison, if we're going to be friends. *Are* we going to be friends?"

"I don't see why not."

Unless, of course, she continued to serve me coffee in a bone china cup. Either the handle was too small for my fingers or my fingers were too big for the handle. I kept wanting to hold it in both hands to make sure that I didn't drop it.

Then there was Allison Springer, whose eyes intently followed my every move, the way my mother's used to when we'd go out to eat after church; as if she feared I'd drop a bowl of soup in my lap and ruin my Sunday slacks along with the family's good name. Not that Allison Springer in any way reminded me of my mother, or that my response to her was in any way son-like.

After we had spent several seconds sorting each other out, she was the first to look away.

She said, "As much as I'm enjoying your company, I do have to be in Madison for a luncheon by eleven-thirty. So perhaps we had better get on with it—whatever it is you came for."

I set my coffee down. I wasn't one of those people who could pat my head and rub my stomach at the same time. And Allison Springer required my full attention.

"Okay, question number one," I said. "Do you have any idea who might have burned that cross in your yard?"

"None whatsoever. Next question, please."

"Does the Senator have any idea who might have burned that cross in your yard?"

"If so, he hasn't told me."

"Then he might have an idea?"

"Not likely."

I didn't pursue it.

"Is that all?" she said, sounding disappointed in me.

"Unless you'd like to tell me why you and the Senator moved to Oakalla in the first place."

She smiled. "You're making things too easy on me, Garth. Jonathan drove through here and fell in love with the place, this house in particular. He's a small-town boy at heart. He's never much cared for Madison."

"Unlike you?" Her smile, I noted, had started to droop.

"I have my reasons," she said.

"I'd like to hear them."

"I grew up in a small town, lived in one until I went to business college. In fact, I even lived in Oakalla for a short while back in the '60s. But that was not a happy experience. None of my small town experiences have been."

"Not happy in what way?" I said.

"That's personal, I'm afraid."

"You're the one who brought it up. So you must feel the need to tell somebody."

Her look said she felt trapped—the old damned if I do, damned if I don't trap. "How much of this is off the record?"

"All of it, if need be."

"Then this is just a social call?" She would have preferred it that way.

"No. A man here in town was murdered last night. I'm trying to find out why."

"Surely you don't think . . ."

"I don't think anything at this point. But a cross was burned in your yard, and the man who carried it away from here is now dead. So if I can find whoever it was that burned the cross, maybe I can find the killer."

"I thought that was Sheriff Jacoby's job." She swallowed hard at the mention of his name, as if it had stuck in her throat.

"You don't approve of the sheriff?" I said.

"I don't approve of the witch-hunt that he's conducting against my husband."

"That's news to me." And it was.

She glanced at her watch and said, "I'm sorry, Garth, but I really do have to go." She stood in case I was hard of hearing.

"You never told me what happened to you here in Oakalla. Your unfortunate experience?"

She stood rigidly, as if at attention, as if the wound still had not healed. "My husband left me—barefoot and pregnant, I believe the expression is."

"And your child?" I didn't remember Jonathan Springer's bio listing any children for either him or her.

"I lost it."

"I'm sorry."

"Are you really?" Both her face and hands were like stone. "An old-stone savage armed" Frost might have said.

"I lost my only child," I said.

That broke the spell. But not by much. "Yes . . . Well . . . That was a long time ago," she said as she picked up my bone china cup and headed for the kitchen.

"When did you say that the Senator would be home again?" I said.

"Tomorrow evening. Why?"

She had stopped with her back to me. I noticed for the first time that Allison Springer had a remarkably well-formed pair of legs. I also noticed how tall she was. Even without her high heels, she would have stood at least five-eight.

"Would you have him stop by my office at the *Oakalla Reporter*? I'll probably be working late."

She turned to face me. Whatever might have passed for friendship between us seemed about to be extinguished.

"If you'll tell me why it's so important that you see him?"

"You said you had no idea who burned the cross in your yard. Maybe he does."

"I said it wasn't likely that he did."

"That still leaves the door open."

"I'll tell him," she said. "But I'm sure he'll have more important things to do than to talk to you about something he knows nothing about. Good day, Mr. Ryland."

The frost in her voice left no doubt that I was dismissed. But as long as I was here, I might as well ask, "The rose? Where did it come from?"

Her eyes went immediately to the table where the pink rose stood in its cut-glass vase. They seemed to soften as they did, take on a whole new light, that of a woman in love.

"Jonathan," she said. "He's bought me one every week for ten years now, since our first night together."

"Lucky you."

"I think so."

I stepped outside where a few flakes of snow had started to fall, chased by a brisk northwest wind that seemed to be on the rise. Another cold front was passing through. If the skies cleared tonight again, it could be twenty below by morning.

Wilmer Wiemer was the owner of the Best Deal Real Estate Company, the Oakalla Savings and Loan, and several properties in and about Oakalla, and anything else on which he thought that he could make a profit. A small, dapper man with silver hair and a TV evangelist's smile, Wilmer and I had forged a friendship over the years, which, if not based on trust, was at least based on mutual respect for the duplicity of the other. But in fairness to both of us, we only lied to each other when it was absolutely necessary, or appallingly convenient.

Wilmer's office was on School Street right next to the Oakalla Mutual Insurance Company and north across the alley from the City Building. The wind pushed me nearly all the way there, until, in the lee of the Lutheran Church, I had a quiet moment to collect my thoughts about Allison Springer and my conversation with her. But the only thought that stayed with me was how much of an enigma she was. I couldn't even decide if she had been beautiful as a young woman (considering how beautiful she was now), since with some women their beauty seemed to grow rather than diminish over time. She was a puzzle, nevertheless, and I wasn't sure how much I liked her, no matter how much I wanted to.

Wilmer Wiemer's office could only be described as spartan. He kept it even colder than I kept mine, which was a couple degrees above frostbite. And the Shaker chairs that he kept for visitors and that he described as comfortable were harder than some of the boulders I'd known along the lakes of Minnesota. Furnishings, too, were at a minimum. Once you got past Wilmer's desk and chair, the photograph of Wilmer's wife on his desk, and the aerial photograph of his farm on his pecan-paneled wall, there wasn't much else to see.

"Garth!" Wilmer smiled broadly as he rose to shake my hand. "It's always a pleasure."

"Likewise, I'm sure." I sat down and discovered that his chairs had grown no softer in my absence.

Wilmer reached into the watch pocket of his double-breasted silk suit, producing a gold pocket watch that had been a fortieth wedding anniversary present from his wife, Clarissa. Clarissa Wiemer was a recluse, who, people said, rarely showed her face in public because she was so ashamed of Wilmer's antics both in and out of the business world. In truth, she had a rare skin disease that tolerated no exposure to the sun.

"You're cutting things a little thin, aren't you, Garth?" Wilmer said as he read the watch. "You're usually in your office by now."

"What time is it?" My trusty Timex was buried under the sleeve of my sheepherder's coat.

"A little after nine."

"I should've been there an hour ago."

Wilmer's smile broadened. He loved to go one up on me, as I did him.

"You make it in there by six every morning, then maybe you can start keeping up with me."

I'd never seen Wilmer in anything but a tailored suit
and a Lincoln Continental. "True," I said, returning his
smile. "Then maybe someday I can get me an office like
this."

"It serves its purpose," he said, undaunted. "So, what
do you have for me today—a deal I can't refuse, or your
usual twenty questions?"

"You're going to give me a complex, Wilmer. You'd
think the only time I came around is when I have a question
for you."

"It *is* the only time you come around. But since I like
your company, I'll take what you offer."

I shrugged. Sometimes I wished I were different, too.
"Twenty questions, I'm afraid."

If that disappointed him, he didn't show it. "Then let's
have it."

"The La Fountaine place—rumor has it that it might
soon be up for sale."

Wilmer frowned, as he took a gold-plated pen from his
shirt pocket and used it to drum the top of his desk.
"Rumor has it wrong, then. That place will never sell now
that Stevey La Fountaine got himself killed."

"Why not?"

"Ellen La Fountaine is why not. Mark my words, Garth.
She'll hang on to that place with her last dying breath." He
stopped drumming long enough to add, "What I want to
know is, if they had to shoot a La Fountaine, why didn't
they shoot her?"

"Then you *are* interested in the property."

"Were. It's all past tense now."

He noticed the pen in his right hand and what he'd
been doing with it. He opened his top desk drawer and
threw the pen inside, then folded his hands tight and rested
them on the desk, as if afraid of what they might do next.

"Rumor also has it that Gilbert La Fountaine's life

savings might be hidden there on the property somewhere," I said.

"Which will amount to about twelve dollars and fifty-
eight cents."

"I hear it could be considerably more than that."

"That's the way the game is played, Garth. You don't
salt a mine with fool's gold."

I studied Wilmer to see what he might be up to. But
as always at such times, he was unreadable. Which was
why, no matter how many times he'd asked, I would never
play poker with him.

"You're saying there's no money?"

"Not from where I sit. Not after five years, which is
how long Gilbert La Fountaine's been dead."

"It's my understanding that his body shop's been locked
up that whole time. And I've been there myself, Wilmer.
There's no other way in, but through that padlock."

Wilmer was nonplussed. "As I have been there, too.
And you're right. There's no other way into the body shop,
but through that padlocked door. Except all that it takes to
open a padlock is a key. Until I knew where that key was,
I wouldn't give a hoot in hell for anything that was supposed to be inside."

"So why were you trying to buy the place?"

"Who said I was?"

"I have my sources."

"Well, they're wrong this time, Garth."

"Ruth's hardly ever wrong, Wilmer," I said, bringing
out the heavy artillery.

Wilmer just smiled. He knew when he held a pat hand.
"She is this time, Garth. You can tell her I told you so. You
can also tell her for me that I wouldn't touch that property
with a ten foot pole." His look soured. "Not that anyone
will ever get the chance now."

I'd gotten about what I'd expected from him, which

was little more than nothing. Still, I hated to leave with that. "You have any idea who might have killed Stevey La Fountaine?" I said.

He shook his head. "Outside of his mother, brother, sister, and art lovers everywhere, I can't think of a single person who might want him dead."

"I think we can eliminate his brother," I said. "With Stevey dead, it makes it that much harder for Hubert to sell the place."

"Unless Hubert's working another side of the street." Wilmer played the devil's advocate, a part he was born to.

"What side might that be?"

"Maybe he doesn't want to sell that property as badly as he lets on."

"Why wouldn't he?"

"Chew on this for a while, Garth. What would happen to that place now if something were to happen to Ellen La Fountaine?"

"Aren't you forgetting Merle La Fountaine?"

"Who's lucky to remember her own name."

"You just said that she was one of those who might want Stevey dead. So which is it, Wilmer? Is she a player in this, or not?"

Wilmer didn't answer right away. He wasn't yet sure how much he wanted to tell me.

He said, "She could be a player. I hear that nurse who's been looking after her is a pretty sharp little cookie. She could have her hand in the pot somewhere."

"What nurse is that?"

"Wendy . . . Bodine, I think it is. The one that has the new sheriff all tied up in knots."

"Tell me more, Wilmer."

"I've told you too much already. It's time for both of us to get back to work."

Wilmer, I knew from personal experience, was a creature of the night, whose rounds stretched from one end of Oakalla to the other, so what he said about Wayne Jacoby and Wendy Bodine could very easily be true. It might also explain Wayne Jacoby's whereabouts last night when Stevey La Fountaine was killed.

"You mentioned art lovers everywhere as possible suspects," I said. "I take it you didn't think too much of Stevey La Fountaine's work?"

"I might have liked it, Garth. If I ever could have figured out just what the hell it was he'd painted."

"I didn't know you were a connoisseur."

"I'm not. But I've been known to buy a painting or two, if I thought I'd get my money back somewhere down the road. So when Stevey became the rage over in Madison, I said why not. Local boy makes good. The least I could do was to help him along. So when they had their annual wine and cheese festival a couple-three years back, Clarissa and I went over. At night, of course, which is the only time she'll travel." Wilmer rolled his eyes. "It was a joke, Garth. Not a soul in the place had a good thing to say about the man or his art. And Stevey's paintings themselves . . . They looked like something an angry kid might do, when turned loose with a brush and a bucket of paint." He snapped his fingers. "Which reminds me, even though it's beside the point. My sources have it there's an outside buyer for the La Fountaine place. Someone in the art community over in Madison, the way I hear it."

"You don't know who it is?"

"No. I was hoping you'd tell me, seeing you've taken such an interest in the place."

"I'll keep my ears open."

"As I will mine."

I rose to leave. Thanks to Wilmer's chair, everything felt numb from my waist down. "Something's bothering me, Wilmer. Are you saying that Stevey La Fountaine wasn't nearly as successful as we've been led to believe?"

"Not from where I stood, Garth."

"Then why all the fuss over him?"

"That's got me puzzled, too. But it answers one question I had. Why Stevey came back here."

"Why was that?"

"To make sure he got his." Wilmer reached for a set of papers on his desk, leaving me to draw my own conclusions about his last statement.

CHAPTER 7

On leaving Wilmer's office, I had intended to go straight to work. However, I made the mistake of looking both ways before crossing School Street and saw a yellow REMC service truck parked in front of the City Building. Charlie Rutan, who drove the truck, was Oakalla's assistant fire chief and a good friend of Danny Palmer.

We met just as Charlie was leaving the City Building. A large, ruddy man with a windburned face and curly grey hair, he wore a yellow hard hat and insulated Carhart coveralls and worked as a troubleshooter for Adams County REMC. We had gotten to know each other through the Community Club's pitch-in dinners and our many fire runs together.

"Morning, Garth," he said, turning away from the wind

so that he could light a cigarette.

"Morning, Charlie. I'm not keeping you, am I?"

"As a matter of fact," he said with his typical bluntness, once he got his cigarette going. "I'm on my way to a service call. I only stopped by here to see if I might have left my gloves in the truck the other night."

"You mean the night the cross burned?"

"That's it," he said.

"You have any ideas on the subject?"

He took a quick drag on his cigarette, then cast a guilty look about, like a kid sneaking a noon smoke at school. "Pauline," he explained. "I promised her I'd quit smoking. She catches me, I'm going to be sleeping on the couch from now on." He glanced over his shoulder again just to make sure before he took another drag on his cigarette. "As far as that cross business goes, I figure the less said the better. Maybe then it'll all blow over and we'll be done with it."

"You're probably right, Charlie. I'll let you go, then."

He took that as his cue to head for his truck.

"One other thing, Charlie," I said. "Did Danny come back here after the fire?"

"Danny Palmer, you mean?" Which in itself was an admission that he didn't want to talk about it, since there was no other Danny on the fire department.

"Yes. That's who I mean."

He turned to face me. His eyes said that the battle lines were already drawn. "No offense, Garth. But what business is that of yours?"

"Danny's a friend of mine, too. He hasn't seemed quite himself lately."

"What of it? Why take it upon yourself to go around asking people about it?"

"Then he wasn't here, is that what you're saying?"

He gave his cigarette a toss in my direction. As the

wind caught it, a shower of fire and ash blew into my face.

"No. That's not what I'm saying," he said. "Danny was here all right, and he was still here when I left."

"Were you the last one to leave? Besides Danny?"

"That's usually the way it is. Him and me take turns closing the place down."

"Whose turn was it Monday night?"

"Mine . . . His, I mean. What the hell difference does it make?"

"You've noticed a change, too, haven't you, Charlie?"

"So what?" He was defiant, determined not to betray Danny Palmer, who up until now had never needed defending by any of us. "Danny ain't in any kind of trouble, if that's what you're thinking. Nothing he can't handle anyway."

"I have your word on that, Charlie?"

His answer was to climb into his yellow REMC service truck and drive away.

Adams County REMC's central office was located in the Y made when School Street split off from Madison Road and continued on south, while Madison Road angled to the southeast. A small brick building that was built originally as an interurban station, it had housed REMC for as long as I could remember. Usually I hardly gave it a second glance on my way to work. Today I stopped there.

Any hope of a quiet entrance ended when I twice banged the venetian blind on my way inside the front door—once as I opened the door, the second time as I closed it. Mildred Purcell, who doubled as receptionist and assistant office manager, looked up from her desk behind the counter and spoke not to me, but to Jenni Whittaker, who doubled as secretary and dispatcher. "I told you we didn't need a bell."

Mildred Purcell was a large,heavyset woman in her late fifties with a mischievous twinkle in her eye and a dimple right in the center of her double chin. Jenni Whitaker was about the same height as Mildred, but ten years younger and a hundred pounds thinner, and likely to change her hair color and style at least twice a year. Both considered themselves lifers there at the REMC office, and while they complained loud and long about being over-worked, it would have taken a small army to remove either one of them from her job.

"Is Hubert in?" I asked.

Hubert La Fountaine's desk was the only one that wasn't open to public view. It was tucked away in the back behind a closed door.

"Who wants to know and why?" Mildred said.

"Garth Ryland. I hear he might have some property for sale."

We all watched as Hubert's office door swung open without a sound.

"I guess he's in," Mildred said, as she went back to her computer.

I crossed the room and closed Hubert's door behind me on my way inside his office. Walleyed and stone-faced, he sat at his desk without saying a word. He was tall and thin, like his sister and late brother, and had thin black hair that only recently had begun to show threads of white, a thin black mustache that he waxed periodically, shiny black eyes that betrayed his intelligence, and the strong slender hands of a pianist or a surgeon. He almost always wore a Western suit, white shirt, and string tie. Of all the La Fountaines, he had the darkest skin color. He was also by far the best looking, and if I took Ruth's word for it, truly his father's son in every way but one. As a con-firmed bachelor, the only skirts that Hubert La Fountaine chased were the Scottish Highlanders as he rode his Appaloosa in Oakalla's annual homecoming parade.

"Did I come at a bad time?" I said, taking a seat in the

captain's chair facing him.

"What is it, Garth? And be brief. I've got a lot on my mind."

"Such as?"

"Such as figuring out how to bury my brother without it costing me an arm and a leg. Knowing Stevey, he got himself killed on purpose just to jab me one last time."

"Was he good at that?" Now that he was talking about Stevey, I didn't want him to stop.

"At what? Putting it to me? He spent his whole life figuring out ways. He and his sister both." He slammed his fist down on his desk. "Damn those two. Talk about your parasites."

"You have any idea who might have killed Stevey?"

"No. But if you find out, I'd like to know, so that I can pin a medal on him before I cut his throat."

"You don't think your sister did it?"

He laughed. "She doesn't have the guts, or the where-withal."

"She was at the house when it happened."

"Doing what?" The smoldering fire in his eyes suddenly became a blaze.

"I have no idea. I just know she was there."

"The little sneak. I know why she was there." But he wasn't about to tell me.

"Ellen hinted that your mother could have killed Stevey. Or had it done." Which seemed the more likely scenario.

"How?" he said with a smirk. "Or haven't you seen my mother lately?"

"Not lately," I admitted.

"Then I suggest that you pay her a visit. It'll put any thoughts of her involvement out of your head."

"You're taking your mother's side, then?"

"I hate my mother, if you want to know the truth.

Always have."

"And your father?"

"What I felt for my father is none of your business. But I will say this about him. He never whined about his lot in life the way my mother did. You'd think she was the only white woman in the world who'd married a black man and then lived to regret it."

"You think of your father as a black man?"

He gave me an unsettling look that was neither sad nor angry, yet seemed both. "I think of myself as a black man. And according to the federal government, I qualify."

"Why?" I was asking for myself now.

"Go read your history books, Garth. Or better yet, today's headlines. Then you'll know why."

"Then does my German blood in me make me a German?"

"Not if you can't see it."

"I can't see the black blood in you."

"Look in my mirror sometime. Then you will."

"And if I did, so what?"

"That's easy to say, from where you're sitting. But not from where I'm sitting." He glanced down at his hands, which lay spread on top of his desk, then back up at me. "But if that was, say 6.25% Chippewa blood in my veins, I'd turn over every rock in sight to prove it. So what does that say about me? Or any of us, for that matter?"

There probably were a lot of ways to answer that question, but since I didn't know any of them, I kept my peace. Then I stood, preparing to leave.

"Your property there where Stevey was shot, I hear it might be up for sale," I said.

I felt a sudden rise in tension, as right before a thunderstorm. "Who told you that?"

"That's the word about town."

"Vultures! Goddamn vultures is what they are!" He

had risen from his chair without seeming to realize it.

"You mean it's not for sale?"

"I mean, who would buy it, even if I could sell it? Not Ellen, and she's the only one who wants it."

"I'm not talking about the house, but the body shop."

Hubert's face darkened to match his eyes. It seemed to take all of his self-control not to strike me. "Out!" he said, pointing to the door. "Get the hell out of here."

So I left.

CHAPTER 8

A light snow fell on me all the way to my office. Pushed by the northwest wind at my back, it raced in swirls down Gas Line Road, scouring the pavement and polishing the patches of ice that had eluded the snowplow. Why, I wondered, had Wilmer Wiemer tried so hard to convince me that there was no money in the body shop, and why had Hubert La Fountaine nearly exploded in rage at the mere mention of it? And as long as I was wondering about things, why had Charlie Rutan been so quick to leap to Danny Palmer's defense? Where there's smoke, there's fire, Grandmother Ryland was fond of saying. In Wilmer's case, I wondered if that also applied to smoke screens?

The phone was ringing when I walked into my office. I expected Edgar Shoemaker and instead got Ben Bryan.

"You didn't hear this from me," Ben said, "but I got it straight from the horse's mouth that Sheriff Jacoby is gunning for you. So if you haven't been minding your p's and q's, now might be a good time to start."

I thought about my morning and all the stops I'd already made. "I think it's too late for that, Ben. Who sicced him on me?"

"Ellen La Fountaine is what he said. She claimed you were up there nosing around her place early this morning."

I wondered how she knew, since I had seen no sign of her? Ellen La Fountaine, it appeared, kept a closer watch on things than one might expect from someone in shock.

"She's not wrong about that. Did he mention her saying anything else to him? Like reporting a missing cross, for instance?"

"No. But when he came by here for the autopsy report, the Sheriff was anything but a happy man, so it might have slipped his mind. You couldn't have missed him by more than a few minutes. He planned on stopping by your office when he left here."

Actually I had missed him by only a few seconds. As I was emerging from the alley beside the cheese plant, he was stopped at the intersection of Perrin Street and Madison Road there in front of Abby's house—Doc Airhart's house, it used to be.

"Speaking of autopsy reports, what did you come up with?" I said.

"Who's asking, Garth the snoop, or Garth the newspaperman?"

"He's one and the same, Ben."

"Not to hear the Sheriff tell it. In either case, I'm not supposed to tell you. According to him, it's privileged information."

"Screw him," I said. "That badge doesn't make him God."

"To his way of thinking, it does. But to answer your question, Stevey La Fountaine took five slugs from what I'm guessing was a twenty-two revolver in the back. I was right in saying that any one of them could have killed him. But the one that punctured his right lung probably did."

"How did he die? In laymen's terms."

"In laymen's terms, he bled to death."

Suddenly cold, I looked up to see the snow pecking at my north window, wanting in. "He was stiff by the time I got there, Ben."

"Same here. What are you saying, Garth?"

"I'm saying that Ellen La Fountaine supposedly called me right after he was shot. If so, he should have still been alive, or warm at least, when I got there."

"I can't argue with that." But neither would he comment on it.

"Twenty-two longs or twenty-two shorts?" I said, when I got tired of waiting.

"Twenty-two shorts. According to a certain former sheriff, who I faxed the information to, the murder weapon was likely a Saturday night special, accurate at the most to ten yards."

"Clarkie, you mean?"

"Who else?"

Former sheriff, Harold Clark, was a bust as a lawman, but a computer genius. "How is Clarkie?" I said.

"Fine. Still loves his job, he says. And gives a lot of the credit to you for putting him on to it."

"He have anything further to add about the murder weapon?" I said. The less said about Clarkie and my role in his new job, the better. I had shamed him into it more than anything else—something of which I was not very proud. Particularly not now.

"No. He'd need to see the spent slugs themselves to take it any further," Ben said.

"What are the chances of that?"

"A snowball in hell's."

"You're the coroner, aren't you?"

"Yes. But Clarkie's not the sheriff."

"Don't remind me."

"Leave it be, Garth," Ben warned. "Don't forget all the grief he put us through, including himself. And while young Sheriff Jacoby might have his faults, not the least of which is the pride that goes before the fall, at least he's trainable."

I was starting to have my doubts about that. But Ben was right about Clarkie. As much as I liked him and wanted him to succeed, he had no instinct for the job of sheriff.

"Anything else you can tell me about Stevey La Fountaine?" I said.

"No. Except I don't think he even saw death coming."

"Do any of us?"

"You know what I mean, Garth. He was ambushed, pure and simple."

"That is kind of scary, when you think about it."

"Real scary, if you ask me."

Ben had no more than hung up when Edgar Shoemaker called.

"Good thing you answered when you did. I was about to give up on you for today," he said.

"I got delayed. What do you have for me, Edgar?"

"Well, you can rest easy about trying to find out where that cross came from. It could've come from about anywhere in town."

"How so?"

"It's made out of old lumber. I'm talking real old, Garth, when a two-by-two was still a two-by-two and a four-by-four was still a four-by-four, not a three-and-a-half by whatever it's shrunk to today. So whoever made it had some old lumber laying around, which, like I said, could be just about anybody."

"New nails or old nails?" I was hoping that if they were new, I could track them down.

"Old nails. And whoever built it wasn't much of a carpenter. Several of the nails were bent over and left that way."

"And you have no idea where it came from?"

"Not a one. Except, I don't think there's just one person involved. Not unless he's stouter than you and I are."

"I carried it to your place by myself, remember?"

"After the fire had eaten it half away. Which brings me to another point. Somebody had soaked it in gasoline before they set fire to it. You take a good whiff of your jacket once it warms up, it'll tell you the same thing."

"Hang on a minute."

I took off my jacket to smell it. Edgar was right. Along with the strong smell of smoke was the faint scent of gasoline.

"Why couldn't they have poured the gasoline on it after they put the cross in the Senator's yard?" I said.

"They probably did. But if that's all they did, it would've burned off, and wouldn't be soaked into the wood the way it is."

"So this wasn't a spur-of-the-moment thing?"

"It depends on what you mean by spur of the moment. They could've built it one day and set it on fire the next. That wouldn't take a whole lot of planning."

"But at least some. Don't you agree?"

"Yes. At least some. If only to get the logistics right."

"But where could someone build a cross, soak it in gasoline, and leave it, if only for a day, confident that no one would see it?"

"About anywhere in town that's cold. Doing it inside your house might be a little risky, even in the basement."

"Thanks, Edgar. You've given me food for thought."

"Then as long as you're chewing, you might as well chew on this. How did they get the cross to the yard in the first place? It surely wouldn't fit in the trunk of someone's car."

"There are a lot of pickups in Oakalla, Edgar."

"But only one's going to have its bed smelling like gasoline. And Garth?" I heard a note of caution in his voice. "The Sheriff was by here, looking for you. I don't think it was to give you a good conduct medal."

"Did he see the cross?" If so, all might be lost.

"If he did, he didn't know what he was looking at."

Relief brought a smile to my face. "Thank God for small favors."

"Did you hear me, Garth? Dudley Do-Right is looking for you."

"Then he should know where to find me."

I spent the rest of the morning into the afternoon working on the *Oakalla Reporter*. Laying it out was always like trying to put a jigsaw puzzle together with a couple pieces missing. I still had my column to write and never knew exactly how long it would be, and there was always some last minute news item, or piece of information, or advertisement, or obituary that couldn't wait until next week. To give me a few more grey hairs, I'd also started a community page on which I printed for free all of next week's coming events for Adams County. It was supposed to be a "first come, first served, sorry, Clyde, you're too late" affair, but I always found myself juggling it to see how much more I could squeeze in. But all of its little headaches were also part of the job's romance. No week, no matter how much I might have longed for it to be, was ever the same as another.

At one' o' clock, I found myself hungrily eyeing the glue on my desk and knew it was time to head uptown for lunch. I'd eaten almost everything in sight, including some crackers of suspicious origin and even more suspect taste, and drunk a gallon of instant coffee, and was feeling like jumping in front of a bus, or pushing someone in front of one, whichever proved handiest. Every time a car had slowed to turn at the intersection of Berry Street and Gas Line Road, I had gotten up to see who it was. But so far Sheriff Wayne Jacoby had yet to make his appearance. I was tempted to go looking for him in order to get whatever might be coming over with, so I could concentrate on my work, but one of Rupert Roberts's maxims was to never go looking for trouble, because it would find you soon enough.

Though the sun now shone dimly through the clouds, a light snow was still falling. From inside the shelter of my office, it had looked a lot prettier than while trudging into it on my way up Gas Line Road. Thank God for stocking caps and insulated underwear. If you couldn't have romance, you could at least have comfort.

Inside the Marathon, Sniffy Smith sat high on his favorite stool, looking out at the drive. A small, soft, opinionated man whose bark was worse than his bite, Sniffy was a retired barber, who now cut hair only on Friday, and that by appointment. I was one of his customers, as were Danny Palmer, Dub Bennett, and a couple others in town. Sniffy only did it as a favor to us, his oldest and best customers. We only did it as a favor to him. It was hard for any of us to admit that the torch was being passed.

"Danny around?" I said, glad to be back in the warm again.

"He should be back any minute. He had to make a wrecker run out to Wyandotte Road."

Whenever Danny had to leave the Marathon for any reason, Sniffy watched the drive and manned the telephone for him, and pumped gas only after he'd done all in his power to avoid it. On a cold day like this one, he would never leave his perch until the customer came into the station after him. Most of the regulars knew Sniffy's tactics, so if Danny didn't appear right away, they'd go ahead and pump the gas themselves. But a few, like Ruth, and Beulah Peters, came looking for Sniffy the instant that they surmised that Danny wasn't there. If Sniffy could bail out and hide in time, he would. But usually they caught him in the act, and after that generally made his life miserable until they left.

I heard my stomach growl. I wasn't sure I could wait for Danny. "Will you give him a message for me?" I said.

"You can give it to him yourself. I think I see him coming now." Sniffy looked hopefully out over the drive.

His hope was rewarded. Danny pulled into the drive a moment later and parked the wrecker beside the station. But before Danny could make his way inside, someone in a black Chevy S-10 pickup pulled up to the gas pumps.

I heard Sniffy give a loud sniff and turned around to see what the problem was. But I couldn't tell whether it was a sniff of alarm, or one of relief that he didn't have to go out into the cold.

"Who's that in the pickup?" I said. Although it was hard to tell from that distance, the person inside appeared to be a most attractive young woman.

"A nurse. She works down at the Lutheran Home."

"She have a name?"

The look Sniffy gave me was, for him, unusually harsh. "I thought you were taken, Garth."

"I am. I wasn't asking for myself."

Sniffy came out with another loud sniff, the way he did whenever he was angry or excited. "Who would you be asking for, then?"

"Just tell me who the hell it is," I said, letting my empty stomach do the talking.

"Wendy Bodine." His feelings hurt, Sniffy made it a

point to look away.

Wendy Bodine? Where had I heard that name before? Then I remembered what Wilmer Wiemer had said about her and Wayne Jacoby.

I watched Wendy Bodine drive away. A moment later Danny came into the station.

"Afternoon, Garth," Danny said, without his usual warmth. "Sniffy tell you that Dudley Do-Right is looking for you?"

"We never got around to it."

"Well, he is," he said, starting for the east bay where someone's car was up on the rack.

"Danny, I have a favor," I said.

He stopped with his back to me. Something was eating at him, and if I were to guess, Wayne Jacoby figured in the equation somewhere. Maybe, like me, Danny didn't want to turn the town over to him until Wayne Jacoby had proved his worth. He'd worked too hard to make it what it was.

"Name it," Danny said.

"Whenever you go out to pump gas in someone's pickup, give the bed a look to see if you can see or smell gasoline."

I saw his shoulders slump. And when he turned my way, he looked completely exhausted. "Garth, do you know what you're asking?" he said. "It's not that I don't already have enough to do the way it is."

"Then forget I said anything."

"Why is it important?" he wanted to know.

I owed him an explanation, but I wasn't sure that with Sniffy there I should give him one. "It has to do with what happened the other night," I said.

"Last night, you mean?" He was referring to Stevey La Fountaine's murder.

"Two nights ago," I said, meaning the cross-burning.

He thought for a moment, trying to read between the lines. Then it seemed all of the color drained out of his face. "Shit," he said.

"Danny, you all right?" Sniffy asked.

"I won't do it, Garth," Danny said, ignoring Sniffy's question. "I won't rat on one of our own."

"Suit yourself." I could feel my face start to burn. It was time to get out of there.

"It's nothing personal, Garth. I just can't do it. After all, I have a business here."

"So do I. But we both live here, too. That makes us citizens first, businessmen second. That is, if we want to keep what we have."

"It won't burn up with a cross," he said.

"I wish I could be as sure."

Sniffy gave a loud sniff, rocked back and forth on his stool so hard that he almost toppled it, then looked at each of us in turn. "Would somebody please tell me what the hell is going on here? You two have been friends forever, it seems."

"We still are," Danny was quick to assure him.

But as I stepped outside into a flurry of snow, I wasn't so sure.

CHAPTER 9

I ate lunch at the Corner Bar and Grill, where the cold seemed to have followed me inside. I didn't know what had happened to the others there, but they seemed to have caught whatever I had, as they spoke to me in monosyllables, if they spoke to me at all. Or perhaps they knew that I was a marked man and wanted to keep their distance, so that they wouldn't be swept away with me when the dam broke. Or maybe I was just hungry.

Lunch did improve my mood some, but it did nothing to clear the skies, and I walked to the far west end of town in a cloud of snow. It seemed that by now we should have had a couple inches of new snow on the ground, but apparently the snow was more style than substance and did little more than whiten what was already there. And annoy me, which seemed its plan all along.

The Lutheran Home had started out as just that—a single three-story brick building where old Lutherans went to die. Over the decades, however, it had evolved into a thriving little retirement community. Its central building (the old Lutheran Home) served as its office and, more or less, as a nursing home for those unable or unwilling to take care of themselves, while its surrounding one- and two-bedroom apartments served those who needed little or no care or supervision. It had also become more cosmopolitan in its clientele. United Methodists were now welcome there, as were Catholics, Baptists, and Jews. No Unitarians, though. After all, you had to draw the line somewhere.

Despite my natural resistance to change, I liked the place. Its present layout made more sense to me than the old one had, and its extended family of staff and residents provided a buffer against that often cruellest of jesters— life itself. The one that teased you with family and friends, health and happiness, then took them all away one by one, until you were left alone.

Dorothy Culp ran the Lutheran Home from her modern office on the main floor of the central building, or the Hotel, as she preferred to call it for reasons of her own. A small, thin, energetic woman with a mop of grey hair and gold wire-framed eyeglasses like those John Lennon had worn, she always looked harried to me, as if she didn't even have time to get all the way dressed in the morning. But she got the job done with a minimum of complaints.

"Who was it again you wanted to see?" Dorothy was shuffling through a stack of 3 x 5 cards like a blackjack dealer, no doubt looking for one she'd lost.

"Merle La Fountaine."

"Why?"

"To let her know her son was murdered, if nothing

else."

"Wendy's already taken care of that."

"Wendy?" I played dumb, not hard for me where Dorothy Culp was concerned.

"Wendy Bodine, Merle's nurse."

"Since when did your residents start having their own nurses?"

She looked up at me for the first time. Her pained expression said that she wished I'd just go away.

"Since we discovered that those with Alzheimer's disease respond better to a loving, caring, *stable* environment. Which Wendy provides." She frowned, looking glum.

"Is something wrong?"

"No. You just reminded me that Wendy will be leaving at the end of the week. Saturday, to be exact. Merle's quite fond of her. I'm not sure how's she's going to react."

"Is this a sudden move?"

"No. I've known for some time that she was looking for other employment. Right after the first of the year, she told me that she'd found something."

"In Wisconsin?"

She went back to shuffling cards again. "Florida, I think. Someplace warm."

"Lucky her."

"That's what I thought."

"How dependent is Merle La Fountaine on her?"

"She's Merle's only company, if that tells you anything."

"You mean Merle's family never visit her?"

She gave me an "are you kidding" look. "Not only do they not visit her, getting any money out of them for her care is next to impossible. The other brother or sister will take care of it, is what they always tell me."

"Who usually does take care of it?"

"Hubert. Though I can tell he begrudges every penny."

"It's my understanding that he and his mother have never been close."

"She's still his mother." End of discussion.

"So is it all right if I talk to Merle?" I said.

"If you'll tell me your reason."

She glanced up at me over the top of her glasses. Not for nothing had Dorothy Culp been made head of the Lutheran Home. Even while shuffling through a king-sized stack of index cards, she had never lost her train of thought, or let me slip one by her.

"I'm curious, that's all," I said.

"About what?"

"The seriousness of her condition. I've been told by someone who should know that Merle is not as bad off as she seems."

"Ellen." It wasn't a question.

"How do you know?"

"She told me the same thing. I told her to get a life. Advice, by the way, that you might consider."

"Then Merle is as bad as she appears?" I said, ignoring her barb, which wasn't the first she'd ever thrown my direction.

"Will you take my word on it?" She studied me a moment. "No, I didn't think so."

In the next breath, she told me how to find Merle La Fountaine.

I was in luck. Merle La Fountaine answered the door of her apartment herself, and for that moment at least, appeared to be having one of her good days, as she smiled broadly at me and waved me on inside.

"Stevey," she said, putting a bony hand to my cheek. "How good of you to come."

I forced a smile of my own and tried not to shrink from her touch. Her marbled hand was as cold as the day outside, while her yellowish eyes, keen as those of a raptor's, bore into mine with a fire I felt in the back of my skull.

"Let me look at you," she said, holding me at arm's length as her fingers dug into my coat. "How long has it been, Stevey?"

Quite a while, it felt like.

"Mrs. La Fountaine," I said. "I'm not Stevey. I'm Garth Ryland of the *Oakalla Reporter*. I used to see you now and again at the Five and Dime."

She dropped her hands, as if I'd burned them. "Not Stevey," she said, backing away from me.

Only then did I notice that the pea green dress that she wore was a ragged twin to that worn last night by Ellen La Fountaine. It was eerie to see her wearing it. Tall and gaunt, like her daughter, she seemed Ellen La Fountaine's apparition, or how she would appear twenty years from now.

"Don't be afraid. I'm not going to hurt you," I said. Then felt foolish for saying it.

"Not Stevey," she had decided.

"Garth Ryland," I answered.

Then, without warning, she started to scream.

I could still hear her on the steps of the Hotel. Only when its thick glass doors closed behind me did her screams stop. I was relieved to find Dorothy Culp still at her desk.

"Well?" she said.

"I think we have a problem."

"Damn." She was already on the move.

I followed her outside. Merle La Fountaine's screams had grown louder, if anything.

"What do you think you're doing?" Dorothy Culp said, as she held out her hand to stop me.

"I'm trying to help."

"You've done quite enough for one day, thank you."

Then I was nearly run over by a blond demon in a white uniform in her frantic effort to reach Merle La Fountaine.

"Wendy Bodine?" I said, as I watched her go.

"Wendy Bodine," Dorothy Culp answered.

Merle La Fountaine stopped screaming the instant that Wendy Bodine entered her apartment. The silence, as they say, was deafening.

"Now you know why I'm going to miss her," Dorothy Culp said.

I had an inkling.

"As for you," she continued, "it might be wise for you to be gone when Wendy comes back. I won't be held responsible for what might happen."

"All I did was introduce myself."

"You'll have a hard time getting anyone to believe that."

"What time does Wendy get off work?" I asked.

"You're not planning on coming back, are you? I'm afraid I can't allow that."

Meanwhile she kept a close eye on the door to Merle La Fountaine's apartment. Had it swung open, she was prepared to rush me off the property herself to avoid a confrontation with Wendy Bodine.

"No. I'd like to talk to Wendy. I'd rather not do it here."

"Talk to her about what?"

"This and that."

"She gets off at five." Dorothy Culp's look was skeptical. "But if I were you, I'd steer clear of her for a while."

"She's leaving Saturday, right?"

"Right."

"Then I don't have a while."

"It's your funeral," she said, as she started back into the Hotel.

CHAPTER 10

At four forty-five, I left my office and started for the near west end of town. In the hour or so that I had spent at work since returning from the Lutheran Home, I had gotten absolutely nothing done on the *Oakalla Reporter*. Either I was thinking about Merle La Fountaine and her ragged pea green dress or I was watching out my north window for Sheriff Wayne Jacoby. I knew he'd be there sooner or later. Sooner, rather than later, I hoped.

It was dusk and still snowing. I could feel it burn my cheeks, see it whenever I passed under a streetlight. More like a snow shadow than a real snow, it was definitely a light hitter, destined to work all day and into the night for something that earlier snows had accomplished in an hour. There was a lesson there somewhere, but I didn't know how it applied to me.

From a phone call to Ruth, I had learned where Wendy Bodine lived, which was on Maple Street, the first house west of Peanut Johnstone and the telephone company, and two houses west of the City Building, if you didn't count the jail. Vera Richardson owned the house, and according to Ruth, Wendy Bodine rented the small apartment that Wilma Conlon, Vera Richardson's mother, had lived in until her death a couple years ago.

As I turned the corner at Maple and School, I glanced over at Clarkie's small white bungalow, which was dark and had been dark for several months now. I missed him. I missed him in the way that you miss the Marmaduke in your life, the one who slobbered on you, ate you out of house and home, and left his big muddy paw prints all over your heart. True, Clarkie was a pain in the ass, but his was a gentle, giving soul, and when I saw him coming, never had to wonder where I stood.

Vera Richardson was a short, plump, jolly old elf, who heard no evil, saw no evil, and certainly spoke no evil. In contrast to her robust good health, her husband, Vernon, had always looked sickly to me, or as Wilmer Wiemer used to say about him, like he had "one foot in the grave and another on a banana peel." He had died of colon cancer a month before Wilma Conlon had suffered her final stroke. That double whammy of losing her husband and mother both would have levelled most people, but Vera went on as if nothing had ever happened, cooking for the school and delivering baskets of baked goodies to the Lutheran Home three times a week. I didn't know exactly why, but I begrudged her for that. Grief, it seemed, should at least give us pause—bring us to our knees, if only for a moment.

I could smell supper cooking as soon as I climbed up on Vera Richardson's back stoop. Unlike the typical house in Oakalla, which was wood frame with a large concrete front porch, Vera had a stone house with only a single step for a front porch. Her back stoop was wooden, three steps high, and led either to Wendy Bodine's apartment or Vera's kitchen, depending on whether you turned right or left on entering the house. If you went straight ahead, you went down into the basement, something that I had no intention of doing.

"Coming!" Vera said in answer to my knock. Then I heard her clump down the two steps to the back door. "Garth Ryland, of all people!" Vera said as she held open the door for me. "Wouldn't Vernon be delighted if he were here."

An avid reader and a sometimes philosopher, Vernon Richardson was the first of Oakalla's citizens to ask me to stop by and visit with him at his home. That visit proved a joy to each of us, so we continued them on a regular basis up until the day he died.

I followed Vera into the kitchen where she had what smelled like a meat loaf in the oven and a pile of potato and onion peelings on the drain board of the sink. The potatoes themselves were on the stove in a pan of water, but not yet cooking. I guessed that the onions were in the meat loaf.

"You had supper?" she said, as she opened a can of green beans. "There's a God's plenty here."

In all of the time that I had known her, I had never seen Vera Richardson stop even to take a deep breath. She would have driven me crazy, but Vernon didn't seem to mind.

"Thanks, but Ruth will have supper waiting for me," I said, as I sat down at the kitchen table. Warmed over tuna casserole, most likely, the way my luck was running.

"Wendy should be home any minute now," she said. "You've met her, haven't you?"

"No. I've never had the pleasure."

Vera dumped the green beans into a saucepan, added some bacon bits, onion salt, and pepper. "I don't know what I'm going to do without that girl. I swear I don't."

"I hear she's leaving Saturday."

"Shh." Vera put her finger to her mouth. "I don't want to hear about it."

Then why bring it up, I wondered? "How long has she lived here?" I said.

"A little over a year now. She moved here in November year before last."

"You ever have any trouble with her?" I said, as I took my coat off and stuffed cap and gloves inside it. It must have been close to eighty in there.

"Trouble? What are you talking about, Garth Ryland? That girl's been like a daughter to me."

And daughters never gave their mothers any trouble? Maybe not in Vera's world.

"I just wondered," I said. "She seems a very attractive young woman from what little I've seen of her. It seems every single guy in town would be perched on your doorstep, wanting to take her out."

Vera didn't say anything. Instead, she went to the oven and opened it to check on the meatloaf. The smell almost brought me right up out of my chair with a fork in my hand.

"Or isn't she interested in men?"

Vera hurried to her refrigerator for a bottle of catsup, as she began making sauce for the meatloaf. "Of course she's interested in men," Vera said in Wendy's defense. "It wouldn't be natural if she weren't."

"But they're not interested in her?"

"Don't be silly, Garth. You said yourself, she's a very attractive girl. I can't bring myself to call her a woman. She looks so young and fresh and all." Vera's smile was wistful, as if she were remembering her own girlhood.

"How old is she?"

"Twenty-six. We celebrated her birthday just last week."

"We?"

She stood on her tiptoes as she reached up into her cabinet for the Worcestershire sauce. "Wendy and I. Who else would I mean?"

"I was thinking of Sheriff Jacoby."

"Oh, him." Vera dismissed him with a wave. "Wendy assures me that it's nothing serious."

"Then he has been here to see her?"

"Of course he has. Where else would he go to see her?" She was now reaching for the dry mustard, which she set down on the counter next to the Worcestershire sauce. "And before you ask, no, I don't know what goes on behind her closed door, or care to know. This is the nineties after all. Young people do things differently now. But I'm not so old, or out of it, that I've forgotten what feelings are. Or that those men who take your breath away, don't always stay for breakfast."

I smiled, even though my ears were burning. Perhaps I'd misjudged Vera Richardson all these years. She wasn't quite the Goody Two-shoes that she appeared to be.

"What about Tuesday night? Was he here then?"

"What night was that?"

I had to think about it myself. "Last night, I guess it was."

"Yes. But that's all I'll say on the subject."

"What about Monday night?"

She squirted some catsup into a mixing bowl, then added the Worcestershire sauce, dry mustard, and a large pinch of brown sugar. "Not that I recall."

"It could have been late."

"If so, I would have slept right through it."

But I noticed that Vera had stopped dead still for the

first time in my memory. She cradled the canister of brown sugar in her left arm with her right hand on the lid, but so far she had made no move to put it away.

"Then he must have been here fairly early Tuesday night."

"What's that, Garth?" She was back in motion again.

"Sheriff Jacoby. You said he was here Tuesday night."

"I also said that's all I had to say on the matter."

"Then answer me this. Does Wendy ever bring her work home with her?"

"What do you mean?"

"I mean does she ever talk about any of her patients?"

"All of the time. That's about all she does talk about."

"What about Merle La Fountaine? Does Wendy ever talk about her?"

Vera frowned as she stood over the mixing bowl. "I'm afraid there's not much to talk about, Garth. That poor woman is as addled as they come."

"You've seen her lately, then?"

"Just the other day."

"What was she like?"

But she never got a chance to answer. At that moment, Wendy Bodine came rushing in the back door. "You don't know how good that smells, Vera," she said as she ran up the steps to the kitchen. "*You,*" she said when she saw me. "You!"

"I thought you two hadn't met," Vera said mildly.

"We haven't formally," I said. Then remembering my manners, I rose from my chair at the table. "I'm Garth Ryland."

I watched as her eyes narrowed, drew a bead on mine. Had Vera not been there, I believe that she would have taken a swing at me.

"I know who you are. Vera, I'll be in my apartment. Call me when it's time to eat . . . If Mr. Ryland's gone by then."

"Actually, Miss Bodine, I came to talk to you," I said.

With her long blond hair, hooded long red coat, and white nurse's shoes, she reminded me of Little Red Riding Hood. But pity the poor wolf who tried to take her picnic basket.

"We have nothing to talk about, Mr. Ryland."

She had about the bluest eyes I'd ever seen. Looking into them was like looking deep into a sky-blue lake, thinking that you ought to see bottom because the water was so clear, only to be disappointed when you couldn't. And her dark creamy skin was that of someone who wasn't afraid of the sun, who could go all winter without ever completely losing last summer's tan, who would sunbathe in the nude without even thinking twice about it.

"I think we do, Miss Bodine. So if you'll excuse us, Vera . . ."

I took her by the arm and began to lead her out of the kitchen. Either I was going to get my chops busted or I wasn't. There was no point in postponing the matter.

She jerked away from me and took the lead down the steps. I then followed her up the steps into her apartment, which was crammed with cardboard boxes in preparation for her move.

"Close the door," she said.

I did as she asked.

The apartment itself was one large room with an adjoining bathroom. There was a gilt-edged full-length mirror on the back of the apartment door, a cherry dresser in the northwest corner, a chest of drawers along the south wall right next to the door. A Jenny Lind bed with a pimpled yellow spread and a large stuffed bear wearing a straw hat sitting on top of it had its headboard flat against the east wall; a nightstand, lamp, and alarm clock were tucked into the northeast corner next to the bed; a large double window with a brown sash that nearly matched the bed covered most of the north wall. The window was bare when we had walked into the room. Wendy Bodine's first act on entering was to pull a white curtain across it. Her second had been to turn on the lamp beside the bed.

If the kitchen had been eighty degrees, it was sixty in here. Still wearing her coat, Wendy Bodine sat down on the edge of the bed facing me. I chose to stand. I felt safer that way.

"You're becoming a royal pain in the butt, you know that, don't you?" she said.

"Some would say I've already arrived."

"You'll get no arguments there." She allowed us both a small smile.

To say that Wendy Bodine was beautiful would not do her justice. There is beautiful, and there is electric. Abby was beautiful, inside and out, someone I never tired of, no matter how tiring life got. Wendy Bodine was electric, someone who, if you allowed her to, could charge all of your senses to the degree that you would have to have her, even if it consumed you. As long as she wanted you, you were hers, no matter who got hurt along the way.

"What are you thinking?" she said.

"That you are a dangerous woman."

"That's funny," she said, even though she didn't seem to see the humor. "I've been told you're a dangerous man. Probably the most dangerous man in Oakalla."

"By whom?" Certainly not Vera Richardson.

She shrugged. "Someone who ought to know." Then she took off her coat and laid it on the bed. "You might as well sit down. I'll keep my coat between us."

I wished she hadn't taken her coat off. I'd never seen anyone look quite so good in a nurse's uniform.

As I sank down in the soft bed, I touched shoulders with her. She was surprisingly soft, and a whole lot warmer than the room around us. No wonder Sheriff Wayne Jacoby missed Ellen La Fountaine's call. This beat the hell out of night patrol.

"Would you rather I move my coat?" she said.

I shook my head no.

"Hard to get?" she asked.

"In love with someone else."

"That's not a problem for some people."

"It is for me."

"For me, too," she said, looking away. "Believe it if you will."

I wasn't sure I did, but didn't say so.

Someone knocked on her apartment door. I looked at Wendy Bodine, who stared anxiously at the door, as if afraid of who it might be.

Then Vera Richardson said, "Supper will be ready in twenty minutes. Is that all right with you, dear?"

"That's fine, Vera, " Wendy said. "I'm sure Mr. Ryland will be gone by then."

I nodded to say that I would be.

"I could have killed you this afternoon. I really could have," Wendy said.

"All I did was introduce myself to her."

"That's not the point. You had no business being there in the first place, even if you did have permission."

"Then you talked to Dorothy Culp?"

"We talked. She actually had some good things to say about you, though I can't recall any at the moment." Wendy Bodine was one of the people who could laugh at you without ever cracking a smile. "So what were you doing there?" she said, now serious.

"Merle La Fountaine's son was murdered last night. But then you already knew that."

"Good riddance is what I say. Why bother Merle about it?"

"Because her daughter, Ellen, suggested Merle might somehow be involved."

"That would be laughable, if it weren't so lame." Her eyes became even bluer when she was angry. But not nearly so clear.

"You're saying Merle can't be faking her illness?"

"She's been my patient for over two months now. I can assure you that she isn't."

"Not even to get back at her kids?"

"By doing what, killing them with guilt? When not one of them has ever been out to see her?"

"Maybe to bankrupt them. It costs money to live in the Lutheran Home, a lot more than it would at home."

She shook her head to indicate how far off base I was. "Merle didn't want to come to the Lutheran Home in the first place. It was Hubert who put her there."

"How? I mean, when? Before or after Stevey came home?"

"I have no idea, since I don't know when Stevey came home."

"But Hubert's been the one calling the shots, ever since Merle's been in the Lutheran Home?" If so, he might have power of attorney, which would put a whole new spin on things.

"That's my understanding, yes."

Again there was a knock at the door. "Ten more minutes to supper, dear," Vera said.

"Mr. Ryland is just about to leave."

I glanced at my watch. The past ten minutes seemed to have gone awfully fast. "Does she do that with all of your male callers?" I said.

Her look made me feel underdressed. "No. You're the first."

"I guess that's a compliment."

"I'm not sure it is."

"One other question." I rose, taking my coat with me. "It's my understanding that Sheriff Jacoby was here last night. What time was that, do you recall?"

"What does it matter? We're both adults."

"But he's also sheriff."

"What difference does that make?"

"A lot, when someone gets murdered, and he's not available to take the call."

"I think it's time you left now." Brilliantly blue, her eyes were as opaque as steel.

"You going to start screaming like Merle?"

"I might."

Another knock on the door. "Five minutes, dear. Time to wash up."

"What about Monday night? Was he here then?"

"I'll pretend I didn't hear that."

"A simple yes or no will do."

"Will that get you out of here any faster?"

"It might."

"Then yes, he was here."

"How long?"

"Most of the night. He left shortly before the fire siren rang."

"What do you mean by shortly?"

"A few minutes. Maybe as long as a half hour. I wasn't watching the clock."

"Were you in and out of sleep?"

"Yes."

"Then it could have been even longer?"

"It could have. I don't know."

"Are you going to miss him?"

"Come again?" Her face, so composed until then, looked wary.

"Sheriff Jacoby. Are you going to miss him when you leave?"

"Parts of him, yes," she said with a smile. "He really does have a nice body."

"That's not what I asked."

"He's been a challenge" was all she would say.

On my way out of the apartment, I nearly ran over Vera Richardson, who was standing just outside the door. Either she was about to announce that supper was ready or she had been there all along. I wouldn't have bet either way.

"Enjoy your supper," I said.

"You really sure you can't stay?"

I looked back into the apartment where Wendy Bodine still sat on the bed with what looked like glass in her eyes. "I'd love to, Vera. But you know Ruth."

CHAPTER 11

It had stopped snowing. I determined that about halfway to my office when my head finally cleared itself of Wendy Bodine. I would never want to fall in love with someone like her for fear of what it might do to me. Twenty-five years from now, maybe. Twenty five years from now she would look a lot like Allison Springer—still blond and beautiful, but without all of that fire to feed. But by then I'd be seventy-five, so who was kidding whom?

I never heard the car behind me. Not until Sheriff Wayne Jacoby touched his siren and nearly put me into the ditch. To make it even more official, he had his bubble light on.

"Get in," he said, stepping out of the car.

I got in. It was warmer inside than out. He joined me.

"Am I under arrest?" I said, only half joking.

"You ought to be. I thought we had an agreement."

"We do. I haven't flashed my badge or any other part of me at anyone the past couple days."

He put the car in gear. "Fasten your seat belt," he said.

"How far are we going?"

"It doesn't matter. Fasten your seat belt."

It turned out that we went only as far as my office, which was two blocks down the road. He parked in the gravel drive east of the building, and we sat there with the lights off and the motor running.

"People are going to talk," I said, trying to lighten the mood a little.

But Sheriff Wayne Jacoby wasn't interested in what I had to say. He said, "Why is it that everywhere I've been today, you've been there first?"

"Maybe because I got started earlier."

He slammed his right hand down on the steering wheel. There in his hat, leather gloves, and leather jacket, neat little black mustache, and green uniform, he looked more Gestapo than county sheriff. It was not an observation that inspired trust.

"Damn it, I'm serious," he said. "I'm trying to make allowances for the fact that you helped out here in the past. But that's over now. Like I told you earlier, this is no work for amateurs."

"I agree. But I'm not an amateur."

"You're not a cop either."

"I won't argue with that."

"So you have no authority to be doing what you're doing."

"I don't need anyone's permission, including yours, to walk around town and talk to people."

"You do if I say so."

"Bullshit."

I'd had enough of Sheriff Wayne Jacoby for one night. I started to get out of the patrol car. But he put his hand against my chest and held it there.

"I'm trying to conduct a murder investigation and you're hindering that investigation. That's obstruction of justice," he said. "You keep it up, I *will* arrest you."

I waited for him to remove his hand from my chest. When he finally did, I said, "Don't you even want to know what I found out?"

"No. I'm not going to prejudice my investigation with hearsay."

"Then tell me what you found out. I don't have any such prejudices."

"Meaning what?" I thought I heard menace in his voice, as if I'd touched a raw nerve. Even in the near dark, I could see his jaw twitch.

"Meaning I'm not proud. I'll take whatever help I can get."

"And I suppose I am? Let me tell you something. If you *don't* take pride in your work, it'll never amount to anything."

"And if you don't learn the difference between pride and arrogance, you'll never amount to anything either. I'm offering you my hand in this. Why won't you take it?"

"Because *I'm* the sheriff."

"Nobody's arguing that fact. Least of all, me."

"No. You're just going around it any way you can."

This was hopeless. But I didn't want to give up on him without a fight. The revolving door we'd had for sheriff lately wasn't doing any of us any good.

"What is it that you're so afraid I'll screw up?" I said. "Or is it bigger than both of us?"

He didn't answer.

"Is it, or isn't it?" I persisted.

"It might be," he reluctantly said.

"So that must mean that Senator Springer is somehow involved."

He turned to glare at me. For a frightening instant, I thought that he was going to reach for his gun.

"Forget you ever said that," he said.

"Then tell me why I should forget it."

"I don't have to tell you anything." Now not just his jaw, but his whole body seemed to be quivering.

"True, but don't forget that the Fourth Estate has some rights, too."

"Damn your Fourth Estate! And damn you!" he shouted. "You don't know when to leave well enough alone."

"Not unless you tell me," I said, trying to remain calm.

"Tell you what? I'm not going to tell you a damn thing."

"Then thanks for the ride."

I started to get out. Again he stopped me. "Stevey La Fountaine was blackmailing Senator Springer," he said.

"How do you know?"

"I know, that's all."

"Not good enough, Sheriff."

His sigh of exasperation steamed the windshield. "A while back I talked to an art dealer there in Madison. She said that Stevey La Fountaine was going nowhere as an artist until the Senator took a personal interest in him. He arranged showings for La Fountaine and got all of his rich friends to buy his paintings. And when the Senator moved to Oakalla, so did Stevey La Fountaine six weeks later."

"There might be other reasons why Stevey came back to Oakalla," I said. "To help put his mother in the Lutheran Home for one."

"That was his cover story. But I don't believe it."

I was starting to doubt it myself—at least until I learned whether Hubert La Fountaine had power of attorney, when he received it, and what all that implied.

"What put you on to blackmail?" I said, thinking that I was missing something in what he'd told me about Stevey. "You had to have a reason."

"The cross," he said. "And the phone calls." His voice changed at the mention of phone calls, became huskier, more intense. I wondered if he'd once been on the receiving end of some himself?

"What about the cross?" I said.

"I believe Stevey La Fountaine put it there in the Senator's yard."

"How could he have? He was in the Corner Bar and Grill almost up until the time it started burning."

"He had help."

"Who? And why?"

"I had the phone company run a check on his calls. He made several the past few weeks to an artist in Madison. The artist is known for his wood sculptures."

"Does he own a pickup?" I said. "I'd check that out before I jump to any conclusions."

"Why a pickup?"

I had to think fast or be left with my foot in my mouth. "Because that cross was heavy. Remember, I helped Stevey carry it home with him. And it was too big to fit in the trunk of a car."

"But not a van. Which is what Stevey's artist friend owns."

Why hadn't I thought of that? You could even *build* the cross in a van and no one would be the wiser.

"Then check the inside of the van for gasoline," I said.

"A can, you mean? He'd be smarter than to leave it there."

"Gasoline itself. That cross had to be soaked in it or it would never have gone up as it did."

"Since when did you become an expert on cross-burning?" The menace was back in his voice.

"I'm not. But I've built a fire or two in my life. And wood isn't as easy to burn as it seems. Not in the snow at ten below zero."

He studied me, looking for a crack in my veneer. The cop in him said that I was lying somehow, but he wasn't yet experienced enough to find the right thread to unravel me.

"You seem to have thought a lot about that cross," he said, still probing.

"As you have."

Something akin to guilt flickered across his face. "It's my job."

We sat in silence for a moment. As we did, I realized what I had missed earlier. Wayne Jacoby had said that he had to talked to an art dealer *a while back* about Stevey. But Stevey La Fountain had been dead less than twenty-four hours now.

"What about the phone calls?" I said.

"What phone calls?" His thoughts were elsewhere.

"You mentioned the cross and the phone calls in the same breath. I wondered what one had to do with the other?"

"The Senator had been receiving crank phone calls before the cross-burning."

"He told you that?"

"His wife did. Though he didn't intend for her to. When I asked if he might know of anyone who might have it in for him, and he said no, his wife said, 'What about . . .' then stopped when she realized that he didn't want her saying anything. When I called him on it, he said he did-n't know what they were about, that the caller had hung up as soon as he answered."

"He might be telling the truth."

"He might not either."

"So what did you find out when you followed up on it?"

"I found out that Stevey La Fountaine was in the phone booth right across from the Senator's house at the time the cross burned. And that he made a phone call from the Corner Bar and Grill about an hour before he was killed."

"Then that rules out the Senator. He was in Madison then."

"How do you know?"

"His wife says he was."

"And you believe her?"

"I have no reason not to. Why? Don't you?" I said.

"Not when I have it from a good source that the Senator was *not* in Madison at the time. But somewhere else."

"Oakalla?"

"I don't know. I haven't had time to check it out."

"Until you do, I'd keep an open mind."

He didn't much like that suggestion. "Why? Why are you trying so hard to defend him?"

"Why are you trying so hard to put him away? You don't like his politics, is that it?" It was a throwaway question, but he took it seriously.

"No. As a matter of fact, I don't like his politics," he said.

"Why? He seems like a law and order type of guy. Aren't you all for law and order?"

"Not for his kind of law and order. Not for yours either."

"I don't suppose you'd like to explain that?"

"You figure it out," he said, turning on his headlights. "And remember what I said. If you interfere in this investigation again, I'll have you arrested for obstructing justice."

"All because he offered you a job?"

"He offered me a bribe. There's a big difference."

"There's a big difference between making a mistake in

judgment and being in league with the devil, which is where you've put him. Me, too, by implication."

"I have my reasons."

"But they didn't start here in Oakalla." I was certain by now.

His look would have frozen the Human Torch. "I never said they did."

I got out of his patrol car and went into the building. He sat there a moment longer, then drove away.

CHAPTER 12

My phone was ringing when I opened the door to my office. I got there just in time to yell *hello* and have someone hang up on me. Wrong number, I guessed.

I intended to go right to work on Friday's edition of the *Oakalla Reporter*. Instead, I sat at my desk doing nothing at all for fifteen minutes before I picked up the receiver and called Abby. I needed to hear her voice. I needed her assurance that all was still right with our world. Just don't let the damn machine answer, I thought. I couldn't stand to hear her voice and her not to be there.

"Hello?"

I was so relieved at the sound of the real Abby that I couldn't speak right away.

"It's Garth," I finally said.

"Garth who?" she said. "The one who never returns my phone calls?"

"I hate talking to your machine."

"Why? It's the same machine I had in Oakalla."

"Except it's not in Oakalla anymore. Neither are you."

"I see," she said, sounding like she really did. "Well, I haven't changed either, if that's what you're worried about."

"That's what I'm worried about."

"Then stop. I'm far too busy to have time for that. And too involved with someone else. Let me rephrase that," she said. "Too much in love with someone else. I'm way past the involvement stage."

"Thank you. I needed that."

"You sounded like you did. What's been going on there anyway?"

Before I could answer, I felt my nape start to tingle. It was always my signal that someone was watching me, and hardly ever wrong.

"Garth? Are you still there?"

"Can you hold on a second? I think someone's looking in my window." From where I sat anyway, it looked like the frost from someone's breath on my north window pane.

"Where are you?" Concern in her voice.

"At my office. I'll just be a minute."

I went to my north window and put my face to the glass to look outside, but couldn't see anyone there. I'd just turned away when the window exploded behind me, showering me with glass. My first instinct was to drop to the floor. My second was to crawl as quickly as possible for the safety of my desk.

"Garth?" I could hear Abby yell. "What's going on there?"

My desk was solid oak and had once sat in the boiler

room of my father's dairy back in Godfrey, Indiana. With it around to crawl under, even tornadoes had seemed less a threat to me.

I reached it without any more shots being fired. Keeping all of it between me and the window but my hand, I felt for the receiver, then pulled it down to me.

"Abby, can I call you back? I think someone just took a shot at me."

"You'd better be kidding."

"I wish I were."

"Do you want me to call someone?"

"Only if I don't call you back in ten minutes or so."

"That might be too late."

"It would be anyway, by the time someone gets here."

"Garth . . ."

"Just keep the faith."

"Ten minutes. Not a second more."

I hated to leave my desk, but there was no other way to reach the door. Crawling wouldn't get it either. There was too much glass on the floor—what wasn't already in my hands.

From a four-point stance, I rocked back and forth on my heels a couple times to get some momentum, then broke for the door, slipping only at the start when my boot skidded on the hard concrete. Once outside my office and into the heart of the building where my printing press sat, I realized that I had little to offer in the way of defense, if someone confronted me, or offense, if I confronted him. But weapons had I none. The pen, you see, is mightier than the sword. That is, until you have to fight a duel with one.

I found a push broom leaning against the wall and carried it with me in my search of the building, then outside when the building proved secure. I felt stupid standing there knee deep in the snow, holding a push broom in my hand, but it was slightly better than the alternative of standing there knee deep in the snow with nothing in my hand. From a distance at least, I might look armed, which might discourage my assailant from having another go at me.

Footprints led to and away from my north window toward Gas Line Road. I wanted to follow them, but my ten minutes were about up. The last thing I wanted was for Abby to call 911, then have Sheriff Wayne Jacoby arrive on the scene.

At that, I'd just reached my office when my phone rang. "Garth? It's Abby. Are you okay?"

I looked down at my bloody palm prints on the floor—the smudges of blood on the desk and broom handle. "Okay," I said. "I think whoever it was has gone."

"You're sure of that?"

"As I can be. But the shot played hell with my north window. I'm going to have to find something to cover it."

"I wish I were there with you."

"I'm glad you're not."

"Thanks, pal. See what you get for your birthday."

"You know what I mean. I don't want someone taking potshots at you."

"I'm a big girl, remember?"

I had to smile. "How could I forget?"

"Call me later?"

"It might be late."

"I'll be up," she assured me.

In the morgue, I found a cardboard box filled with old fliers that I dumped, then flattened and carried back into my office with me. It didn't fit the window perfectly, but it would stop most of the cold air now pouring in. Then I used duct tape, the universal bonding agent, to hold it in place.

What bothered me the most when I finished was that

I could no longer see out the window. It was little consolation that neither could anyone see in to take another
shot at me. "Windows to the soul," someone once said
about eyes. Both my eyes and soul required a window.

Surveying all of the glass on the floor, I wondered how
it could have come from just one pane. The window had
probably shattered because of the cold. Had it been a
balmy summer night, I might have escaped with a small
hole in it—and perhaps in me, since I believed that the
shattering glass could have deflected the slug. Though it
was also possible that my assailant was just a bad shot.

I called Ruth before I left to let her know I was on my
way home.

"What's the occasion?" she said. "You don't usually
call."

I told her, then said, "So if I'm not there in say a half
hour or so, come looking for me."

"Why don't I come looking for you now?"

"Because there's no sense in us both getting shot."

"We have a sheriff, you know."

"I know." I hung up.

The night outside was cold and still, the sky gradually
widening as the clouds drifted away to the east. I followed
the footprints away from my north window as far as Gas
Line Road where I lost them. I picked them up again a
block west of there where they veered through a patch of
newly fallen snow onto the sidewalk. At the intersection of
Perrin Street and Gas Line Road, I spent several minutes
trying to find their direction from there, but had no luck.
Neither could I determine the size or the sex of my
assailant by the size of the footprints. They were perhaps
a half inch shorter than mine, but that might not mean
anything. Small people sometimes had big feet and vice
versa. And the soles of most boots no longer came marked
with a m or an f.

All the lights were on at home when I got there. Either Ruth was throwing a party or something had happened since I'd called.

"What goes on here when I'm away?" I said as I came in the front door.

Ruth sat on the living room couch with a magazine in her hands and a hammer in her lap. With a joyful woof!, Daisy came racing in from the kitchen to greet me.

Ruth gave me a frosty look. "I was hoping you'd tell me. No sooner was I off the phone with you than Daisy began to raise a ruckus in the basement, wanting out. I let her out and she made a beeline for the back door, and from there to the garage. The next thing I knew, headlights came on and a car took off down the alley, hell-bent for election. So then I had to go out and drag Daisy back inside because she's clawing her way up the back gate, determined to chase whoever was here."

"Which way down the alley?" I said.

"North."

Daisy shot past me as I went out the back door and headed straight for the back gate, where she did her best imitation of Spiderman, as she tried to climb it. Little did she realize that she could easily jump it, and had jumped higher obstacles when grouse hunting with Doc Airhart and me. Or maybe she did realize, and wanted me to save her the trouble.

"Come on, Daisy," I said, picking her up and carrying her inside, where I put her in the basement. "Tomorrow is another day."

Then I went back outside and around to our south kitchen window to see if any footprints remained from Monday night. They were still there, but clouded by today's snow, so it was hard to tell if they matched the ones that I'd followed on my way home. Their size was about right, though, as they appeared a little smaller than my own.

Back inside the house again, I went into the downstairs bathroom and returned with tweezers, needle, cotton and a bottle of alcohol. Meanwhile Ruth had moved to the kitchen and put on a pot of coffee. I got the message. It was time for a council of war.

"What's that for?" Ruth said, as I set the things from the medicine chest on the table and went to hang up my coat.

I showed her the palms of my hands.

"Go wash the blood off."

The next fifteen minutes were a lot harder on me than they were on Ruth. She never even pretended that it hurt her a lot more than it did me, as she pinched, pulled, and dug the slivers of glass from my hand. But she was good at it, and in the end her single-minded concentration and determination saved more pain than if she had tried to be gentle.

"Thanks," I said when the last shard was out.

"You're welcome."

It seemed folly to dab at each cut in turn, so when she was finished, I went into the bathroom and washed my hands with alcohol. As my father was fond of saying about such particularly excruciating moments, it sure took my mind off of sex for a while.

When I returned, Ruth had poured us each a cup of coffee and set mine on the table. "So what gives?" she said as I sat down. "First, I get a phone call with no on there; then somebody parks in our alley with their motor running and their lights off."

Daisy whined from behind the basement door, as if she were wondering the same thing.

I took a sip of my coffee before answering. Everything considered, I felt I owed myself that much.

"What time did you get the call?" I said.

"I don't know for sure. A while before you called."

"As much as an hour?"

"Maybe even longer. I wasn't keeping track."

I took another sip of coffee. Now that the initial shock had worn off, my hands were starting to hurt.

"That doesn't make sense to me," I said. "Why come by here when they knew you were home?"

"They?"

"It's just a figure of speech."

"Maybe they weren't calling to find out whether we were home. Maybe *they* were calling to find out if *you* were home."

She waited to let that sink in, but tonight I wasn't a very quick study. "And?" I said.

"And when they found out you weren't, they called the *Oakalla Reporter* to see if you were there."

Bingo! I remembered the call that I thought was a wrong number. "It's possible you might be on to something."

She gave me her Cheshire cat smile.

"So here's what I want you to do," I said, hoping to slip one by her in the heat of the moment. But I should've known better.

"It's not that late, Garth. I'm not that tired."

"Damn it, I need help, Ruth." I held out my hands to prey on her sympathy. "This is personal now."

In her wisdom, she said, "When is it not personal when it has to do with Oakalla?"

"Not just Oakalla this time. Me too."

She thought a moment, then said, "So which are you really after, the new sheriff, or the one who took a shot at you?"

"I don't know that they're not one and the same."

"I think you do."

"Hear me out, Ruth. Wayne Jacoby came into this job

with a chip on his shoulder. Not only against me, but
Senator Springer as well. With me, it might just be general
principles, and I'll admit I haven't given him any reason to
think otherwise. But with Senator Springer, I know there's
more to it than that. Wayne Jacoby admitted as much to
me tonight."

"Be that as it may, I don't see how that is any of your
concern."

"Somebody took a shot at me, Ruth. I must be stepping
on somebody's toes, which means I'm involved whether I
want to be or not."

"Not if you don't keep at it. Tonight might have been
just a warning."

I'd also considered that possibility, but wouldn't admit
it to her. "What will it take for you to help me?" I said.

She sat back in her chair, put both hands around her
cup of coffee and said, "Tell me about your day."

"All of it?"

"All of it." Her brows rose in questions. "Unless
there's something you think I shouldn't hear?"

"Okay," I said. "Here goes."

When I finished an hour later, she took a moment to
digest what I had said, then leaned forward and put both
elbows on the table. "What do you mean by 'electric'?"
she said in reference to Wendy Bodine. "How can anybody
be electric?"

She had fastened on the one thing that I had hoped
she would ignore. But knowing her, I shouldn't have been
surprised.

"What I mean by electric is that there's a sensuality
about her that goes beyond reason. You don't really care
what she is, only what she projects."

"Which is?"

"I thought I explained that."

"Not to my satisfaction."

"Sexiness, for lack of a better word. You don't necessarily want to marry her, but you sure as hell would like to sleep with her. It even goes beyond that, but I don't know how to put it."

"Just like that?" She clapped her hands.

"Just like that."

She grew very quiet, and thoughtful.

"What is it, Ruth?"

"Nothing."

"What do you mean, nothing?"

"That's what I mean, nothing."

"Then you won't help me?"

She leaned back in her chair. "On the contrary, I don't see now how I can't."

CHAPTER 13

My night didn't go as planned. After I called Abby, I had wanted to go straight to bed and fall into a deep sleep that would last at least until dawn. I went right to bed after my phone call, but sleep was hard to come by. First, my mind wouldn't stop talking to itself; then my hands started to throb. When sleep finally did come, it was a restless sleep, filed with dreams that kept running in circles, repeating themselves. Neither good dreams nor bad dreams, but tireless, relentless, monotonous dreams, the kind you have when you're coming down with something.

I awakened sore and chilled, feeling like I had boxing gloves for hands. But on closer inspection, once I got the rocks out of my eyes, they didn't look as bad as they felt.

"So what are you up to today?" Ruth asked after I had

made my way downstairs.

She had fixed scrambled eggs, bacon, and toast for breakfast, and already had the catsup and the strawberry jam on the table.

"Today, come what may, I'm spending at my office, working on the *Reporter*. What about you?"

"I plan to work on some things."

I smiled. I was hoping to hear that.

At six that Thursday evening, I left my office for the first time. Except for my column, which I had yet to write, the *Oakalla Reporter* was all ready to go. I'd also managed to sweep the glass up off the floor and in so doing found what I assumed to be a .22 short slug. It was so flat that at first I mistook it for a piece of gum, until I bent down to scrape it up. Examining it, I was amazed at how anything so bland looking could do so much damage to the human body. But then I suppose that the same thing could be said for a land mine.

When I stepped outside for the first time in eleven hours and saw that it was dark again, I realized that i'd spent the entire day without once looking at the sky. Had it been grey, white, or blue, or some variation thereof? Neither had I watched at the window, since I had no window, to see what direction the wind was blowing or what might be in the air. I was reminded of my college days at the University of Wisconsin - Madison, when, insulated and isolated from everything but myself, I never noticed the weather until the snow filled my shoes. Since then, I had often wished for that same security, that same cocksure ignorance that no matter what I did, everything would turn out all right in the end.

Sometimes I ate in the barroom of the Corner Bar and Grill and sometimes I ate in the dining room, separated from the barroom by two wooden swinging doors, like those of the saloons of the Wild West. Tonight I ate in the bar because I wanted to talk to Hiram.

Hiram came all the way across the barroom to take my order. Normally I would have sat at the bar or in Abby's and my booth, but tonight I wanted our conversation to be as private as possible.

"What will it be, Garth?" Hiram said.

"The usual." Which on Thursday was a fish sandwich, slaw, and a Dr. Pepper. "And Hiram, when you get a minute, I need to talk to you."

"Let me put your order in first."

Unlike nearly every other town in Wisconsin, which seemed to have a bar for every block, Oakalla only had the Corner Bar and Grill. How it had evolved that way, I never knew, never really cared to know, since I liked having only one place to go whenever I wanted a sandwich and a beer, or maybe pork steak and dressing with pea salad on the side. Not great food, but good enough. Not great atmosphere either, but comfortable, like that old University of Wisconsin sweatshirt that I could no longer read the lettering on. Would competition have changed the Corner Bar and Grill, its "come as you are" mentality that made it Oakalla's natural gathering place and watering hole? Again, I didn't know. Hopefully, would never have to know.

Hiram brought my slaw and Dr. Pepper. "Fire away, Garth. I think everyone's set for now."

"Stevey La Fountaine," I said. "From the start, was he in here about every night?"

"Every night we were open."

"And he usually closed the place, right?"

"Right. He'd come in about now or a little later and stay until I'd run him out, which was usually about two or so."

I took a drink of my Dr. Pepper. It wasn't Leinenkugel's, but then not much else was.

"Did you ever see him make any phone calls?"

Hiram shook his head no. "Nope. Not that I recall."

"You're sure?"

"Well, I'm in and out of here, Garth, but usually not for very long at a time."

"What about the night he was killed? Didn't he make a phone call then?" Which was what Wayne Jacoby had told me.

"I can't rightly say, Garth, now that you mention it. He was on the phone when I came up from downstairs, but he hung up right away and said loud enough for everybody in the place to hear that it was a wrong number."

"But you don't know how long he was on the phone, or even if he made the call?"

"Nope. I'd run out of beer in one of the kegs and gone down to the cooler for another. Whatever happened did so while I was gone."

"Is there anyone in here tonight who might have been in here then?"

Hiram glanced at all of the regulars sitting around the bar. "Chances are they all might have been here then. But I'll have to ask."

"Try to be discreet. I'd rather that Sheriff Jacoby didn't know that I'd been asking."

Hiram looked doubtful. "I'll do my best, Garth. But discreet this place is not."

I hadn't mentioned the downside of having only one bar in town, which was that everybody knew everybody else's business. Or thought they did. What they didn't know was sometimes frightening, as Rupert Roberts took pains to show me several nights running when I first came to town.

A moment later I saw Hiram leaning over to talk to Phil Wettschurack, who was at the north end of the bar. Soon it grew quiet in there, as the other regulars strained to hear what they were talking about. When Hiram returned to my table, he brought my fish sandwich with him.

"Phil says that the phone started ringing, and when no one in the bar would answer it, Stevey, who was the closest one to it, got up and answered it himself."

"Was he on there long?"

"Long enough for Phil to know it wasn't a wrong number."

Why did that bother me? It bothered me because the phone call could have come from anywhere—either in or out of Oakalla.

"How long after that did Stevey leave?" I said.

"About an hour, give or take a few minutes. He kept checking the clock, and the next thing I knew he was on his way out."

"Which door?"

Hiram hung his head to one side and squinted. "The one here in the bar, I think."

"And the night the cross burned?"

"He went out the front door. It made me wonder later."

"About what?"

"Why he went out that way when it was below zero outside. It been me, I'd have taken the shortest way home."

It made me wonder, too.

"Especially after what happened earlier," Hiram said.

He had my attention. "Go on."

But someone at the bar was waving at Hiram, wanting another drink. "I'll be right back."

I'd managed to eat most of my fish sandwich by the time he returned. Perch, it tasted like. Good, whatever it was.

"I asked Phil while I was at it," Hiram said. "He thinks Stevey went out the bar door, too."

"So odds are, he was directly on his way home the night he was killed."

"Odds are."

I stuffed the last of my sandwich into my mouth and washed it down with the last of my Dr. Pepper. "About Monday?" I said to Hiram, who appeared deep in thought.

"How did he know to call here?" he said to me.

"Who?"

"Whoever shot Stevey La Fountaine. How did he know to call here for him, unless he knew Stevey's habits pretty well?"

"Why does that bother you?" I said, because it obviously did.

"Because the word is out that the Sheriff thinks the Senator did it. But how would the Senator know Stevey well enough to know where he'd be?"

I didn't say anything in the hope that Hiram wouldn't press me on it, and was rewarded when he said, "Anyway, what happened Monday night was that Hubert La Fountaine came into the bar late, got Stevey over in this corner, and read the riot act to him about something."

"How late?"

"Close to midnight, I'd say."

"You have any idea what the problem was?"

"I only caught bits and pieces. I'd be afraid to say for sure."

"Then give me your best guess."

Someone at the bar was waving for Hiram again, but Hiram didn't see her, and I ignored her. "I think it had to do with that property of theirs," Hiram said. "You know, the one on Fair Haven Road where Stevey was living. Hubert was accusing Stevey of double-crossing him and Stevey kept denying it."

"Do you know if Hubert has power of attorney on that property now that his mother is incompetent?"

"Stevey said something to that effect. He claimed all that power was going to Hubert's head, making him a worse Scrooge than their father ever was."

"Was this during their argument?"

"Afterwards. After Hubert had left."

"Do you know when Hubert got power of attorney, before or after Stevey came to town?"

"I have no idea, Garth. I didn't even know he had it until Stevey mentioned it. Why don't you talk to Wilmer Wiemer? He might know. He knows everything else about that sort of thing."

Maggie Gray had given up on Hiram and gone after her own beer. She acted as if she'd done it before.

"What happened after that?" I said.

"Stevey started acting funny. You know, not at all like himself. Usually a train could go through here, and it would be something if Stevey even gave it a look. He wasn't in a stupor or anything, but pretty much keeping to his own thoughts. But after Hubert had that talk with him, it got him all worked up, so that he'd talk to anybody who would listen about what a sorry lot his family was, Hubert in particular. Then he slammed his fist down on the bar—he'd run everybody else out of here by then—and walked out the front door."

"And how long after that did you say the fire siren rang?"

"Five minutes or so. Long enough for me to finish cleaning up in here."

"Then Stevey *could* have called the fire in?"

"I thought he had?" Hiram was surprised that it could be any other way.

"According to Stevey, the fire siren started ringing the minute he walked out the door."

"No. That's not the way I remember it happening at all. Besides, Stevey was still in the phone booth when I got there. That's why I was so sure he called it in."

"Doing what in the phone booth?"

Hiram seldom smiled. But when he did, you knew you were in for a treat. "He wasn't changing clothes, if that's what you're thinking."

"No big *S* on his chest?"

"None that I could see."

"Then it appears Stevey was lying. I wonder why?" I mused aloud.

"Good luck finding out," Hiram said, as he went back to tending bar.

My next stop after the Corner Bar and Grill was not one that I wanted to make. Its purpose was one of the things that had kept me awake in the night, and no matter how hard I tried to deny the obvious, I still came to the same conclusion. But had I never met Wendy Bodine, I never would have believed it.

I was relieved to find Danny Palmer alone in the Marathon. By day, he usually had company in the person of Sniffy Smith and some of the other retirees in town, like Dub Bennett and Harvey Wiggins, but who at night wandered off into other haunts, likely the back room of the Corner Bar and Grill where they would play euchre until it was time to go home.

As a rule, Danny saved his biggest jobs for night when he was officially closed, and there were no customers or "helpers" to distract him. Tonight he had someone's engine torn apart. A mechanical dropout, who, in my father's words, couldn't figure out the mechanism of a potato masher, I was always amazed when Danny did something like that, and even more amazed when he put it all back together with no parts left over. His only failure in all of the years that I had known him, was my car, Jezebel, alias Jessie, who despite Danny's best efforts, ran strictly at her own convenience.

"What's it like outside?" Danny asked. "The last time I was out, it felt like it was warming up."

Now that he mentioned it, it *had* felt warmer outside. Softer, too, if I could explain that.

"The stars are out," I said. "And you're right, it does feel a little warmer."

"Maybe we're headed for our January thaw." Danny had stopped turning bolts to wipe the grease off his hands. "Or a snow. It always warms up before it snows."

"Usually anyway."

He picked up a zip-lock bag of what looked like fried chicken and sat down at the well-worn wooden desk where he figured his bills and did most of his ordering of parts. "You want a piece?" he offered, as he opened the bag.

"Thanks. But I just finished supper."

I glanced around the station where he had spent so much of his life, first as an attendant, then as a mechanic, then as part owner, and finally as full owner. Cool and always drafty, the station smelled of grease and oil, exhaust fumes and cigarette smoke, and there was never quite the right light to work by, no matter what the day outside. But Danny rarely complained, and when he did, he had good reason. And it was his abiding presence, his good humor and infectious energy, that gave the place its life—something that it had been missing lately.

"What are you thinking, Garth?" he said. "I know it can't be good."

"I'm thinking that I'd hate to see you lose this place, or the other way around."

"I don't think there's much danger of that." But he wasn't as convincing as he intended to be.

I said, "We've been friends for how long, going on fifteen years now? So we know each other pretty well, right?"

"Right."

"And we both admit that Jessie is bigger than both of us . . ."

"Bigger than life itself, I'd say. What other car do you know that can think for itself without a computer?" He said between bites on a drumstick.

"So why don't we admit that Wendy Bodine is also bigger than both of us and go on from there?"

He dropped the drumstick back into the plastic bag and zipped the bag closed. "I wasn't hungry anyway."

"You look like you could use it." By my estimation , he'd lost close to ten pounds the past couple months, which was ten more than he could afford to lose.

"No. I don't have much of an appetite for anything anymore, Garth."

"Because she's leaving Saturday?"

"That and because I'm in love with her."

That was what I was afraid of. "So what are you going to do?"

"There's nothing to do, Garth. It's over between us. It was as soon as Dudley Do-Right hit town."

"But not if you had your druthers?"

"No. It was her decision, not mine."

"You were fully prepared to run off with her?"

Danny looked like he wanted to cry. "Yes."

"And leave Sharon and the kids behind?"

"That pretty much goes without saying, doesn't it?" He sat back in his chair and glanced outside, as if looking for a way to step outside his pain. "I know what you're thinking. It's Amber Utley all over again. But that was a fantasy. This is real."

Amber Utley had starred in some of my fantasies, too—at least until Abby Pence-Airhart had arrived on the scene and rewrote the script. But Danny was right. Though both were young, blond, and beautiful, there was a vast difference between Wendy Bodine and Amber Utley.

I likened it to the difference between a lynx and a tabby.

"So you haven't spent all of your time admiring her from afar?"

His look said, "What do you think?"

"I'll pray for you."

"Garth, this is serious."

"I know it's serious. I met the woman—eye to eye in her apartment. You're not telling me anything I don't already know."

"When were you in her apartment?" His was not a happy face.

"Last night. I was trying to get a fix on Merle La Fountaine, among other things."

"What does she have to do with anything?"

"Her son was shot to death a couple nights ago. Remember?"

Danny got up and began to pace. "Shit, Garth, has it come to that? I really had forgotten."

Love can do that to you. Good love, bad love, both can steal your mind. But especially the rollercoaster of bad love, which, when you catch your breath again, always leaves you anxious for the next ride.

"Will you help me out in this, Danny? I'm at a loss right now."

"Help you out in what?" He'd stopped in front of his overhead door and was looking out at Jackson Street.

"The Wayne Jacoby saga. I need to learn more about him." And perhaps Wendy Bodine in the process.

"What can I tell you about Wayne Jacoby, except that I think he's an asshole?"

"When did he start sleeping with Wendy Bodine, for starters?"

"How would I know that?"

"By calling his house to see if he answered. By calling hers to see if she answered."

He put both hands on the overhead door and rested his head there a moment on the cold glass. "I never thought I'd stoop to that, Garth. It made me feel like a stalker."

"Don't be too hard on yourself, Danny. We've all been there at one time or another. At the edge, I mean. Ready to jump off, if necessary, to show her just how much we love her."

He returned to his desk and sat down. He didn't believe me, but that was okay. It seemed so long ago that I had trouble believing it myself.

"I don't know exactly when they did start sleeping together, Garth. He'd no more hit town, it seemed, than she was saying goodbye."

"Did she give you any warning?"

I could tell by his look that she apparently had. "She said it wouldn't last, it couldn't last. I was a family man, and even if I could ignore that, she couldn't. Also, from the first, she kept dropping hints. Like, were all the winters here as bad as last winter? And how could I stand it, not being near the ocean? Things that made me think that she never intended on staying here."

"Where is she from originally?"

"Florida, I think. At least that's where she's headed now."

"What brought her up here?"

"I don't know, Garth," he said, starting to pace again. "I think she said that she had a favorite aunt in Madison, who talked her into coming up after her parents died. From what I understand, they had her pretty late in life, so it wasn't as much of a shock as it might have been when they did die. Anyway, she tried living and working in Madison for a year, but when that didn't work out, she came here. She loves her job, she says. But she really misses Florida."

"Who wouldn't, considering our weather lately?"

He just shrugged. He was trying to make his peace with it, but reason wasn't one of the things he wanted to listen to.

"Is that where you went after the fire Monday night, to her place?" I said.

His hesitation made me wonder if he was going to answer. But then he said, "Yes, but she wouldn't let me in. She said that if we started up again, we might not be able to stop."

"Did you believe her?"

"I wanted to."

"What about that wrecker call you had yesterday, or was her showing up here right afterwards just a coincidence?"

"Not a coincidence," she said. "I'd said all I had to say, but apparently she hadn't. She might as well have saved her breath, though."

"Why is that?"

His face was strained, as he tried not to cry. "She said she loved me. Would always love me. And maybe someday I'd understand." He could no longer hold back the tears. "If she loves me so goddamned much, then why is she leaving without me? And why did she ever take up with an asshole like Dudley Do-Right?"

"Maybe to help you get over her."

"Well, she's doing a piss-poor job of it."

I had to look away. Seeing tears on Danny's cheek was too much like seeing them on my own. Some of us, though I don't know why, are supposed to be above all that.

"Monday night," I said, "had you tried to call her earlier?"

"Yes. I kept getting her machine."

"Because Wayne Jacoby was there with her?"

"That's what I thought anyway. There was no reason for her not to be home. Why are you asking?"

"She said he was there until about a half-hour before

the fire. I was double-checking."

"Why?" he persisted.

"Because I can't be sure that he didn't burn the cross himself."

"Why would he do something like that? I mean, I don't like the man and all, but I have my reasons."

"He has it in for Senator Springer," I said as I prepared to leave. "When I know why, maybe I can answer that question."

"I've always liked the Senator myself. I'll probably vote for him if he runs for governor."

"Same here. But his chances aren't looking too good right now." I stopped at the door to put on my gloves and stocking cap. Warmer or not, it was still a long way from balmy outside. "By the way, you notice the smell of gas in the bed of anyone's truck today?"

But Danny didn't appear to be listening. In fact, it seemed to take all his strength just to hold himself up.

CHAPTER 14

I spent the next few hours writing my column—feeling the whole time that Ruth was there looking over my shoulder, shaking her head. She had said more than once lately that it was time to get off my soapbox, that if I kept up my harping, whether people agreed with me or not, they were soon going to turn a deaf ear.

For once, I agreed with her and had been fully prepared to write on something innocent and nostalgic, like attics, and the lasting pleasures and treasures that they hold for those of us who like to visit them every now and again.

Then, while rummaging through the morgue for items for my "It Happened When?" monthly column, I found quotes from a speech made in 1927 by Glen Frank, then president of the University of Wisconsin, on the subject of education. He scorned the conception of schools as a cure-all for social and economic ills and pointed out that the community is the most important unit in the educational system of the nation. Then he said, "Real education never has nor never will come of organized mind factories . . . We are doomed if we depend on our school system alone to save us. The school and the social order must be saved together or sink together."

Had I been able to ignore Dr. Frank's remarks, I would have had a hard time ignoring those made nearly thirty years later by Bishop Fulton Sheen on sparing the rod and spoiling the child . . . "Schools are geared today to the imparting of information rather than to education. There is a world of difference between information and education. Information is the filling of the mind with knowledge, very much the same way as water is poured into a glass. . . Education on the contrary has its roots in the words 'educere' and means the drawing out of the powers of the mind and heart and will. . . The imparting of information requires no discipline, no character formation, no obedience, but only a passive reception."

Both Dr. Frank and Bishop Sheen had said a lot more, but the gist of what they said, and the heart of my column was that in order to educate children, you needed: (1) discipline within the school and (2) a community surrounding and embracing it.

More and more money for education, as the politicians and the professional educators would have us believe, wasn't the answer. If it were, the hundreds of billions of dollars that we'd spent over the past thirty years would have solved the problem by now, or at least improved it. Neither was the answer in bigger and better buildings, the computers in every classroom, and the administrators on every level that the money would be spent on—instead of on hiring the very best teachers, where it would do the most good. Neither could we pray our way to better education any more than we could pay our way to it.

My solution? Give the schools back to the communities from whence they came and let us on the local level run them as we saw fit. Did that open up a new-old can of worms, like separate and unequal? Unfortunately. But how many schools were equal now and just what did that mean anyway—that now we all could have drugs in our lockers, bars on our windows, and riots in our cafeterias? Did returning the schools to the local level include private and parochial schools and tax credits for education? I surely hoped so. The government didn't make our shoes. I didn't know why we expected it to make our kids. Did my solution mean that all the problems of education would now be solved? No. But the problem would be just that, a local problem, instead of a national crisis, as it was now. And the children of Oakalla only would have to suffer the fools of Oakalla, instead of the fools of Washington and/or Madison, too.

When I finished writing my column, it was after eleven, and I was about to call my printer when Senator Jonathan Springer walked in my office door. He wore his camel's hair coat with a green plaid scarf folded carefully inside it and tan leather gloves that matched his coat. His blond hair looked frosty in my office light. The rest of him, including his grey-blue eyes, looked tired.

"Have a seat, Senator," I said, putting my ancient Underwood back on its shelf. "Coffee?"

He shook his head no as he sat down. "Is that new?" He was looking at the cardboard over my window.

"The cardboard isn't. Its placement is."

"That's what I meant. What happened to your window?"

I sat back down at my desk. "You just get into town?" I said.

"You're my first stop." When he saw the confusion on

my face, he added, "Allison said you wanted to see me."

Then I remembered. I had wanted to ask him about the cross-burning. But that seemed eons ago.

"As a matter of fact, I did want to see you," I said. "Any ideas about who burned that cross in your yard?"

"I thought I'd already covered that territory." He removed his gloves, but left his coat on.

"Not with me, you didn't."

"Then I'll tell you the same thing that I told our illustrious sheriff. I have no idea who burned that cross in our yard."

"What about the crank calls? You have any idea who was making them?"

"I might," he said, staring at the cardboard, which was doing a poor job of keeping the cold out. "If you'll tell me what happened to the window?"

"Someone took a shot at me and missed. But that's not public knowledge," I said. "Our sheriff doesn't even know."

"Why would someone take a shot at you?" he said.

"Hard to say. Maybe they don't like my writing."

"It would seem to make more sense just to cancel their subscription."

"That's what I thought, too."

Neither spoke for a moment as he continued to stare at the cardboard, while I continued to stare at him. Now that I thought about it, he looked more than tired to me. He looked defeated, like a man who had just lost a hard-fought election.

"You were about to tell me about the phone calls," I said.

"Was I?" He seemed to be having a hard time pulling his gaze from the cardboard window. "How do you stand it in here, not being able to see out?"

"I don't stand it very well. But since I'm the one who'll

have to replace the window, it will have to wait for a warmer day."

"That might not be until spring. Why don't I replace it for you?"

"You mean have it done?"

"I mean do it myself this weekend. I should have Sunday free."

"Why would you want to?"

He turned to look at me. I saw sadness in his eyes. "Because I feel somehow responsible. I asked you to sit on this thing and you did. Then someone takes a shot at you."

"One might not have anything to do with the other," I said. "I haven't spent all of my time 'sitting' either."

"Still, I'd like to do it."

He seemed so determined that I hated to turn him down, even though I really didn't want to be bothered with it. "Then I'll help you," I said. "How about two o'clock Sunday afternoon? I'll meet you here with the glass and the putty."

"It's a deal," he said with a smile.

I wished I didn't like the man so. It would have made things a lot easier all the way around.

"We still have something on the table," I reminded him.

He sat slumped in the chair, now looking at the west wall at some point between me and the window. "I don't know who was making the phone calls," he said. "But they've since stopped."

"Since Monday night or Tuesday night?"

"Since I was last home, which was Tuesday morning."

"What exactly was said in these calls?"

"Nothing, for the most part. They'd hang up as soon as I'd answer."

"Except?"

"Except one night Allison and I were in different parts

of the house when the call came. She was already in bed,
I think, and I was reading the paper. By the time I got to a
phone, she'd already answered. 'Nigger lover,' someone
said. Then hung up."

"A man or a woman?"

"I don't know. A serpent's voice, it sounded like. Full
of venom."

"Not Stevey La Fountaine's voice?"

"No. I would have recognized it."

He calmly sat back in his chair and waited, like a man
before a firing squad, as if he already knew what was coming
next, but was helpless to get out of the way. I wished he
weren't so perceptive. It would have made me feel less a
heel.

"The rumor is that you had been bankrolling Stevey
La Fountaine. Is there any truth to that?"

"Yes. But it's not a rumor. It's a well-known fact in
Madison."

"Why? My sources say he was no good as an artist."

"Your sources are wrong."

I waited to see if he was serious. He seemed to be.

"Have *you* ever seen any of his work?" he asked.

"No," I had to admit.

"Do, the next chance you get. And I don't mean all the
pap he put out for sale, because he thought that's what the
public wanted. But the good stuff he kept for himself.
There's a world of difference between the two."

"Have you any of his good stuff?" Because I didn't
remember seeing anything extraordinary on my visit to
his house. Except for Allison Springer, who was in her own
classic way a work of art.

"Yes. It's hanging in my office in the State House."

"And everything that you did for him was only because
you liked his work and wanted to promote it?"

His face tightened in anger as he reached for his gloves

to put them back on. "Yes. That was my only reason. Who says differently?"

I was tempted to tell him, but that would be going too far in the name of friendship. "It doesn't matter. It was said, that's all."

He stood, his eyes taking in the window once more. "Sunday at two," he said.

"I'll be here."

CHAPTER 15

Sometime after two A.M. my printer and I put the *Oakalla Reporter* to bed, and it was after three when we finished loading them into his old green Pontiac station wagon, and he took off for the post office. As always, he offered me a ride, and as always, I refused. I needed the walk home to help me unwind, to let my shoulders droop and my mind settle—to think about nothing but the stars overhead and how big it all was; and how I would always be amazed at that, and sorry that I would never get the chance to see clear to the other side.

It seemed that I'd no more hit the bed and rolled over when I smelled coffee perking downstairs. As long as they were busy, which included all of yesterday, my hands gave me no problem. But the minute that they stopped, something akin to rigor mortis set in, and I awakened feeling as if I'd gone fifteen rounds with a concrete post. Unlike yesterday morning, they had swollen to near bee sting proportions, and made any needlepoint that I had planned today seem out of the question. Next time I might just let them shoot me. It would be a lot less painful.

"Morning," I said to Ruth, who was busy at the stove fixing biscuits and gravy. "What's it like outside?"

"Dark, the last time I looked."

"The stars still out?"

"Why don't you see for yourself."

I heard Daisy whining at the basement door and let her out. But instead of heading straight for the kitchen as I thought she would, she wanted outside. Just to run, it turned out. I smiled, wondering what it would feel like to have that much energy again.

Neither Ruth nor I said much during breakfast. We had home-canned apples along with the biscuits and sausage gravy and two cups of coffee apiece. Once our bellies were full and our brains had started to purr, we felt more like talking.

"So what did you learn yesterday?" I said.

Ruth was letting our dirty dishes sit. That meant she had a lot to tell me.

"Where do you want me to start?" she said.

"Allison Springer. Did she actually live here once, as she said she did?"

"According to Mary Beth Robinson, she did. She lived in that little house right north of the Marathon."

"Where Ellen La Fountaine is living now?"

"Where Ellen La Fountaine *was* living before her brother got himself shot and she moved back in her old house."

"I thought Marvin Heckel, Merle La Fountaine's father, owned that place?" I said.

"He did. But after he moved across the street, he'd

rent it out from time to time."

"When did Allison Springer live there?"

"Late 1960s, early 1970s, somewhere in there. She was only there a year or two at the most, Mary Beth says."

"How did Mary Beth happen to know her?" I asked.

"She did Herman's and Mary Beth's taxes one year. She was as sharp as they come, according to Mary Beth, for someone so young. She saved them a bundle of money."

"I wonder if she did Marvin Heckel's taxes, too?" I said. "Maybe as a way of helping out with the rent."

"I can try to find out, if you think it's important." She had her doubts.

"You never know, Ruth. Give it a try."

Dark had given way to dusk outside. The night was no longer flat against the window.

"Where were we?" she said, as she drank the last of her coffee.

"You were about to tell me all you knew about Allison Springer."

"There's not much more to tell. Her husband ran out on her, and when she could no longer pay the rent, she left town."

"Why did he run out on her?"

"Mary Beth said that he was quite a bit older than she was, and somewhat of a philanderer. And mean besides. He would have kept the poor girl chained to his bed, if he could've gotten away with it. When she stood up to him and threatened to take him to court, he decided to cut his losses and run."

"Then he had money?"

Ruth's look said she wasn't so sure. "That's kind of iffy, Garth. He liked to spend what he had, so there might not have been much left over."

"Did he leave her barefoot and pregnant, as she claims?"

"Next to barefoot, if not. And Mary Beth always thought that she was pregnant. She wasn't showing yet, but she had all of the symptoms."

"Does Mary Beth remember what her last name was then?"

"Taylor, she believes it was. Or Tatum. One or the other. Why?"

"I think I'll have Clarkie check her out."

"For a police record, you mean?" She didn't see the point.

"That, and the fact that she says she lost her baby. What if she didn't lose it, but had an abortion, which was illegal then? How would that play on the Senator's family values record?"

"He's never come out against abortion."

"He's never come out in favor of it either. And a lot of people who've voted for him lately are against it."

Ruth still was skeptical. "How could Clarkie find out if she had an abortion, even if it were an issue? He's good with a computer, but he's not that good. He can't find something that's not there."

"No. But he could find out if someone named Allison Taylor ever miscarried. There should be a hospital record of it somewhere."

"Not if she never made it to the hospital."

"But if she did, we can rule out one of the reasons that Stevey La Fountaine might have for blackmailing Jonathan Springer."

Ruth rose to pour us another cup of coffee. I didn't necessarily want another cup, but right now I needed it just to get through the morning.

"You still think Stevey was blackmailing the Senator?" she said.

"Until I can prove otherwise. Wayne Jacoby wouldn't have told me that for nothing."

"He might have to throw you off the scent."

"The scent of what?"

"Whatever is really going on."

"I don't think he's that smart, Ruth."

"You've been fooled before," she was quick to point out.

"And I'm not alone."

Ruth returned to the table. Meanwhile the day continued to unfold. Though dark and fuzzy now, in a few more minutes the trees across the way would start to take shape.

"You were right about Wilmer Wiemer," she said. "He does have his finger in the pie. But you'll never guess whose pie it is."

"Then why don't you tell me." It was too early to have to think that hard.

"Hubert La Fountaine's."

"You're right. I never would have guessed. Are you saying that Wilmer is trying to buy Hubert's own property from Hubert for Hubert?"

"That's what Mildred Dixon says."

"How does she know?"

"She works for Wilmer part-time in his real estate office. That's why you can't say anything to anyone, or Wilmer's bound to know where it came from."

"I don't see how I can get around it, Ruth, if I'm going to do anything with it."

"I'm just telling you what Mildred said. If it gets out, I'll never hear the end of it."

Now a deep dusky blue, the sky would begin to lighten as the sun approached the horizon. From all appearances, it was going to be a beautiful day. I planned to soak up as much of it as possible.

"Why go to all of that trouble?" I said to Ruth. "I'm talking about Hubert La Fountaine. Why not simply make your brother and sister an offer on the place?"

"Because in the first place Ellen wouldn't sell out to him, if she had a say in the matter, which she does. She likes things just the way they are—her on the inside and everybody else, including Hubert, on the outside."

"Even if Hubert has power of attorney, which I think he does?"

"I was getting to that. If, through Hubert's power of attorney, the property *is* put up for sale, Ellen has a right to demand fair value for her share. And don't forget whose property it is in the first place, which is Merle La Fountaine's. By law, she should get at least half and everybody else is in for a third, now a half with Stevey dead, of what's left. So it's not as simple as you make it seem. If it goes up for sale, Ellen can insist on the highest bid, which might not be Hubert's. So by using Wilmer as a front, Hubert is hoping to put one over on Ellen."

"There's something else we might consider," I said. "Wilmer might be planning to put one over on everybody. I wouldn't put it past him."

"I thought you said that Wilmer said the property wasn't worth buying?"

"He did, but I'm not sure that I believe him, seeing how intent everyone is on getting that property for himself. Then there's the matter of the fight that Hubert had with Stevey. I'm not sure where it fits in, if anywhere."

"What fight?"

I told her what happened at the Corner Bar and Grill.

"Maybe Stevey changed his mind," Ruth said, "and decided to throw his lot in with Ellen."

"That would be a revolting development, if you were Hubert," I said. "But why would Stevey change his mind at that late date?"

"Maybe she made him a better offer."

Dawn was now upon us. There was a pink glow to the sky not there before, and right at the horizon, the sun sent up a single bright orange plume, like a distant fire.

"Maybe she did," I agreed. "Stevey didn't seem a man to stand on principle."

"Speaking of which, I read the paper you brought home with you."

"And?"

"Like I said, it's time to get off your soapbox."

"You don't think it was worth one last shot?"

"If you'll let it rest there."

"I plan to."

"Good" was all she said.

Deflated, I went over my column in my mind to see where I might have gone wrong. I decided that it was better not to ask. When it came to Oakalla, Ruth and I had widely differing opinions. I wanted to recapture its past innocence and, in my mind, glory. She wanted to keep it moving on to keep the rust off.

"I found out something about Sheriff Jacoby, too, if you're interested," she said.

"I'm interested."

"Well, according to his Aunt Mae, this happened a short while before he got out of the service, and it's not supposed to go any farther."

"Than what?"

"Me."

"And why did you say you were asking?"

"I didn't say. She doesn't have much use for the boy herself, but she'd hate to start a family feud over him."

"I'll try to be discreet."

"Why don't you like him?" she asked right out of the blue.

"Like whom?"

"Wayne Jacoby. As much as you like lost causes, why don't you like him?"

"Who says he's a lost cause? If I really believed that,

I *might* have to side with him on general principles."

"His Aunt Mae. She says he won't last on this job because all he's ever wanted to do was be in the Army. But that got ruined for him. According to her, he ruined it himself."

The sun had finally made its appearance, a ball of molten gold that soon burned to white. When I looked away, it was with regret.

"How so?" I said.

"He got brought up on charges for mistreating a black man, one of the soldiers under his command."

Sunrise was forgotten as I leaned forward to ask, "Mistreating him in what way?"

"Giving him all of the dirty assignments. Singling him out for discipline when there was no reason for it. This, you understand, was the testimony of the black soldier, who, according to Wayne's Aunt Mae, was a real troublemaker from the word go."

"According to Wayne?"

"According to a lot of other people, too."

"So what happened?"

"The charges against him were dropped. Nothing ever would have come of it if a local newspaperman hadn't picked up the story and run with it. He found some other black soldiers, formerly under Wayne's command, who said that while he wasn't the worst of the lot, he wasn't the best either. The long and short of it was that it cost Wayne his career in the Army."

"The Army booted him out?"

"No. They just let it be known that he'd seen his last promotion for a long while."

"Where did this happen?"

"Fort Leonard Wood. Mae said that if I wanted to, I could read all about it in the *Saint Louis Post-Dispatch*."

"I thought a *local* newspaperman uncovered the story?"

"He did. But then the St. Louis paper picked up on it."

At least that explained Wayne Jacoby's hostility toward me, but it did nothing to explain his hostility toward Jonathan Springer.

"We're missing something somewhere, Ruth."

"I think you're right. But it all seems to keep coming back to that cross."

"If we were to believe our Bibles, Ruth, it always does."

I helped Ruth clear the table, then called Clarkie at home and got his answering machine. I decided to leave a message. It would be evening at the earliest before he could get started on what I wanted him to do, and if I missed him then, depending on where he was spending his weekend, it might be Saturday or Monday.

My only fear was that his machine would run out of tape before I finished, or not record the message at all. An admitted Neanderthal, I mistrusted all of the ballyhooed electronic wonders of our age and personally could think of nothing, except perhaps for breaking rocks in the hot sun, I would rather not do than sit in front of my computer, surfing the net. Not that I would ever deny anyone that pleasure, but I hoped that for some of us at least, it would never pass for surfing the Pacific.

"I'm off," I said to Ruth a few minutes later.

Elbow deep in suds, she could have cared less. "To give you fair warning, if you need anything, I won't be here. I've got to drive Aunt Emma up to the Rapids to see her doctor, then go grocery shopping when I get home."

"Nothing serious, I hope."

Ruth's Aunt Emma, a former Army nurse and a practicing alcoholic, was pushing ninety, if she wasn't already there. Every year she confounded her doctor by living to see him once again. Ruth said it was because she was too stubborn to die on anything but her own terms.

"Her yearly checkup," Ruth said.

"Well, give her my best."

"Just remember what I said. If you get into any kind of trouble, I'm not going to be here to bail you out."

Since Ruth was sometimes psychic and always mother hen, I didn't know which influence was operating today. "I don't plan to go that far, so I don't see how I can get in too much trouble."

Famous last words.

CHAPTER 16

Ellen La Fountaine apparently wasn't expecting company so early in the day. Looking more mannish than I remembered her, she wore baggy navy blue pajamas, thin white socks, no shoes, no make-up, and no smile. "What do you want?" she said.

"To take a look inside. Hubert said it was okay."

"Hubert doesn't live here."

Something had happened since we had last talked two and a half days ago. Whatever coyness that she appeared to have then was long gone. I felt that she could be whatever she needed to be at any time she chose.

"Neither do you live here, according to your mother."

"You talked to her, then? I told you she was faking it. I was right, wasn't I?"

She had opened the door just wide enough for me to

step inside. I didn't think I'd get a second chance.

"It's warmer in here," I said, as I slipped past her.

"I'm not dressed!" she said, putting both hands to her chest.

"If you won't tell, I won't tell," I said, pulling off my cap and gloves, while putting some distance between us.

"I'm not prepared to offer you anything," she said, following me into the house.

"That's fine. All I want to do is look around. At Stevey's things mainly."

"Why Stevey's things?"

"I hear he was a good artist. I might be interested in buying one of his paintings."

She laughed. It sounded like the caw of a crow. "Stevey, an artist? Whoever told you that?"

"Senator Springer. He seems quite taken by Stevey's work."

Her eyes came to life. In their hard-edged brilliance, they reminded me a lot of her mother's. "That's because they're lovers, don't you know?"

"No. I didn't know."

"Does that surprise you?"

"About the Senator, yes. Perhaps not so much about Stevey."

"I think Stevey was killed in a jealous rage."

"By whom?"

"The Senator. Or Stevey's roommate."

"I didn't know Stevey had a roommate." Except perhaps the ghost of his father.

"Not here. Back in Madison. He has an art studio there."

"Tell me more," I said.

"There's nothing more to tell. Both he and the Senator wanted Stevey. One of them couldn't have him, so he shot him."

I guessed that it could have happened that way, but I

had my doubts. "How do you know Stevey and the Senator were lovers?"

"I overheard Stevey talking to him on the phone one time. He didn't know I was anywhere about, and there he was, in this hush-hush conversation with someone. Calling him 'dear' and 'sweetheart', and whining in that sickening voice of his, the way only Stevey could whine when he wanted something." When she suddenly snapped her fingers, I thought I heard bone on bone. "Oh yes! Something else Stevey said was 'I know we agreed it was over and done with, but I'm not through with you yet.'"

"And when you made yourself known, Stevey said that it was Senator Springer that he was talking to?"

"Not in so many words," she said. "But when I asked him who was that on the phone, he said, 'my benefactor.' Well, who was Stevey's benefactor, if not Senator Springer?"

Since I didn't have a good answer for her, I didn't offer one. "You seem to know a lot about Stevey's business," I said. "So maybe you can tell me why he and Hubert had a falling out last Monday night?"

Her smile could have cut glass. "Haven't you heard? There's no honor among thieves."

"What were they trying to steal?"

"This place. Right out from under my nose."

"And they were in it together?"

"As always. Both of them against me. But it didn't work, you see. Because I'm still here."

"And Stevey's dead."

"Yes. But through no fault of mine." She made a sweeping gesture with her right hand. "Look around all you like. I'll be in the kitchen."

"Actually, if you could tell me where Stevey's room was . . ."

"The basement was Stevey's domain," she said before I could finish. "Appropriate, don't you think?"

"In what way?"

"That's where all the vermin live, isn't it?"

"Not always. Sometimes they live in the attic."

"None that I have ever known." She left, but went up the stairs rather than into the kitchen.

I've never liked basements, not even my own. They're usually cool, damp, dark, and smelly. Also, I'm claustrophobic and basements have a tendency to shrink in direct proportion to the time that I'm in one. The La Fountaine basement was no exception to the rule. If anything, its cobwebs were longer, its shadows thicker than most. And the dank smell in the air seemed to have been there for years, a holdover from the days when the shelves were lined with canned fruits and vegetables, sweetmeats and sausage, when there was still coal in the bin and fire in the furnace. It seemed the rancid scent of dreams gone bad and lives gone sour, and I tried not to breathe too deeply, not to take too much of it into my lungs, for fear that it might settle there, too.

Apparently Stevey La Fountaine had slept and worked in a small walled room, set off from the rest of the basement and equipped with a space heater, a mattress and comforter, an easel, paints, brushes, and canvasses, a two-hundred-watt bulb that gave out heat as well as light, and a canvas lawn chair speckled with mildew. What clothes he'd brought down there were all piled in one corner with the pockets of all the pants turned inside out, as if someone had been going through them. The rest of Stevey's things were also in disarray, as if they, too, had been searched. Someone also had slit every one of his paintings and run a hand inside, bulging the canvas. Searching for what, I wondered?

Both Wilmer Wiemer and Jonathan Springer were right about Stevey La Fountaine, the artist. Stevey's abstract paintings, of which there were several, made no sense to me, would never make sense to me, even if I'd been given a paint-by-numbers description of exactly what it was that I was looking at and why I was supposed to see it. But maybe that was my fault, not Stevey's, since abstract art made no sense to me, no matter how great the artist. And for me to appreciate a work of art, it had to make sense to my mind's eye. Not only make sense, but make me want to stand there and look at it over and over again. Not while trying to figure out what the hell it was, but being drawn into and beyond it by its power to rouse my wonder and imagination.

Only one of Stevey's paintings did that for me, one that I judged to have been of Gilbert La Fountaine as a young man. Wearing only bib overalls, no shirt or shoes, he was bent over polishing what appeared to be a newly restored 1967 Mustang convertible. His face was reflected on the fender of the car. A handsome face, it showed intense concentration, as his neck, arms, and shoulders rippled with hard brown muscle glazed with sweat.

The man, neither white nor black, but a sublime mixture of both, dwarfed the car, which itself was larger than life. I knew I had seen that man before, glimpsed his passion and his power, in fact looked directly into his fierce brown eyes, but I couldn't remember where.

On the floor of the basement beside the painting was a cruder, obviously older sketch on white tablet paper that looked like it had been done by a child. The outline of the painting was there in the sketch, but none of the details and certainly none of the power. Glancing from one to the other, I was struck by two observations. Over the years, Gilbert La Fountaine might have shrunk from the giant he was then, but not in his son's eyes. Only his painting had escaped the slasher's knife.

But I left the basement no wiser than before. There I had hoped to find an empty container of gas and evidence of a cross. Instead, I found the portrait of a man who might very well have been hung on one.

Ellen La Fountaine still wasn't in the kitchen where she'd said she would be. Neither was she anywhere downstairs that I could see. So I took the opportunity to look around.

Even before I pulled open that first drawer, I had an inkling of what I might find. I wasn't disappointed. The drawer had been searched recently. The scramble of its contents told me as much, as did the mixed dates of its shuffled papers, which if left to themselves, would still have been in chronological order.

"What do you think you're doing?"

Ellen La Fountaine would have to start wearing wooden shoes. That way I could hear her coming down the stairs.

Ellen had changed from her pajamas into orange slacks and what appeared to be one of Gilbert La Fountaine's old white dress shirts, complete with gold cuff links and a paisley tie. I was struck by the bright, bold colors in the tie, which seemed those of someone once very much in love with life.

"Did you find what you were looking for?" I said, beating her to the punch.

"No. Did you?"

"Yes, as a matter of fact. I'd like to buy that portrait of your father."

"It's not for sale." She left no room for doubt.

"But you said Stevey had no talent."

"Who said Stevey painted that portrait? There are others of us in the family with talent, you know?"

Not that kind of talent, I was willing to bet. "So are you saying that it's yours?"

"I'm saying that whoever's it is, it's not for sale."

"Then get it out of the basement before it's ruined."

"Why? I think that's the perfect place for it."

I studied her to see if I could find her meaning. I saw nothing there that I could read. Either she was crazy or very close to it. There was no other way to explain her actions.

"Did you hate him that much?" I said.

"Who?"

"That's what I'm asking you."

"If you're talking about Daddy, he was the one thing in this life I did love. And I won't share him with anyone."

"Then why not just burn the painting?" Instead of, as Frost wrote about the woodpile, to ". . . leave it far from useful fireplace/ to warm the frozen swamp as best it could/ With the slow smokeless burning of decay."

"That would be too easy," she said.

I nodded, thinking that it was time for me to go. "The other night, when Stevey died, what were you doing here?" I said.

"Sheriff Jacoby knows. And he says that I don't have to tell you anything if I don't want to."

"Stevey's body was stiff when I got here. He must've been lying there for a long time before you called."

"He was."

"But you said you heard the shots."

"I did."

The next question was an obvious one, but I didn't ask it for fear that I might discover how deep Ellen La Fountaine's hatred for her brother ran. Instead, I said, "Did you know that you and your mother have the same green dress?"

"I know." Then she giggled, like a schoolgirl at her first dirty joke.

CHAPTER 17

Since it was on my way up-town, I stopped by Edgar Shoemaker's welding shop. As usual, Edgar was chewing on a dead cigar and the air in there was as thick as Ruth's fried chicken gravy. I stood a moment, watching Edgar work, as he welded the corner of a steel frame that he was building. I never ceased to marvel at his skill, as I did with anyone who was really really good at what he did. They made life worth living, I thought, those inveterate craftsmen of excellence, and gave the rest of us something on which to feast our world-weary eyes.

"Is that you, Garth?" Edgar said, as he shut off his torch and lifted his welding mask.

"It's me. Could I use your phone a minute?"

"Help yourself. I'll be done here shortly."

He relit his torch and went back to work. I called Ben Bryan.

"Garth Ryland here," I said when Ben answered. "I have an unusual question for you. Did you happen to look in Stevey La Fountaine's pockets before you did the autopsy on him?"

"That's standard procedure, Garth."

"Then did you find anything of interest?"

"I found a nearly empty wallet. That's about all. Why do you ask?"

In total concentration now that he was about done, Edgar had sparks flying everywhere around the shop with no thought to where they might land. I stretched the phone's cord as far as I could to get out of their way.

"I believe Stevey had something that Ellen La Fountaine wanted; or at least she thought he had it and has been searching for it ever since."

"Funny you should say that, Garth. Both of Stevey's front pockets had been pulled partway out and left that way. I couldn't figure out how he could have done it, even by accident, there on the steps, as slick as they were."

"Did you mention that to Sheriff Jacoby?"

"That and the fact that she was right there when Stevey was killed, without even a good excuse for being there. But every time I bring her up, he says she's not a suspect."

"Did he search the house for a gun?"

"He said there was no reason to, since she wasn't a suspect."

"Did he say what her excuse was for being there?"

Finished, Edgar flipped up his mask and stood back to admire his handiwork. If only he really could see it, as he had before fate and a hot piece of steel conspired to rob him of most of his sight.

"No. He didn't say. He said it wasn't important."

"Thanks, Ben. Anything else I should know?"

"Don't cross him, Garth. He's a man on a mission."

"What do you think?" Edgar asked about the frame that he was building, as soon as I was off the phone.

"I think you keep getting better with age. What's it for anyway?"

Edgar ran his gloved hand over the weld he'd just made. "Floyd Cash wants a new stand for his oil drums. His old one rusted out on him."

"I think he'll be satisfied," I said.

"I think he will, too."

I put my cap and gloves back on. It was time to hit the road. "You're absolutely sure that cross was soaked in gasoline before it was burned?" I said.

"No. It could've been soaked in kerosene, or diesel fuel. But it was soaked in something. Of that, I'm certain."

"Thanks, Edgar. I'll be on my way."

He used his welding torch to relight his cigar. "What's it like out there today?"

"Pretty. The prettiest day we've had in weeks. It feels a lot warmer out, too."

After sucking hard on his cigar, he finally got it to go. "Hear there's a snowstorm blowing in here tomorrow." He spat on the floor. "From what they're saying, it's going to be a bad one."

"Then it probably won't amount to much," I said.

"Just thought you'd like to know."

From there I walked uptown to the Oakalla REMC building, where Hubert La Fountaine had his office. For the first time that January, I felt overdressed with my stocking cap on.

"Is Hubert in?" I asked Mildred Purcell.

She and Jenni Whittaker exchanged glances. I knew those glances by heart. They were reserved for personas non grata.

"Never mind." I opened the gate and let myself into the office. "I'll see for myself."

Mildred Purcell gave Jenni Whittaker a shrug. "We tried," she said.

The door to Hubert's office was closed. Not hearing him in conversation with anyone, I decided to let myself in there, too.

"Good morning, Hubert," I said.

"I have nothing to say to you, Garth. So don't ask me any more of your questions."

Today Hubert wore a black jean suit, a white shirt with yellow stripes and black pearl buttons, and a black string tie. I imagined that his boots, too, would be black, if I could have seen under the desk.

"I just came from your old house," I said, taking the nearest chair. "Ellen sends her regards."

"I'll bet she does," he muttered, while doing his best to ignore me.

"She said you and Stevey had a falling out over that property there. 'There's no honor among thieves,' I believe were her exact words."

His eyes fastened on mine. No pupils that I could see. Just two cold black orbs. "She should know."

"There was another thing she passed on to me," I said, trying to draw him out. "She's about to run out of fuel there and wondered when you might be refilling the tank?"

"Goddamn it, Garth. I know what you're trying to do and it's not going to work. So you might as well be on your way before I have to call the sheriff."

"He's gotten to you, too, huh? I can't say I'm surprised."

"The hell he has," Hubert said. "This is between you and me."

"So what did I do to tick you off?"

When he didn't answer, I figured it either had to do with

Wilmer Wiemer, or my conversation with Hiram last night at the Corner Bar and Grill. Not knowing which, I tossed the dice and said, "What is it to me if you want to buy your own property without anybody knowing about it?"

Snake eyes, Garth. That was the wrong thing to say.

"Who have you been talking to?" Hubert was merely annoyed at me before. He was incensed now. But at least I had him going.

"I told you, I just came from your sister's."

"Sister, my ass. She's not smart enough to figure that out."

"She was smart enough to go through Stevey's pockets while he was dying," I said. "Knowing she'd never get a chance later."

He didn't take the news well. "Looking for . . ." *What,* he was about to say. "God damn her. I wondered what game she was playing. Now, by God,I know!"

"Which is?" I said.

"Go to hell." Then he punched a number on his phone. "Mildred? Call the sheriff for me, will you please?"

I rose and opened his office door to see if he was bluffing. He wasn't. "You might as well tell me what you and Stevey had your row about at the Corner Bar and Grill late Monday night," I said. "Seeing that I'm probably not going to get a chance to ask you again."

"Mildred!" he yelled.

"I'm trying as best I can," she answered, while frantically thumbing through the phone book.

"I'm going," I said. "Save yourself the trouble."

"It's no trouble," Hubert bit off the words. "I can assure you."

Walking down the alley beside the cheese plant, I noticed the wind for the first time that morning. Barely a breeze, it blew straight from the east into my face. I hadn't watched a weather report all week, so I didn't know what was supposed to be brewing to the west of us. One thing I did know, however, was that an east wind in January was never a good sign.

I wondered how long Wayne Jacoby had been following me. He pulled his patrol car in front of me about a block down Gas Line Road, and stopped.

"You're under arrest," he said, as he got out of his patrol car. "For obstructing justice."

His right hand rested on the butt of his revolver. He appeared to be serious.

"So that's the way it's going to be," I said.

"That's the way it is," he answered.

Our ride to the jail took less than a minute. All he had to do was to make a U-turn on Gas Line Road, drive a couple blocks, and we were there.

"Empty your pockets," he said, once we were inside the City Building. "You can get it all back when you get out."

Then he read me my rights, even though I told him that it wasn't necessary.

"Don't I get at least one phone call?" I said before he led me away.

"No. Not today."

It didn't matter. Ruth wasn't home anyway. Rupert Roberts was in Texas, and Abby was in Detroit.

Oakalla's jail was a solid, low-to-the-ground brick building, built in the same style as the City Building during Oakalla's centennial year, 1958. It sat between the City Building on the east and the phone company across the alley to the west. It had six cells in all, though I had never known them to be full all at once, except during the Kangaroo Court hours of Homecoming, when there was usually a waiting line. The most it usually housed was one or two a night, and it was empty more often than not. But still it served as a reminder that even in Oakalla people sometimes drove drunk, or stole from their neighbors, or beat up on those they did, and didn't, love.

"How long do you plan on keeping me here?" I asked, as Wayne Jacoby opened the front door of the jail.

"Don't worry. You won't starve," he said, referring to Peanut Johnstone, who, along with running the phone company, was the jailer, and his wife, Edith, who did the cooking for the jail.

"That's not what I asked."

"You'll get out when I decide to let you out," he said. "I don't know how long that will be."

"You're not worried about false arrest?"

"I believe I'm within my rights. Now, let's go." He gave me a not-so-gentle shove inside.

"Who called you, Ellen or Hubert La Fountaine?"

"That's none of your business."

Inside the jail, it seemed only a hair warmer than it was outside, and without the sun shining down, really not warmer at all. There was, too, in its darkness and dampness, its melancholy that got under your skin and stayed there, a sense of doom. Without a clear grasp of the future, or perhaps even with one, it would be easy to abandon all hope once you entered here.

"It doesn't bother you that Ellen La Fountaine was on the scene when Stevey died, or that she let him bleed to death before she called for help?" I said.

"You don't know that," he said.

"I do know that. It's you who seems to be ignoring it."

His jaw began to twitch. We were on dangerous ground. He gave me another shove to get me moving again. "Ellen La Fountaine is not a suspect."

"Why not?"

"That's my business."

I stopped to face him. "Your business is to get to the truth of the matter, not hang Jonathan Springer out to dry."

"And your business is to stay out of my business," he said, opening a cell door.

Wayne Jacoby had six cells to choose from. He chose the one that had previously been occupied by a drunk and that Peanut Johnstone hadn't yet had time to clean. The reason that I knew it was a drunk who had stayed there was the sweet wine smell to the vomit.

"You don't have any rooms with a view?"" I said.

He gave me my third shove of the day. "Get in."

There are sounds and there are sounds, but there is nothing quite like the sound of a cell door closing on you. It doesn't matter who you are or whom you know, how much money you have or your position in life. When that cell door closes on you, you're on the selfsame level with prisoners everywhere—abandoned and alone.

A quick look around my cell told me that, no matter what its duration, it was going to be a long stay. Vomit covered the bed and the toilet, the only two places on which to sit down, and the floor itself had also received several volleys, so I had to be careful where I walked. Also, with no running water in the cell, by necessity the toilet was like that of Grandmother Ryland's privy—same hard wooden seat, same grab-you-by-the-throat smell, but without the four walls and a roof to keep it all inside. And someone, either the drunk or Wayne Jacoby, had done away with the toilet paper. Not that I had any great yearning to use it, but it would have been nice to have had something with which to wipe the vomit off my boots.

Since my coat and stocking cap were out of the question, I used the blanket on the bed, which was already a little crusty anyway, and not likely to win a good-housekeeping award. Then, after wiping off the mattress to the best of my ability, I rolled up the blanket and set it in the far corner where I wouldn't have to smell it. But as the mattress warmed up, I noticed a urine smell coming from it, one that attached itself to my clothes and stayed there.

When you are busy with life, as I was most of the time, you'd give almost anything for the luxury of standing in the shower until the water ran cold, or watching a sunset from beginning to end, or not caring that your last vacation was in 1981, or that there is a foot of snow on your sidewalk, waiting to be shoveled. Time is something that belongs to someone else, that elite of society of haves and have-nots to which you've never belonged. Then bam! when you suddenly have time on your hands, the first thing that you do is look for something to do. Why? I wished I knew. It would have helped keep me from going crazy there in my Oakalla jail cell.

All that I could think about was getting out. Every minute that passed seemed like an hour, and every hour that passed seemed like a day. In his search of me, Wayne Jacoby had overlooked my watch. But since it only added to my misery, maybe he had done so on purpose.

When noon, then one P.M., came and went, it became obvious that Peanut Johnstone had no knowledge that I was in jail. Either that or he had been warned off by Wayne Jacoby, which was more likely the case. Otherwise, Peanut would have brought me one of Edith's potpies, or one of the many other dishes that she was so famous for. It also became obvious that Wayne Jacoby didn't care how long I stayed in jail or what the consequences to either him or me were. As Ben Bryan said about him, he was a man on a mission. To an ex-military man, which Wayne Jacoby was, that meant succeeding at any cost.

But he wasn't crazy. Of that, I was fairly certain. So he wouldn't let me die there, or even go beyond a couple days. He would, however, make me pay for my real or imagined transgressions.

At five, even though I couldn't see it, I knew that the sun had already set and that night would soon be upon me. At five-thirty, I knew that it was dark, or nearly so. It was then that I got up and began to pace around my cell, like an animal his cage. There was no purpose to it, except to help relieve the tension that was building up inside me. I wasn't sure how much longer I could survive in here before I started banging my head against the door. The walls, it seemed, never very far away to begin with, had begun to close in on me.

Then I heard someone's ragged breathing and realized that it was my own at the same time that I heard the outside door of the jail open. Wayne Jacoby, I bet. Back to torment me. Frantically searching the cell for any kind of weapon, I found nothing but a blanket crusted with vomit. Balling it my hands, I stepped into the nearest shadow and waited.

But instead of Wayne Jacoby, there came Peanut Johnstone jangling his keys with Ruth marching in step behind him. Shit! I thought. She's been arrested, too. In frustration, I hurled the blanket into the toilet and tamped it down with my foot.

But without a word, Peanut opened my cell and let me out. And without a word, Ruth took me by the arm and led me outside, where we got into her yellow Volkswagen bug and drove home.

There, I stood a moment just looking at the stars. "Does Sheriff Jacoby know about this?" I said to Ruth.

"Not unless you told him."

Good, I thought. Now I'm an escapee.

Daisy met me at the back door, where I greeted her with a hug, before she raced past me out into the backyard. Ruth had a big pot of vegetable soup cooking on the stove and shortbread in the oven. Once inside the kitchen, all that I wanted to do was to stand there in front of the stove and feel its heat.

"Take your coat off," Ruth said, "before you get too warm."

"I'm not sure I'll ever be too warm again." But I did as she said.

After hanging up my coat, my next stop was the kitchen cabinet, where I took out my bottle of Old Crow and without measuring it, poured some into a water glass. Ruth watched me closely the whole time, as if unsure about what might happen next. "Bottoms up," I said just before I drained the glass.

"That won't help," she said.

"Says you." I had to get the taste of the cell out of my mouth.

"Was it that bad?" she said.

"Let's put it this way. I never want to do it again. How did you find out where I was?"

Ruth began filling our bowls with vegetable soup. "Alice Conner told me. At least she said she saw you getting into the Sheriff's car. When you didn't come home or answer the phone at your office, I figured out the rest."

"How did you persuade Peanut to let me go?"

Ruth had that look in her eyes that said a train was coming, so you'd better get off the tracks. "I didn't persuade him of anything. I told him that if he didn't have you out in five minutes, I'd have his hide."

"And he believed you?'"

"I wasn't kidding, Garth."

"Lucky for me, you weren't."

"I know. Now, let's eat."

CHAPTER 18

Fear can do strange things to you. It can energize you, make you almost superhuman, as you prepare to flee or to fight. It can drain you, make every nerve and muscle shut down until it immobilizes you, leaving you a sitting duck. It can drive you inside yourself, torment you with mind games that substitute for action and, in the end, for life itself. Or it can motivate you to excel because your fear of failure is even greater than your fear of punishment or banishment or death. Or it can do a lot of other things to your mind and body, while you try to pass them off as something else.

That next morning, with dawn a river of red in the east, I stood at the kitchen window, unable to decide what direction my fear would go. The only thing that I could be certain of was that I never wanted to go back to jail again.

It was not just a matter of preference, but one of survival.

"So where to today?" Ruth said.

She had come down the stairs without my hearing her. She must have been taking lessons from Ellen La Fountaine.

"I haven't decided yet. It's been a while since I've been out to the farm. I thought I might drive out there."

"I thought Sheriff Jacoby had your wallet and keys?"

"He does. But there's a key to the house in Grandmother's root cellar. And I always leave Jessie's key in her ignition in the hope that someone might steal her."

"Fat chance of that."

"Better than none."

She took the coffeepot off the drainboard and began to fill it with water. "You call Abby last night, like you said you would?" she said.

"I called, but I got her machine."

"You leave a message?"

"No. I didn't feel up to it."

"It's still early. You might catch her this morning."

"I might, but I'm not going to."

"Why not?" she asked.

"Because she can't help me on this one, Ruth. Nobody can, but me. And I don't even know what I'm afraid of except that I can't stand to be locked up. Even as a kid, I fought it with blood in my eye, whenever they tried to put me in our imaginary jail."

She added coffee to the pot and set it on the stove. "Cream of Wheat okay with you today?" she said.

"Do you understand, Ruth? Because I'm not sure I do."

"Do you want a banana with that or huckleberries?"

"Ruth, are you listening?"

"You said that it was your decision, that no one could help you out."

"But what am I so afraid of? It's not like I've never

faced trouble before. And didn't blink then."

"I'm not a psychiatrist, Garth. Don't ask me to be one."

"But what is it about jails? Answer me that."

The sky was all red now, from one horizon to the other. Blood red was the only way to describe it.

"Okay, you asked for my opinion and I'm going to give it to you. Then we're going to sit down and see where we are in this because I've learned something that might shed some light on the matter."

"Why didn't you say something last night?"

"Because you were too busy feeling sorry for yourself."

She was right. The minute that I had finished eating, I had gone into the living room to build a fire. And there I had sat in front of it long after its ashes had gone cold and Ruth had gone to bed. Only then had I tried to call Abby, and that was more an act of desperation than an act of love.

I sat down at the table while Ruth rummaged through the cupboard in search of the Cream of Wheat. We had Cream of Wheat about as often as we had fried mush or oatmeal, which about once a year, or as often as I could stand it. With any luck, the bugs would have gotten into this box as they had to some in the past.

Perplexed, because she had the memory of an elephant and knew that the Cream of Wheat should be here somewhere, Ruth gave me the evil eye when she couldn't find it in the cupboard.

"I didn't touch it. I swear," I said.

Then she smiled in triumph. As a way of defeating the bugs, she had put the Cream of Wheat in the refrigerator.

"Look what I found," she said, holding up the box.

"Lucky me."

"It's good for you."

"That's all it is, then."

Ruth set the Cream of Wheat on the stove and went
to her special larder in the utility room for a jar of huckleberries. Ruth had canned the huckleberries years ago
when she and Karl were still on their farm, but they were
every bit as good now as they were then—perhaps even
better, sweetened as they were with time. After turning
down the fire under the coffee, which had started to perk,
she sat down across from me at the table.

She said, "First of all, there's no sense beating yourself over the head with this. Karl was about the bravest
man I ever knew, and he was scared to death of spiders.
Black widow, wolf spider, daddy longlegs, they were all the
same to him, and there was nothing I could do to convince
him otherwise. Once he saw one in the house, whap! It
was either dead, or he didn't rest until it was. He even
turned the whole kitchen upside down one day, looking for
what turned out to be a piece of black yarn that had blown
across the floor. So we all have our weaknesses, Garth.
Karl's was spiders, mine is snakes, and yours is jails, or
anything with or without four walls that you can't get out
of. But it's not something worth worrying about. It's there,
we know it's there, and that's that. I'll try to stay away
from snakes and you try to stay out of jail."

"But that's what scares me, Ruth. I'm not sure with
Wayne Jacoby as sheriff that I can stay out of jail. Not and
go about doing things the way I'm used to doing them."

"You have had it your own way for a long time around
here," she said. "I can see why it would be hard to change
now. If change is in order," she made it a point to add.

"Are you saying it's not?"

She got up to pour us each a cup of coffee. I got up to
put the sugar and half-and-half on the table. We sat back
down.

"I'm saying that sheriff or not, Wayne Jacoby way
overstepped his bounds yesterday. If he does that again,

then you have every right to go after his badge."

"By then it'll be too late. I'll have been back in jail again."

"One more time won't kill you."

"I'm not so sure, Ruth. I was ready to make a break for it when you came in last night. Had it been Wayne Jacoby instead, I'm not sure what I would've done."

"So stay away from him as best you can from now on."

"I thought I was. But Ellen La Fountaine must've blown the whistle on me. Either she or Hubert did."

Ruth blew on her coffee to cool it. I did the same. "Why? Do you have an answer for that?"

"There's got to be money involved, and lots of it. That's the only way to explain it. Once Merle La Fountaine left for the Lutheran Home, it's been open season from then on."

"So that's what Stevey came home for? To keep Ellen away from the house and the money, until he and Hubert got control of the property?" she said.

The sky had gone from red to white, as the sun broke through the clouds. But its stay would be short lived, as another flotilla of clouds was descending upon it.

"Maybe. And maybe he came here to blackmail Jonathan Springer, as Wayne Jacoby claims. That's my problem, Ruth. I can't see the beginning or the end of this, at least far enough to know what's what. And if Jonathan Springer is a crook, or worse, as Wayne Jacoby believes, I might be doing the citizens of Wisconsin a disservice by getting in his way."

"There's no chance that Wayne Jacoby is just trying to make a name for himself?"

"That, or trying to redeem himself through the Senator."

"In whose eyes?"

"Maybe his own."

"You want to explain that?"

"If I could."

Ruth took her coffee with her to the stove where she measured out the water for the Cream of Wheat into a saucepan. I watched the sun wither under a fusillade of tiny white clouds, fired like grapeshot from the ever-advancing flotilla.

"You said you learned something that might have a bearing on all of this," I said.

"I did. But I wonder now how important it is."

"Why don't we try it on for size and find out?"

She stopped measuring Cream of Wheat long enough to say, "You remember you asked me to find out if Allison Springer, then Allison Taylor, ever did Marvin Heckel's taxes for him. She didn't, but she did do Gil La Fountaine's taxes for him."

"You're sure?"

"Mary Beth Robinson is, and I've never known her to be wrong about something like that."

"Do you think it's possible that Allison Springer knows about Gilbert La Fountaine's money?" I said.

"She would have to know something about it to do his taxes."

"Enough to come back here one day and try to get some of it for herself?" Even as I said it, I didn't believe it.

But Ruth's thoughts were somewhere else. So when she said, "That remains to be seen," I didn't know which one of us she was talking to.

Breakfast didn't take long. Cream of wheat never did. Neither was its empty bowl something over which I chose to linger. The huckleberries were good, however. I remembered with a smile that they, along with Graham crackers and milk, were my Sunday night supper when I stayed with Grandmother Ryland.

"So you're still planning to drive out to the farm?" Ruth said, disappointed in me.

"Until I can think of something better to do."

"Then why don't you take Daisy along? She needs to get out and run."

"I'd rather not, Ruth."

"I'd rather you would."

So Daisy was the first one inside when I opened Jessie's driver's side door. Jessie was the brown Chevy sedan that I had inherited from Grandmother Ryland along with her eighty-acre farm and the money to buy the *Oakalla Reporter*. Jessie and I had survived more crises together than most Hollywood movies, but while in a moment of weakness I would admit to being fond of her, I wouldn't go beyond that. She had failed me too many times to earn my heartfelt love. I did respect her, however. As temperamental as she was, I would have been a fool not to.

"Don't get too excited," I said to Daisy, who sat erect in the passenger seat all ready to go. "We're not out of the garage yet."

"Woof!" was her answer.

I pumped the accelerator a couple-three times and turned on the key. *Ruh, ruh, ruh* . . . fire! *Ruh . . . ruh . . . ruh.*

I turned off the key and waited a couple minutes before I tried again. Meanwhile Daisy sat there stoically, as if certain that I was going to pull this off.

"I told you not to get your hopes up."

"Woof!"

Afraid I'd flood her, I kept my foot off of Jessie's accelerator this try. *Ruh, ruh, ruh* . . . fire! fire! *Ruh . . . ruh . . . ruh.*

"One more time and that's it," I said to Daisy. "And don't be so damn trusting. That's a bad habit to get into."

"Woof!"

"You'll see."

I turned the key one last time. Fire! fire! fire! *Ruh . . .*

ruh . . . ruh.

"Goddamn it, Jessie!"

I jumped out into the garage, intending to kick the first thing in sight. It turned out to be a five-gallon gas can. My foot was already in motion before I realized that the gas can didn't belong to me. In my effort to avoid it, I lost my balance and fell to the garage floor, where Daisy immediately pounced on me, thinking that this was all in the game.

"Get off!" I said, shoving her to one side. "And buy yourself some Certs first chance you get."

On my feet again, I took a moment to examine the gas can. Covered with a thick, oily layer of dust, it appeared that it had been sitting unused in someone's shed for a long time. I removed the cap and smelled inside. "Come on, Daisy," I said, slapping my leg. "We're going for a walk."

I should have brought along her leash, but before Doc Airhart died, he had taught her to heel. Sort of. Her idea of heeling was not to get more than twenty feet ahead of me. But traffic was light that Saturday morning, and we managed to reach the Marathon without incident.

"What do we have here?" Sniffy Smith said, as he jumped down from his stool to pet Daisy, who nearly bowled him over in her excitement.

"Is Danny around?" I said, not seeing him anywhere.

"He's next door. He'll be back in a minute."

Danny kept a lot of his spare parts in the house next door. The house had come with the property and had never been lived in as long as I had been in Oakalla.

"What are you doing with that thing?" Sniffy said. "I hope you don't plan to put gas in it."

"Take a whiff and tell me what you think."

"Whew!" Sniffy said, giving a couple loud sniffs as he put the lid back on the can. "If that stuff was any older, you could sell it at the antique shop."

"That's what I thought. But I wanted a second opinion."

Then Danny Palmer returned to the Marathon, carrying wiper blades and an oil filter. "Here, let me take those," Sniffy said. "Garth has something that he wants you to smell."

Danny gave me a questioning look until I pointed to the can. "Be my guest," I said.

Staring at the can as he might a jack-in-the-box, Danny kept his distance.

"Go ahead," Sniffy said. "It won't bite you."

Reluctantly, Danny bent over to smell inside the can. His opinion made it unanimous. The gasoline in the can, which to me smelled like lacquer, was years old.

"You weren't planning on using that?" Danny said to me.

"No. I just wondered if it would burn."

"I don't think here's the place to find out."

"Good God no!" Sniffy said.

"How about out back?"

"I don't see the harm in that."

Sniffy grabbed a book of matches and followed me out there. The can was about empty, but I managed to make a small puddle in the snow. The speed at which it burned surprised both of us, and cost me a few hairs on my hand.

"Well, I guess that answers that question," Sniffy said.

"I guess it does."

Back inside the Marathon, Danny and Daisy were playing tug of war with one of Danny's rags. It was the happiest that I had seen him in weeks.

"You have any bolt cutters here?" I said to Danny.

"No. Mine are up at the City Building. I leave them on the fire truck."

"You have a key to the City Building?"

He pointed to a hook beside the door. "It's the one on the ring by itself."

"Stay," I said to Daisy, who was too busy wrestling with Danny to pay any attention.

CHAPTER 19

The two-block walk to the City
Building took all of five minutes, if that. It was a walk that
I had made hundreds of times before without a second
thought. That day, however, my heart was pounding before
I ever stepped out of the door of the Marathon.

There were two ways that I could go to get to the City
Building: Jackson Street to School Street or Perrin Street
to the alley that ran behind the hardware and beside the
cheese plant. Since I didn't yet know Wayne Jacoby's
habits, I had no idea where he was most likely to be at this
time of morning. But what I didn't want to happen was to
meet up with him and run the risk that he would put me
back in jail again. In a few short days, I had gone from
leading citizen to second-class citizen, and I didn't much
like the feeling.

I vetoed the alley beside the cheese plant for two reasons. One, once I was in there, there was no way out. Two, it would take me right past Adams County REMC where Hubert La Fountaine worked.

I was a half block up Jackson on the south side of the street when I saw Wayne Jacoby's patrol car turn the corner at the four-way stop and come toward me. I didn't wait to see what might happen next. I ducked into the hardware, waved to Fritz Gascho, its owner, and headed for the basement. From there, I went underground to the cellar of the Corner Bar and Grill, climbed the stairs into the bar, which was empty except for Robby Rumaley, who looked like he'd been there all night, pushed through the swinging doors into the dining room, and was outside again before anyone in there seemed to notice me. Keeping my head low and my eyes straight ahead, I tried to make myself as small as possible.

Once at the City Building, I went into the office in search of my keys and wallet but couldn't find them. Apparently Wayne Jacoby had locked them in the office safe.

I found Danny's bolt cutters behind the seat of the Number One fire truck. Outside again, I went north on School Street until it became Home Street, then north on Home Street as far as the alley behind the Five and Dime before I turned east. That route took me a half block out of my way, but I was rewarded when I saw Wayne Jacoby's patrol car leave the Marathon and head west just as I reached Fair Haven Road. He hadn't seen me, I didn't think. At least he didn't make a U-turn on Jackson Street and come my way.

"Your buddy was just in here asking about you," Danny said, as Daisy came running up to me.

"I'll bet. Where did the gas can go?" I didn't see it anywhere about.

"Are you looking for this?" Sniffy said, as he emerged from the back of the station, carrying the gas can. "We didn't think Dudley Do-Right should see it just yet. Not until we found out where it came from."

"I found it in my garage this morning, but that's not where it came from. I have an idea, though."

"What's your idea?" Danny said, looking solemn again. It must be hard, I thought, to pump gas for the man who's screwing the woman you love.

"Gilbert La Fountaine's body shop," I said.

"I don't see how it could have come from there," Danny argued.

"Why not?"

"Just because," he said, suddenly at a loss for words.

"What Danny is trying to say is that Gilbert La Fountaine's body shop has been locked up since the day he died," Sniffy said. "All of us in the north end know that."

I wasn't certain that was what Danny was trying to say, but I let it pass. "What if someone found the key to the lock?" I said. "What would stop him from going inside?"

"Nothing, I suppose," Sniffy agreed. "What do you think, Danny?"

Danny nodded at the bolt cutters. "I think that if you plan on using those, you'd better get going," he said curtly. "Dudley Do-Right told me he had to go to Madison for the day."

"Has he taken you into his confidence now?" I said, not quite understanding his brusqueness. Then I remembered that today was the day that Wendy Bodine was scheduled to leave town.

"He said he was leaving me in charge. If there were any emergencies, to call the State Police."

"Didn't you find that ironic?"

Danny's look seemed one of total resignation, and defeat. "To be honest, Garth, nothing surprises me much any more."

On our way to the north end of town, I left Daisy at home for fear of what we might be getting into. Sniffy, who insisted on carrying the gas can, kept glancing at the sky every few seconds, as if searching for divine guidance.

"What's up, Sniffy?" I finally asked.

"We're supposed to have a shit-kicker coming. But I don't see any sign of it yet."

"How bad of a shit-kicker?" I said.

"About as bad as it gets. We've got a low pressure coming up from Texas and a blast of cold air coming down from Canada, and they're supposed to get together right about here."

"I'll believe it when I see it."

"That's what Danny said."

When we were two houses south of Ellen La Fountaine's, we made a right along a row of Lombardy poplars that separated Elden Schiery's place from that of John and Bess Gunkle. After approaching the body shop from the back side, we rested there a moment against the east wall. I didn't tell Sniffy, but already I could feel snow in the air. When I smelled it, I would know for certain it was on its way.

"Now what?" Sniffy said. "We can't very well cut our way inside from here."

"I'm going around front to try to cut the lock. You keep watch and whistle if you see anyone coming."

"I can't whistle worth a shit, Garth. Especially not when my mouth feels like I've been eating crackers all day."

"Then holler at me. I won't waste any time getting out of there."

"What do you hope to find in there, Garth?"

I took the can from him. "The place where this came from. Among other things."

After a long look at the house to see where Ellen La

Fountaine might be, I quickly made my way to the front of the body shop and cut the brass padlock. But it was a good thing that the bolt-cutters were top of the line, or I never would have gotten the job done.

I found a light switch to the right inside the door and was surprised when an overhead bulb came on. Considering Hubert La Fountaine's reputation for pinching a penny, I expected the electricity to be turned off. At that, though, the bulb didn't put out much light, so I supposed that Hubert could have overlooked it.

Cold in there, I discovered, as I made my way along the north wall to where Sniffy stood guard outside. I could see every breath I took. And quiet. I could hear my boots scrape the floor every step of the way.

Then I stopped, did a double take, and smiled. Two five-gallon gasoline cans stood about an arm's length apart against the wall of the body shop. The ring in the dust on the concrete floor between them was a perfect fit for the can I carried, so I set it down inside the ring and went on.

"See anybody?" I said through the wall.

When Sniffy didn't answer right away, I thought perhaps he'd deserted me. But a loud resounding *sniff!* soon set me straight.

"Jesus Christ, Garth, you just scared the stuffing out of me. What was your question again?"

"Have you seen anybody about?"

"You'll be the first to know. So hurry up. I'm getting cold standing here."

Along the east wall I found a pile of old lumber that included four-by-fours and two-by-fours, like the ones used to build the cross. I was on to something, I knew, when I began to find a bent nail every few inches. But the outline of the cross there in the middle of the floor still shocked me. I had hoped to find some real evidence of it, but was not prepared to encounter its bare bones lying

there on the cold concrete. Kneeling, I touched my hand
to the cross and felt something wet. Gasoline, it turned out
to be. Old gasoline, by the smell of it.

I had what I'd come for, and it was time to leave. No
good could come of staying longer. However, I was intrigued by a white cabinet built into the shelves on which
Gilbert La Fountaine stored his paint, body putty, and all
the other compounds that he used in his work. A chipped
corner told me that the cabinet was built of solid oak. Its
door was equipped with a stainless steel hasp and staple
and secured with a brass padlock similar to the one I'd cut
earlier.

The problem, as I saw it, was that, considering the
way the winds in Oakalla were blowing, if I didn't open it
now, I might never get another chance. This dilemma was
somewhat balanced by the fact that I carried only the one
replacement padlock I'd brought from home, which wasn't
even brass and which had to go on the outside door. So
unless I could come back later and set things right, whoever
came in here next would know that I'd been here, or at
least that someone had. And odds were he'd come looking
for me.

"No guts, no glory." "A faint heart never won a fair
hand." "Carpe diem." "He who hesitates is lost."

There's a saying to support every foolhardy act known
to man.

Balanced by "Look before you leap." "Fools rush in. . ."
"Sorry, but you're dead, Fred."

I cut the lock anyway.

Imagine my dismay on discovering that the cabinet
was empty at the exact instant that Sniffy yelled his warning to me. Already on the run, I reached the outside just
in time to see Ellen La Fountaine step off of her back stoop
on her way to the body shop. The chance that she might
be armed didn't occur to me until I heard the shotgun's

blast pepper the corrugated steel door behind me. But by then I was around the south side of the body shop and heading for the row of cedars that served as a windbreak along the north edge of Howard Ruckel's property. A few steps later I caught up to Sniffy.

"Good," I said as we slowed our pace. "You made it."

"What's good about it?" said Sniffy, who was too winded to sniff his indignation. "We're both going to be in jail before long."

"Who says?"

"Dudley Do-Right. He threatened both Danny and me this morning, said that if any of the rest of us even thought about taking up with you in this, he'd put us in jail right along with you. Including, and these are his words, not mine, that housekeeper of yours."

"I won't tell him, if you won't."

"Hell, Garth. Our tracks are all over the place back there. Even Clarkie could figure that one out."

"Not if Ellen La Fountaine can't identify us."

"What are the odds of that?"

Not good, I decided, after looking back and seeing her standing at the edge of the cedars. My only consolation was that her shotgun must be a single-shot.

CHAPTER 20

"**W**hy don't you ever think before you do these things?" Ruth said when I reported back to her. "You should have known she'd be watching that place like a hawk."

Sniffy had stopped off at home to hide out. I had gone on alone from there.

"I really didn't think she'd see us," I said in my defense. "I thought she'd still be too busy looking for the key."

"What key?"

"The key to the padlock I cut. It's what she's been after all along, would be my guess."

"Well, one thing's for certain. She's not going to need it now."

"For the good it will do her. There's no money in there. None that I could find anyway."

Ruth was in the process of chopping onions and cubing potatoes. Lunch was still two hours away, but she liked to give her soups plenty of time to simmer.

"You'll have a hard time convincing anyone of that," she said.

"You're my witness. You saw me come home empty handed."

"I also saw you come home with a pair of bolt cutters. How do I ever get around that under oath?"

"It'll never get that far."

"Don't be too sure, Garth. It's already gone a lot farther than I ever thought it would."

I got up from the kitchen table and went into the living room. I didn't need her to cheer me up. Then when the phone rang a few minutes later, I refused to answer it for fear of who was on the other end. But with both her hands full, Ruth refused to answer it as well.

"Hello?" I said at the end of the fifth ring.

"Garth, it's Clarkie. I was about to give up on you."

I smiled in relief. Never had Clarkie's monotone sounded so good to me. "I was in the bathroom," I lied. "What do you have for me?"

"Not much, I'm afraid."

"Then give me what you've got." I hoped that I didn't sound as desperate as I felt.

"Sorry, Garth. I'd rather not just yet. I've made some phone calls to Mississippi and I'm waiting for an answer from there."

"Why Mississippi?"

"That's where Senator Springer went to school. East Central at Larue, Mississippi. It's a small private school down there."

"Probably so he could play baseball year round," I said.

"What's that, Garth?"

"Nothing, Clarkie." I was thinking that if that line

drive hadn't shattered Jonathan Springer's kneecap, prob- ably neither one of us would be in the mess he was in right now.

"Anyway, I should have something by early this evening, if you're planning to be around."

That, I supposed, would depend on when Wayne Jacoby came to arrest me. "I'll try to make it a point to be," I said. "But it would help if I knew in what direction to head this afternoon."

"Sorry, Garth," he said for the second time. "No can do."

"Are you saying there's some pressure being put on you by your fellow officers in blue there in Madison?"

"You might say that, yes."

"And you think they'll have changed their minds by this evening?"

"They tell me their business will be finished by then."

"Business with whom?"

"Sorry, Garth," he said for the third time.

"Can you give me anything? Anything at all?"

"Not where Senator Springer is concerned. But I can tell you there's no record of an Allison Taylor ever being in a hospital here."

"What about an Allison Tatum or Trailer?"

"Her either."

"Somehow that doesn't surprise me."

"But . . ."

"But what?" I asked when he didn't continue.

"Wait a second. Let me pull it up on my computer. What was the name of the man who was killed?"

"La Fountaine. Stevey La Fountaine."

"That's what I thought, but I just wanted to make sure." I waited while he played with his computer. "Here it is. A Merle La Fountaine was admitted to Saint Mary's Hospital on December 17, 1970, and released three days later."

"Admitted for what? Does it say?"

"No. Those records are confidential. I had to cut some corners to get what I did."

"Thanks, Clarkie. It might mean something." Though I was hoping for a lot more.

"Later, then." He hung up.

"What was that all about?" Ruth asked, as soon as the receiver hit the cradle.

"Merle La Fountaine was admitted to Saint Mary's Hospital in Madison in December 1970, and released three days later. Do you make anything of that?"

She had melted some butter in a saucepan and would next add milk before she stirred in the onions and potatoes. Salt and lots of pepper would follow.

"No. Do you?" she said.

I shook my head no. "Clarkie also said that there was no record of an Allison Taylor ever being admitted to an area hospital at that time."

"Maybe she used her maiden name."

"If so, that ends the hunt right there."

"Maybe not. She told you practically everything else about herself. If you ask, maybe she'll tell you that."

"Not everything, Ruth. She didn't tell me why Stevey La Fountaine was blackmailing her husband."

"You're sure that's the case now?"

"Clarkie seems to think it is. Although he didn't say so in so many words."

"Then I'd keep an open mind. It's served you well in the past." She put the lid on the saucepan and turned down the fire. "Which reminds me. Wilmer Wiemer called. He wants you to call him back."

"Did he say what he wanted?"

She was reaching for the meat grinder. "I just told you."

"Wilmer, this is Garth Ryland," I said on reaching him. "Ruth said you called."

"Garth, I just wanted to thank you for losing a client of mine. Hubert La Fountaine informed me as of this morning that he was going to take his business elsewhere."

"You don't sound too broken-hearted about it," I said.

"It was a crazy deal anyway, if you want the truth of the matter. Trying to buy your own property, while at the same time trying to keep it a secret. Whoever heard of the like?"

"Pardon me for saying so, Wilmer, but I still believe there's a great deal of money involved."

"Gilbert La Fountaine's life savings, you mean?"

"It has to be somewhere, Wilmer. The principals involved are trying too hard to get it."

"Well, I'll tell you where it's not, and that's in that body shop that Hubert was, still is I guess, trying so hard to buy."

"You've looked, then?" I'd be damned if I'd give him the satisfaction of telling him that he was right.

"I didn't have to look. I told you before. Gil La Fountaine's been dead for five years now. Anybody with an ounce of brains would know that money wouldn't just sit there that whole time without somebody in town going after it."

"It would, if it were locked up."

"Believe it if you will, Garth. I don't."

I glanced outside where a cardinal was huddled in the evergreen under the dining room window. He looked so forlorn and out of place sitting there I wondered if Sniffy was right about the storm we had coming in.

"Then where do you think the money is?" I said.

"Like I told you, in someone's pocket. Or was, anyway." Never one to shun the limelight, Wilmer now knew that he had my attention.

"Continue," I said.

"Well, I made some calls to Madison for you to see what I might learn. You'll never guess whose name popped up."

"Jonathan Springer," I said.

As I waited for Wilmer's response, I was certain that I was right. "Where did you ever come up with that?" he said.

Where had I come up with that? Then I remembered. Allison Springer had once done Gilbert La Fountaine's taxes for him. If she somehow knew about his money, then that piece of property would be a good short-term investment, particularly with an expensive election coming up.

"Stevey La Fountaine. That's who was after the property." Wilmer said. "I guess insanity runs in the family."

"If not, greed surely does."

"But where Stevey thought he'd get the money for it, I have no idea. Neither he nor that boyfriend of his has a pot to piss in."

"What boyfriend?" I said, to learn what he knew.

"The guy in Madison that owns the art studio there in the low-rent district downtown. Where Stevey was living before he came back here."

"How do you find out all of these things?" I said in amazement.

"I made it my business, Garth. You've got to cut yourself every angle you can, and even a few you can't."

"Thanks, Wilmer," I said. "I owe you."

"It's not the first time. Probably won't be the last."

Along with the potato soup, we had Ruth's homemade ham salad for lunch. She put hers on crackers. I made a sandwich out of mine.

"So where are you headed this afternoon?" she said.

"I plan to visit Merle La Fountaine again and maybe stop by the Senator's house on the way back."

"Why Merle La Fountaine?" Ruth said, spooning some ham salad onto a soda cracker. "Your last trip there should have been enough for you."

"Ellen still insists that Merle's faking it. I know Ellen might be crazy, but I just want to be certain about Merle."

"To what end?"

"Hell, Ruth, I don't know. I'm at a loss right now. But I can't sit around here and do nothing."

"It seems to me, considering your track record of late, that would be the smartest thing to do."

"But that's not the way I'm made."

She put the cracker in her mouth. To hear what she had to say, I had to wait until she finished it, since to her one of life's cardinal sins was to talk with your mouth full.

She said, "You were singing a different tune earlier today. In fact, if that car of yours had started, we wouldn't even be having this conversation. What happened to change your mind?"

"Think about it, Ruth. How much more trouble could I be in?"

She shrugged. "Point well taken. But if the hammer falls again today, I'm not going to be here to bail you out. The girls and I are going bowling late this afternoon or early this evening, depending on when Wanda gets her hair done."

Wanda Collum, the youngest of the "girls," as Ruth called them, had turned seventy in June. "Where are you going bowling?" I said.

"We haven't decided yet. Wanda wants to try that new alley up at Glover. Liddy Bennett wants to go to the Rapids as always."

"I'm not sure that's such a good idea. In Sniffy's words, we've got a shit-kicker of a snowstorm coming."

She bristled at the thought of staying home. "I've never seen a snowstorm yet that could keep me from where I wanted to go."

"You're driving, then?"

"Who else?"

Then there was no use asking if I might borrow her car today.

A half hour passed. We had finished eating several minutes ago, but Ruth was still chewing on a thought.

She said, "One thing you might not have considered is that whoever built that cross had to have a key to get inside the body shop."

"That did occur to me, yes."

"And if they had a key to get inside the building, they might have had a key to get inside that cabinet," she continued, taking little note of my sarcasm.

"So what you're saying is, find the maker of the cross and I might find the money?"

"Unless it was Stevey La Fountaine who built the cross."

Leave it to Ruth to complicate matters.

CHAPTER 21

There wasn't even a wrinkle in the clouds when I left for the Lutheran Home later that afternoon. Stretched in a flat grey sheet as far as I could see, they hadn't yet begun to lower, but when I stopped to check the wind, which had been from the east for two days now, I thought I smelled snow.

Avoiding Jackson Street, since I didn't know when Wayne Jacoby might be returning from Madison, I took the back way to the Lutheran Home. As a kid, I had spent many a summer day exploring Oakalla and once knew it by heart. No longer, though. I kept bumping into outbuildings where there used to be none and houses where there used to be fields and reality where there used to be only the grandest of notions. Part of the gain of growing up was in seeing people and things as they were, instead of how you fancied them to be. Part of the loss, too.

I doubted that Dorothy Culp would allow me to see
Merle La Fountaine again, so I didn't bother to ask her.
Instead, I went straight to Merle's door and knocked. At
least she didn't call me Stevey this time when she opened
it. But her smile of obvious joy went quickly to a look of
fear and confusion. Shit, I thought. Here we go again.

"May I come in?" I said.

Merle wore the same long ragged pea green dress that
she had worn the first time that I had gone there. I wondered if it was the only dress she had and why she and
Ellen had come to own two exactly alike. Ellen might tell
me if I persevered, but I doubted that Merle ever would.

Merle held on to the door a little tighter and made no
move to let me in, as her bright yellow eyes studied me
with interest, yet wariness, like a crow an owl decoy in the
meadow below. I could only stand there in the cold and
await her decision.

Then she threw the door open and began to back
away. I waited for her to get all the way to the couch before
I entered.

"Not Stevey," she said, once I was inside.

"No. Not Stevey. Garth Ryland."

At least she didn't scream this time. But I saw no recognition on her face.

The apartment was as hot as Vera Richardson's kitchen
had been. I took off my stocking cap and gloves and unbut-
toned my coat, but I was still too warm. Soon I'd started to
sweat.

The beige couch on which Merle sat had white doilies
on its arms and a beige, brown, and orange afghan folded
once and draped across its back. A beige overstuffed rock-
ing chair with a pull-out footrest sat facing the color tele-
vision across a brown shag carpet, and of the three framed
prints on the walls, two were of irises, the other of lilies.

From what I could see of the kitchen behind the couch, it was small with just enough room for one person. I couldn't see Merle's bedroom, but assumed that it and the bathroom were to my left down the hall.

"Are you up to answering a couple questions?" I said.

She just stared at me.

"Twenty-six years ago, do you remember ever being in the hospital?" I said.

She appeared to have heard me. So I waited for her answer. Finally, "Yes."

"Do you remember what was the matter with you?"

She thought a moment, and was about to shake her head no when her face suddenly brightened. "Yes!"

I waited.

"Wendy," she said at last.

"Wendy Bodine?"

She nodded.

"What about her?"

"Had her there. In the hospital."

"You gave birth to her there?"

She nodded emphatically.

"Then she's your daughter?"

"Yes. My only one."

"What about Ellen?"

She scowled. "She's not my daughter."

"Then whose daughter is she?"

"The stork's."

"Are you saying the stork brought her?"

Her scowl deepened. "*Yes.*"

"What about your two sons, do you claim them?"

She folded her arms and wouldn't look at me. "I have no sons."

"You do know that Stevey was shot to death?"

"I have no sons!" she repeated, much louder this time.

"And your husband, do you claim him?"

The look on her face was one of pure anguish. "Yes." It was barely a whisper.

"Do you know where his money is?"

"Stevey took it."

"When?"

She appeared confused by the question, but then she said, "Long time ago."

"Years, you mean?"

She didn't answer. I saw by the weary look on her face that I had already lost her. But I wouldn't complain. I'd gotten more than I had expected.

"Thank you, Mrs. La Fountaine. I'll be going now."

If she heard, it didn't register.

I didn't know who was more surprised, Wendy Bodine or I, when we nearly collided on Merle La Fountaine's doorstep. "What are you doing here?" she said sharply.

"I might ask you the same thing?"

Today Wendy Bodine was out of uniform. In her jeans, ski boots, and bulky red jacket, with her Chevy S-10 loaded and a tarpaulin over the bed, she looked ready to hit the slopes.

"I'm here to say goodbye. So if you don't mind . . ." She started to go inside.

I put my hand on her arm to stop her. She didn't resist, but I could feel her coil inside her coat. One wrong move, and I'd be bent over, looking for the family jewels.

"Take your hand off me, please," she said through clenched teeth.

"When you tell me why Merle La Fountaine insists that you're her daughter. Her only daughter." I dropped my hand, hoping that the question would hold her.

"Because I am," she said with tears in her eyes.

"In spirit, you mean?"

"What else would I mean?" She opened Merle's door and went inside.

I needed to call Ruth before she left to go bowling. Since the nearest phone was inside the hotel, I went in there.

"The answer is no," Dorothy Culp said when I walked into her office. "Whatever you want from me, the answer is no. I almost lost my job over you."

"I just wanted to use your phone."

"There's a pay phone in the hallway between the men's and the women's restrooms." She pointed to show me the way.

I felt for the coin purse that I had carried for the past thirty-five years, the hard red plastic one that used to say "Ryland Dairy" on it before the writing rubbed off. I discovered that Wayne Jacoby had taken it, too.

"Do you have a quarter I could borrow?"

Whether to reclaim her quarter in case I struck out, or to keep me in sight, Dorothy Culp followed me part way to the phone where she could watch me and the front door at the same time. I hoped that earlier she hadn't called Wayne Jacoby, who would now be on his way.

"Is there a problem, Dorothy?" I said.

"If it snows and blows like they say it's going to, there will be."

Relieved, I called Ruth and asked her my question.

"No, Garth. No matter what she says, Merle La Fountaine is not that girl's mother. Up until she got sick, she hardly missed a day's work there at the Five and Dime. Hardly a one in the last thirty years. I'd have known if she were pregnant. All of us in Oakalla would have."

"She missed three days of work that we know of, when she went to the hospital in Madison."

"It wasn't to have a baby, Garth. You can forget that."

"She seems sincere," I persisted.

"So does every crackpot I've ever known. You can't judge the message by the messenger. Surely, you've lived long enough to know that."

I could tell by her tone of voice that she was starting to get frustrated with me. Either that or she was ready to go bowling.

"Okay, then. I'll let you go," I said. "But have you listened to the latest weather report?"

"No. I've been too busy doing dishes and cleaning the house. And answering the phone," she emphasized.

"Then I'm not your only caller?"

"Let's put it this way, Garth. You're not the only person in town who's worried about the snow."

"You might listen to one of us," I said.

"When you start listening to me." She hung up.

I saw my first snowflake when I stepped up onto Jonathan and Allison Springer's front porch. Unwilling to risk being seen by Wayne Jacoby, I had returned from the Lutheran Home the same way that I had gone, which was what I liberally termed the "back way," since it avoided Jackson Street altogether. It was two blocks farther that way, most of it into a forehead-numbing east wind, but under the circumstances, it seemed a small price to pay.

The first thing that I noticed when Allison Springer let me inside was that the pink rose on the dining room table had started to droop. Jonathan got her a fresh one every week, she had said. He would have to bring her one today, or their string would be broken.

We sat at the dining room table where Allison Springer served us each coffee. She didn't forget this time, but brought my cream and sugar along with the coffee. The only thing for which I could fault her was her choice of cups. My fingers were still too big for the handle, especially now that they were swollen from the glass.

"So," she said, "for what reason do I have the pleasure of your company today?"

Her voice was cheerful enough, but Allison Springer

looked tired, as if, like me, she had put in a hard week. Neither did her light grey sweater help her looks any. It went well with her dark grey jeans, but made her face appear pale and drawn. And her makeup did nothing to hide the circles under her eyes.

"You look like you've been burning the midnight oil," I said, ignoring her question.

"Does it show?" She seemed to take no offense. "I guess that's one of the hazards of being over forty. You don't look twenty-five any more."

"So they tell me."

"How old are you really?"

"A couple-three years older than you."

"You don't look it," she said.

"I don't feel it most days. Today I do."

"Jonathan says wait until we get to be his age. Then we'll really have reason to complain.

"You love him very much, don't you?"

"To use the old cliché, more than life itself."

"Enough to kill for him?"

"Of course," she said smoothly without missing a beat. "If the situation demanded it."

"Have you killed for him?"

"No. Did you have someone in mind?"

"Stevey La Fountaine."

She laughed in my face. "Forgive me. But I didn't know you took your art so seriously."

"Are you saying that Stevey was a bad artist?"

She took a sip of her coffee. Her hand seemed to fit the bone china cup a lot better than mine.

"I'm saying that Stevey La Fountaine was a drunk. Like all talents, he had his moments, but in the end couldn't sustain them."

Who can? I thought. As the saying went, only a mediocrity was always at his best. Out loud, I said, "So you do agree with Jonathan that he had talent?" And me, if I judged by the one painting of his father.

"When he wanted to exercise it, yes. And when he wanted to be a bastard, he could be that, too."

"Was he gay?"

She looked disappointed in me. "What does that have to do with anything? You're not homophobic, are you?"

"Claustrophobic," I said with a smile. "That's the only phobia I have."

"When why the question about Stevey's sexual preference?"

"He was overheard talking to your husband on the phone, using words like 'dear' and 'sweetheart.'"

"Not *my* husband," she said with certainty. "Maybe somebody else's."

"How many benefactors did Stevey have? Because the person that Stevey was talking to was also his benefactor."

"Who told you that?"

"Ellen La Fountaine."

"Then she's lying, if she says that Jonathan and Stevey were lovers."

"Why did Jonathan go so far out on a limb to support Stevey?" I said.

"He felt sorry for him, I think."

"Why?"

"Because Jonathan *was* quite taken with Stevey as an artist, and didn't think that he had gotten a fair shake in life. He couldn't see that a lot of Stevey's problems were his own doing."

"Unlike you?"

The look she gave me spoke of life's lessons learned the hard way. "Jonathan is the dreamer in the family. I'm the practical one. He believes that if your heart is in the right place, things will always turn out all right in the end."

"Good for him, I guess."

"Not so good for me, though," she said with a sigh.

"Because he keeps proving you right?"

"Because he keeps proving me wrong. I was one of the very few who never clapped for Tinkerbell."

Had I clapped? Probably. I was a sucker for happy endings.

"Is there any chance that Stevey was blackmailing Jonathan?" I said.

"You've been talking to our new sheriff, I see," she said angrily.

"He seems to think he has something going."

"Well, let him try to prove it. That's all I can say. You, too, if you're so inclined."

"I'm not. But Sheriff Jacoby doesn't strike me as a man who blows smoke."

"Only when it's to his advantage," she said.

"What's the advantage in alienating the man who in all likelihood will be our next governor?"

"It's a way to redeem himself. Surely you believe in redemption, Garth. It saves us from all our past sins."

"Even murder?"

"Who said anything about murder?"

"Somebody murdered Stevey La Fountaine."

"Jonathan didn't. I can assure you of that."

"Not even to save your reputation?"

She gave me a steely look. "Explain yourself, please."

"I've made some inquiries. There's no record of your being in any of the area hospitals when you say you lost your child."

"That's because I wasn't in a hospital. I couldn't afford one. I was in a cheap motel bleeding down a toilet."

"That must have been very scary for you."

"You have no idea."

"I'm sorry."

"Sorry for asking, or sorry it happened?" For whatever

reason, my answer seemed important to her.

"Both," I said.

"Then you're forgiven."

She stood as a signal that my time there was over. As I got up from the table, I realized that I hadn't taken that first drink of coffee.

"Merle La Fountaine," I said.

"What about her?"

"I understand that you used to do Gilbert La Fountaine's taxes. I just wondered what your opinion of his wife is?"

"I have no opinion of his wife. I hardly knew her."

"Just asking."

"Why?"

"As with you, I'm trying to figure out what she's capable of." I started walking toward the front door. She followed.

"She couldn't be capable of much, according to what Stevey told us," Allison Springer said. "She's in the Lutheran Home, isn't she, with Alzheimer's?"

"Yes. But according to her daughter, Ellen, she's faking it."

"I don't think that's a disease you fake."

I had forgotten about the snow. When I looked out the window, I was surprised to see that the sidewalks were white again.

"Did Stevey ever talk to you about his family?" I said.

"Stevey and I seldom talked about anything, his family included. But I don't think there was any love lost among any of them."

"What about Gilbert La Fountaine's hidden fortune? Did Stevey ever mention it?"

"Only in passing. He said that whoever inherited the family estate would be a rich man someday."

"I'm assuming that he intended to be that man."

"Why do you say that?"

"His choice of words for one thing. 'Man' seems to leave his mother and sister out. For another thing, I have it from a good source that he was trying to buy the place for himself."

She smiled. "With what? Most of the time Stevey could barely afford to buy his paints."

"Maybe he was planning to come into some money."

Her anger returned. "Blackmail, you mean?"

"There's always that ugly possibility."

"I like your choice of words. Blackmail is a very ugly possibility," she said as she closed the door on me.

CHAPTER 22

It was dark and snowing hard. I could see it in the street lights every time I got up to look outside. Ruth had already left when I got home, so I fixed myself an Old Crow and ginger ale, pulled a chair up by the phone, and tried to call Abby. I got her answering machine instead, and was so disappointed that I decided not to leave a message.

The phone rang about an hour later. I was on my second Old Crow and ginger ale and not giving a damn about much of anything. I knew I should eat some supper, but as surely as I got it all fixed, Wayne Jacoby would arrive at my front door to arrest me again. A fire would have gone well with the Old Crow, and Daisy would have enjoyed a walk in the snow, but it all seemed pointless somehow. The fat on the fire had been rendered to lard, and the sand in the hourglass had dropped long ago.

"Hello?" I said, not sure of my voice.

"Garth, it's Clarkie. I haven't caught you at a bad time, have I?"

"No. I just had a frog in my throat."

"Sorry to take so long with this, but like I hinted earlier, I was catching some flak for even messing with it. It's sort of an in-house thing. At least that's the way the people around here feel."

The snow was coming down harder. I could barely see across the street now.

"I guess you can't blame them for that."

"Anyway, here's what the deal is. A few months ago, a man by the name of Julian Carter was arrested by then Dane County Deputy Sheriff Wayne Jacoby and his partner for DWI. He'd been to one of those crossroads bars north of the city and was on his way back when they stopped him. Well, it turned out that the man was gay, which is neither here nor there, but for his part he didn't want to be locked up in a drunk tank with a bunch of rednecks who might take offense to him. So Julian Carter offered Wayne Jacoby and his partner a deal. If they'd let him go with a slap on the wrist, he'd give them some really juicy stuff that would put a well known state senator away for a long time. It turned out that Julian Carter was Stevey La Fountaine's roommate, and that they'd just had a lover's quarrel, which was why Julian Carter was out getting drunk in the first place."

There was then a long pause.

"Is something wrong, Clarkie?"

"I can't believe I'm telling you all of this with a straight face. I've come a long way from high school."

"I'd like to think we both have."

"Anyway, since Julian Carter had brought it up, Wayne Jacoby and his partner felt obligated to ask him what sort of evidence he had on the state senator. That's when he started to backpedal and said that he didn't exactly have the evidence, but knew that his roommate had been blackmailing the senator for several years now. He offered as evidence all of the showings that the senator had arranged for Stevey La Fountaine and the fact that the senator had footed the bill for Julian Carter and Stevey to travel around the country for a year, doing whatever it was they wanted to. The van he was now driving was a present from Stevey, bought with the senator's money. No deal. Wayne Jacoby and his partner told Julian Carter. That was all hearsay. There wasn't a prosecutor in the state who would act on it. Then go after the evidence, Julian begged. When you get it, I'll corroborate it. Still no deal, they said. So Julian Carter went off to the drunk tank and later got his license suspended for a year, and thought that was the end of it. So did Wayne Jacoby's partner, who really didn't care to learn what the senator had done because he liked his voting record. Wayne Jacoby, on the other hand, decided to follow it up on his own, and my sources say it took him first to Mississippi and then to Oakalla, where he is now."

"So he followed Jonathan Springer here?"

"From all indications, yes."

I didn't much like the scenario, but then there wasn't much about Wayne Jacoby that I did like.

"What haven't you told me, Clarkie? In other words, what took Wayne Jacoby to Mississippi, and why did he make a special trip to Madison today?"

"He made a special trip here because Julian Carter happened to be back in the drunk tank on another DWI. He stands to lose his license for good this round, plus he might be looking at some prison time."

I glanced out the window. The house across the street had all but disappeared. Only its porch light told me it was there.

"So he was only too eager to cooperate?" I said.

"You got it. Especially with Stevey La Fountaine dead. He said that he couldn't hurt Stevey any more than he already had."

"He blames himself for Stevey's death?"

"That's the word I got. Which was why he was out tying one on last night."

There might be something to Julian Carter's guilt, or it just might be loneliness talking. There was no way to know unless I talked to Julian Carter myself, which, if Wayne Jacoby had anything to say about it, was never going to happen.

"What's the smoking gun, Clarkie? Just what does Wayne Jacoby have on Jonathan Springer?"

"There seems to be a paper trail, if that's what you're asking. The Senator's wife sold her farm south of Madison right before Stevey La Fountaine and Julian Carter took their cross country trip. That's the big item. But once they start digging, I imagine there'll be others."

"That might be a coincidence, Clarkie. No prosecutor's going to risk his career for something like that."

"There's something else, Garth," Clarkie said, his voice sobered by the enormity of what he was about to say. "You asked about Mississippi. While he was going to school, Senator Springer was involved in a lynching down there. He was arrested, but the case never went to trial."

"The lynching of a black man?" I could feel myself frantically grasping for handholds, the way a sliding mountaineer does when there is nothing but ice beneath and the abyss below.

"Yes. He and several of his fraternity brothers were involved."

"What fraternity?" I prayed to God it wasn't my own.

"Wayne Jacoby will have to tell you that. He has all the details. I'm just reporting what my sources told me."

Though it was hard to think, I made myself think. Finally I found something to which to cling.

"There's only one problem, Clarkie. How would Stevey La Fountaine ever find out something like that? He doesn't have the resources that Wayne Jacoby has."

"It's my understanding that it's a matter of public record. Besides, according to everybody that knew him, including Julian Carter, Stevey La Fountaine was a master at finding your weakness and living off of it."

"I don't know, Clarkie. I still think there's more to it than that."

"Wayne Jacoby doesn't think so. And the last time I looked, he was sheriff of Adams County." I could hear "poetic justice" in Clarkie's voice.

"Thanks for your help, Clarkie. I owe you once again."

"The debt's paid, Garth. It was the minute I took this job."

"You don't want your old job back?"

"Not in a thousand years. Not for a million dollars." He hung up.

I had no more than put the receiver down when Danny Palmer called. "Garth, I just caught the squeal. We need all the volunteers we can get, and the way it's snowing, that won't be many."

"What's the problem?"

"Merle La Fountaine is missing. They brought her her food at six. When they went back at six-thirty to check on her, the door to her apartment was standing wide open, and she was gone. If she's outside in this weather, she won't last an hour."

"I'll be there as soon as I can."

"You'd better bundle up. The wind is starting to blow."

Indeed it was. Not only could I no longer see across the street, I couldn't even see my next door neighbor's house a few yards away.

CHAPTER 23

There are snows and there are snows. Some you ignore because, despite the temporary inconvenience, they don't amount to much. Small at heart, more like sand than snow, they "strut and fret their hour upon the stage, then are heard no more." Others command your attention simply by their beauty. Large-flaked and easy going, they usually fall straight down on bare ground, cover the grass and cling to the trees, and leave the world awash in white. They are most often, though not always, April and October snows, and serve as a reminder that winter in Wisconsin is never very far away.

Still other snows invite you to put on your gloves and a pot of hot chocolate and come out and play. Sledding snows, as I like to call them, they are neither too fierce nor too deep nor too wet to enjoy. Too busy having fun, you don't realize how cold or how spent you are, until evening falls and burns your cheeks, and you start that sad-happy trudge toward home.

Then there are those rare storms that rivet you with their fury and make you pay them homage whether you want to or not. In unrelenting volleys which if they pause at all, do so only to catch their breath for another blow, they shake the house, rattle the nerves and the windows, and fill the outside corridors with thick white smoke that barely looks like snow. Inside, you thank God that you don't have to go out. Outside, as I was that night, you bend low to the ground and try to keep the wind at your back.

Exactly ten of us had gathered there in Merle La Fountaine's apartment. The rest of Oakalla's volunteer army were either looking after their families or too far away from town to make the trip in. Had it been a child who was lost, there would have been too many of us to count. But apparently, in most eyes around Oakalla, Merle La Fountaine didn't rate the risk.

Sheriff Wayne Jacoby in his hat, black fur earmuffs, and leather jacket was giving us our instructions. The earmuffs matched his gloves and mustache perfectly. Maybe that was why he kept them on inside.

Starting with Danny Palmer and Lanny Morrison, he began to assign pairs of us different sectors of town to search. As we went out two by two, it didn't take long for me to notice that Wayne Jacoby and I were the only ones left in there. The thought of being his partner appealed to me less than going out into the storm in the first place.

"You might as well go home, Ryland," he said, as he put on his gloves. "You're not needed here."

"You need every man you can get," I said.

"Not you."

"Have it your way, then," I said, starting for the door.

"I'll go looking on my own."

He made a move to stop me, but was an instant too late. I had him jammed up against the door with both of his arms pinned at his side.

"Don't borrow any more trouble than you're already in," he said.

"And don't you be a bigger fool than you already are. You need foot soldiers, and I'm volunteering."

"It won't change anything," he said as I released him. "No matter how this plays out, you're still going back to jail."

"Be that as it may . . ." I said, as I stepped around him out into the snow.

Wayne Jacoby had deployed his squad much as I would have done by giving them each a quadrant of town to search. The most logical assumption was that Merle La Fountaine would head for home, and that was the direction that Danny Palmer and Lanny Morrison had gone. The least logical assumption was that she would head for Baker's Four Dozen, the woods just north of the Lutheran Home, so that was the direction that I went. It seemed to me that either in or out of her right mind, Merle La Fountaine might fly in the face of logic.

Baker's Four Dozen was a small tame woods compared to Mitchell's Woods northwest of town and the Lost 1600 southeast of town—both of which required a compass or a strong sure sense of direction to navigate. Formerly a Christmas tree farm that had been allowed to grow up in brush for the past few years, Baker's Four Dozen encompassed about fifty acres in all, most of it pine and fir, and most of the trees between twenty and thirty feet tall. Where trees had been cut and no saplings planted was where the weeds and briers had taken over, making it a virtual deer haven in there, and a great place to hunt, if you didn't mind being shot at close range by a high-powered rifle.

Consequently, those of us in Oakalla, even the die-hard nimrods, usually avoided it at all cost during deer hunting season, preferring to leave it to the out-of-towners, who didn't know any better. Though fatalities were few, near misses were almost an everyday occurrence, so the standing joke around Oakalla was, only the born to run and the born again ventured into Baker's Four Dozen.

The flashlight that I had brought from home was no help out in the blowing snow, so I kept it off until I reached the edge of the woods and a windbreak. There, I turned it on, then turned my back to the wind for a moment to let my face thaw out and to knock some of the snow from my coat, particularly the patch that was leaking ice water down my throat.

Then I took something from my pocket and held it under the light. It was a pink terry house-slipper that I'd found half buried in snow in a rut at the edge of the drive in front of Merle La Fountaine's apartment. Since it was neither water-soaked nor frozen, I had to assume that it hadn't been there for very long. But did it belong to Merle La Fountaine? I'd only know that if I found her.

I came upon my first footprint a few yards inside Baker's Four Dozen in the lee of a dwarf spruce that had grown out instead of up and somehow escaped the pruning axe when the woods was thinned for market. The way the wind was blowing, even here with acres of woods between it and me, there was no way to tell how long ago the print had been made. It could have been an hour, or five minutes ago. I guessed an hour, because while I couldn't find any others to match it, it was still there when I decided to move on.

But I'd only taken a couple steps when a thought made me turn around and go back to it. Putting my own foot next to it for size, I discovered that, if I allowed for what the wind had covered up, it was very nearly the size of my own. I took no comfort in that discovery. The print reminded me too much of those that I'd found outside my north window.

My next find was one of pure dumb luck. I'd come into a cut-over area where the briers grew so thick that I could see no way through it until, searching for a way around it, I came upon a deer path that seemed to split it in two. At that moment, however, the whole area exploded in a white gust of wind that rocked me back on my heels. Groping for something to hold on to, my left hand caught on a brier that wouldn't let go. Rather than lose my glove and maybe my fingers to frostbite, I waited out the gust until I could see to free myself. In doing so, a few seconds later I discovered that my glove was wrapped around a frayed piece of soft green cloth, very similar in color and texture to the dress that Merle La Fountaine was wearing the last time I saw her.

Still on the deer path, I stepped into a small stream that seemed to lead ever deeper into the thicket. The stream should have been frozen solid at that time of year. But I'd picked the place where it bubbled up from a spring and likely the place where the deer had been coming to drink now that running water was in short supply.

For once, I wished that I had listened to Ruth when she suggested that I buy better boots. Not that my right foot was very wet or in any immediate danger of freezing. Still, it was a concern, especially when I saw all that snow coming down, and no end to my search in sight.

When the stream bent left into a small, level clearing that I took for a marsh, the deer trail continued straight up a ridge and back into the firs and pines. Even without the wind and the snow, I would have had a hard time knowing my direction in there. With them, the ever-swirling snow that seemed to come from everywhere at once, and always overhead, imperious and incessant, the wind's mind-

numbing roar, I began to doubt myself even when I knew
which way I should be going. Neither did I know what was
beyond Baker's Four Dozen. Farm fields, I assumed, but
there was no guarantee of that.

Stopping to rest and again clear some of the snow
away from my throat, I noticed, even after knocking them
together, that one boot was a whole lot heavier than the
other. It was the one in which I could barely feel my toes.

At the top of the ridge, I had a decision to make. I could
keep going, or turn back. If I kept going, I might find Merle
La Fountaine's frozen body, which was the best that I could
hope for by now. That was the good news. The bad news
was that I could get lost and find nothing but trouble.
Neither appealed to me, so I kept on going. My rationale
was that I already knew what was behind me, so there was
nothing to gain by backtracking.

But as my father was fond of saying (with me directly
in his sights), a smart man will change his mind, but a fool
never will. The wind at the top of the ridge blew so hard
that it seemed to flatten my face, smashing even the bones
as it poured into my brain. That was when I could still feel
my face, still see the shape of my thoughts. When everything started to get black and fuzzy and each ankle had a
sandbag attached to it, I knew that I had to turn around.
But that in and of itself wasn't easy. Groggily, like a race-
weary jockey whipping a spent horse, I kept slapping at
my right leg until I finally got it to swing around and start
back the other way.

I had to get off the ridge, and I didn't care how, so I
took the nearest game trail, which led me straight down to
the marsh that I had skirted earlier. I knew I shouldn't go
through it, but I wasn't sure that I had the wherewithal to
go all the way around it. *Think!* I told myself. *You have to
do something.*

As I stood there trying to put two thoughts together, I

glimpsed something large that came down off the ridge to my right, before it was swallowed in a gust of wind and snow. A deer, I first thought, then dismissed the idea. No deer in its right mind would be out in this weather. It would be curled contentedly under its electric blanket with a big bowl of buttered popcorn, watching reruns of *Bambi*. Or at the very least be bedded down in the deepest pine thicket that it could find.

With my right foot now numb and the fingers of both hands nearly that way, I hated to walk the twenty yards or so that it would take to find out what I'd seen. But if by some miracle she were still alive, I couldn't miss my chance at Merle La Fountaine. Rescuing her wouldn't keep me out of jail, but it might help me sleep at night.

Not a deer. Not Merle La Fountaine either, unless she'd picked up some hiking boots somewhere. The footprints looked a lot like the one I'd found earlier by the dwarf spruce, and now that I had a set of them to study, even more like the ones outside my office window. Though they led straight into the marsh, even the coward in me said that it would be a shame to miss the opportunity.

The marsh was small, about an acre in all, and no more than fifty yards wide where I was crossing. Each step that found frozen ground seemed a small victory to me, who hated wet feet to begin with and frozen feet even more. The thought of ice water rushing into my one dry boot brought a chill that stayed with me all the way to the other side. Thinking that I was in the clear, I rushed the last couple steps and found another spring with a soft bottom. I pitched forward into the snow, as my feet temporarily stayed put in the muck behind me. When they did come out of the mud, they were as black as my thoughts. The hell with it all, I was getting out of here while I still could.

The tracks, though, where the wind hadn't drifted them shut, seemed to lead south, the direction that I wanted to go. So I went that way. Really cold now, with snow up my sleeves and snow down my throat, and two clubfeet and the feeling going in my hands, I soon began to second-guess myself. Baker's Four Dozen had to be larger than fifty acres. Either that or I couldn't be going in the right direction, or I would have been out of there by then.

Turn around! A voice inside me screamed. You're going the wrong way. But logic said otherwise, because the wind was still at my back. I stopped, unable to resolve the clamor within. It was then that I realized why some people freeze to death with help or shelter not far away. You can't be reasonable if you can't think. And you can't think with someone screaming in your ear, even if it's you doing the screaming. Thought requires calm. Calm in the face of adversity requires the hardest kind of discipline. Once I determined that yes, I was in fact going the right way, it was just a matter of putting one foot ahead of the other.

I was almost there. I could see the lights of what I took to be the Lutheran Home as a large white blur not far ahead. As the woods thinned and the wind once more had free reign, I found fewer and fewer tracks to follow. Even my own tracks seemed to disappear almost as fast as I made them.

I'd given up on finding either Merle La Fountaine or the person ahead of me. I'd given up on redeeming myself or avenging myself, however things might have turned out. Jail even was starting to sound good to me. At least I couldn't get in any more trouble there. Peace at any price? As Vince Lombardi was fond of saying, fatigue makes cowards of us all.

So when I came upon an unnatural hump in the snow, I rationalized it as just another drift in my eagerness to be warm again. It took a lifetime of eating peanut butter-and-jelly sandwiches-crust first to make myself stop long enough to see what was there. Wayne Jacoby, it turned out, lying face down in the snow, with, as I soon learned, a bullet in his chest. If that were not enough of a surprise, I discovered that he was still alive. Just my luck, I thought. Now, I've got to carry the son of a bitch from here.

CHAPTER 24

Danny Palmer and I sat in the second-floor waiting room of the Adams County Hospital. Danny was the one who had driven Wayne Jacoby and me to the hospital in his wrecker, since it was about the only thing that could get us there that night. Wayne Jacoby had bled all over me and to a lesser extent all over Danny's wrecker, but I supposed that couldn't be helped. The cold, which is every shot man's friend, had acted as a coagulant, keeping Wayne Jacoby's bleeding in check, until we got him in the warmth of Danny's wrecker, where the flood gates opened. Fortunately, we didn't have far to go, or despite our best efforts, Wayne Jacoby would have bled to death.

He was in recovery now and his prognosis was good. The slug, which since had been removed, had struck him

high on the right side of his chest, collapsed a lung and
nicked an artery, which was what had caused most of the
bleeding. The slug had continued on from there to lodge
against the skin of his back, bulging it slightly—like a boil
or carbuncle, the surgeon said as he handed the slug to
me. Wayne Jacoby would want it back, of course, but in
the meantime it was mine to keep.

"What time is it?" Danny said. "It seems like we've
been here all night."

I glanced at the big round clock above his head. "One-
fifteen."

"Is that A.M. or P.M.?"

"A.M., I believe. At least it's still dark outside."

"You couldn't prove it by me."

"Why don't you go home and get some sleep? You've
done more than enough for one night anyway," I said.

"Even if I go home, I won't get any sleep," he said.
"Some idiots are bound to be out in this storm, and as sure
as they are, they'll get hung up somewhere and call me."

"Speaking of which, I'd better call home to make sure
that Ruth and the girls made it back okay."

"Where were they?" he asked, alarmed.

"I really don't know. Either Glover or the Rapids."

Five minutes later, after borrowing a quarter from
Danny, I'd been to the pay phone and back. "No one
answers at home," I said to Danny, as I gave him back his
quarter. "That must mean they're holed up somewhere."

"You'd better hope that's what it means," he said.
"They might be stuck in a drift."

Though I had tried to put that thought out of my mind,
I knew it was a possibility. Ruth, in her infinite stubborn-
ness, might try to make it home in spite of all warnings to
the contrary. That was what I loved about her, though, her
indomitable will. She drove me to the brink sometimes,
but she never faltered when I most needed her.

"She'll be all right," I said. "She always is."

Danny nodded, acting as if he believed me.

An hour later the surgeon came in and said that Wayne Jacoby wanted to see me. Danny had fallen asleep in his blue plastic chair, so I didn't bother to wake him. He needed what sleep he could get. In the days ahead, with the roads drifted and the cold at hand, with Wendy Bodine gone for good, I doubted that he would be spending much time in bed.

Wayne Jacoby had changed dramatically from earlier that evening. Without his hat, gloves, and boots, his uniform and gun, and a couple pints of blood, he seemed to have shrunk several inches, and turned a whole lot younger, and paler. He looked about eighteen lying there. Even his mustache looked like peach fuzz.

"Is it still snowing?" he said.

"Some. It's mostly wind now."

Reluctant to approach him for a lot of reasons, I stood at his west window, watching the wind blow. Now in the northwest, it scooped a cloud of snow from the field beyond and dumped it in the hospital parking lot, recognizable only by its battery of blue lights, and their poles, which stuck up out of the white froth, like pilings from an angry sea.

"What do you see out there?" he said.

"Deliverance," I said, as I turned away from the window.

"For you?"

"I was thinking of Merle La Fountaine."

"That's a strange choice of words."

"Only to the uninitiated."

If he could have shrugged, he would have. He didn't understand me any more than I did him.

"I understand that I have you to thank for saving my life," he said.

"It was an accident, more or less."

"Still . . ."

We left it there. Anything more might have implied an intimacy that neither of us wanted. It was enough that I was still wearing his blood on my clothes.

"Who shot you, do you know?" I said.

"Senator Jonathan Springer," he said mechanically, without hesitation, as if he had rehearsed it beyond a doubt.

"You're sure? We were in the middle of a snowstorm, remember?"

His eyes momentarily found their fire again, before drifting away to the window, where the wind was busy knocking. "I know what I saw."

"Then tell me all of it," I said.

"That is all of it. I saw him coming at me and wouldn't let him pass, so he shot me at nearly point-blank range. I never heard the shot. I didn't even know I'd been hit until my legs gave out from under me, and I was face down in the snow."

"Was he wearing his camel's hair coat?"

He glanced at me, then back to the window again. I saw no certainty in that look.

He said, "I don't know what he was wearing."

"Then how do you know it was Jonathan Springer"

"I just know, that's all."

"And you couldn't be mistaken?"

He gave me a weary look, said nothing. A moment later the surgeon came to the door and held up two fingers. That meant I had two minutes left to find out what I needed to know.

"What happened in Mississippi?" I said. "I know there was a lynching and Jonathan Springer was supposedly involved . . ."

"Not supposedly involved," he interrupted. "He was arrested, along with eleven of his fraternity brothers."

"What fraternity?"

"The Knights Exemplar," he said, his voice filled with contempt.

"I never heard of it."

"That's because it was a secret arm of the KKK."

"Bullshit."

That lighted his fire again. "It's not bullshit. If you'd been in the service like I was, you'd know it was anything but bullshit. Those kinds of groups are everywhere, even in Oakalla, if you'd look hard enough."

I didn't say anything. I wanted answers, not an argument.

"So who did he lynch?" I said.

"An old black man on his way home from church. Twelve of them were arrested, but not one of them was ever brought to trial."

"Why not?"

He rolled his eyes. The answer had escaped him, seemed beyond him.

"And the cross, you've definitely linked it to Stevey La Fountaine?"

He closed his eyes. He was too tired to keep them open. "No. Not beyond a shadow of a doubt. But I know that's where it came from."

"So you found traces of gasoline in Julian Carter's van?"

"No. No gasoline . . ." He drifted off momentarily, then opened his eyes again. "But he had plenty of time to wash out the van."

"*Had* he washed out the van? Did he admit to it when you talked to him yesterday that yes, he and Stevey had burned the cross?"

"I never asked him." Then I saw his jaw begin to twitch.

It was time to leave. My two minutes were up three minutes ago. "When are they coming to arrest Jonathan Springer?" I said.

"As soon as I can get someone here."

"I want to be there when it happens."

He shook his head. "We're even, the way I see it. No jail for you, no deal from me."

"You owe me that much."

"I don't owe you a damn thing."

I shrugged. "Have it your way."

"You won't get around me on this. Don't even try."

"I don't plan to. But maybe the people of Oakalla might be curious as to where you've been spending your nights."

It took him a moment to run that through his computer. When he realized what I was referring to, he didn't like it a whole lot.

"I haven't been spending my nights anywhere, but at home or on patrol."

"Your late evenings, then."

"You're a bastard, Ryland." Had he been able, he would have come up out of his bed after me.

"I'm just saying that the citizens of Oakalla will be better served now that Wendy Bodine has moved to Florida."

At the mention of her name, all the fight seemed to go out of him, as he slumped back against his pillow. "Do whatever you want," he said. "Come Monday, it won't matter anyway."

"What happens Monday?"

"I'm resigning."

The thought didn't please me as much as it should have. "To do what?"

"I'm going to try to reenlist, maybe join my old outfit. I don't understand life out here. I never have. You, the senator, most of the people in this town, you live by your own rules and to hell with everybody else. In the army at least, I knew where I stood. Here, it changes from day to day, sometimes from minute to minute."

"I thought a career in the army was closed to you?" I said.

"Oh, I can still have a career," he said bitterly. "I just won't advance as I should."

"Then why put yourself through it again?"

"Because army life at its worst is better than this."

"Oakalla, you mean?"

"Yes. That's what I mean. I left here once to join the army. Now, I know why."

"You realize, don't you, that your charges against Jonathan Springer are never going to stick? Once you resign, that's it as far as your case against him goes, if you ever had one to begin with."

When he looked at me, without guile or remorse, without doubt, or even the need for it, I thought I finally understood Wayne Jacoby. It was payback time and Jonathan Springer just happened to be in the way.

"It won't matter. By then, his career will be ruined."

"Just like yours?"

"I wasn't a racist. I wasn't what they made me out to be. And even if I was, at least I never lynched anybody."

"Have you ever considered the fact that maybe he didn't either?"

He closed his eyes and settled into his pillow. "I know what he is. That's enough for me."

"Thanks for the ride," I said to Danny Palmer, as he stopped his wrecker in front of my house.

"No problem," he said, looking more tired than he had before he slept.

"You better head home," I said. "Sharon will be worried about you."

"I'll think about it." Then he said, "You never found Merle La Fountaine?"

"No. You either?"

"No. Where do you suppose she got to?"

"We can always hope that she's holed up somewhere here in Oakalla. If so, we'll be hearing about it before long."

"And if she isn't?"

"Then she's probably dead."

"Shit," he said.

As I looked out my window, I saw that the snowdrift in front of the house was as tall as the porch. "I agree," I said.

CHAPTER 25

Ruth called at six that morning. Unable to summon the energy to climb the stairs to bed, I'd slept in my clothes on the couch. I awakened when the phone rang, feeling as if I'd just gone over Niagara Falls without the barrel.

"Where are you?" I said.

"The bowling alley in Glover."

"Good. I was afraid that you'd try to make it home."

There was a long pause on her end. "We did try to make it home. We got as far as the roadblock, where they told us we could either go back to the bowling alley or spend the night in jail."

"You made the right choice, believe me."

Another long pause. "Have you ever tried to sleep in a bowling alley, Garth? On league night?"

I had to smile. "I don't suppose they provided cots?"

"They didn't even provide ear plugs. To make matters worse, Liddy Bennett has taken up snoring in her old age. When Liddy wasn't wheezing and snorting, Wanda Collum was trying to sing herself to sleep. I swear, if I hear one more verse of 'She'll Be Coming Around the Mountain,' I'm going to run that roadblock and take the consequences."

"Well, I didn't have the best of nights either."

"What happened?"

I told her.

"It could be worse, I suppose," she said when I finished.

"I don't see how."

"You're still here, aren't you?"

She yawned. I yawned. I could hear bowling pins flying in the background.

"What time did they start up there this morning?" I said.

"Start up?" She was indignant. "Those fools have never stopped."

"So what time do you think you'll be home?"

"As soon as they open up the roads between here and there, we're on our way."

"I don't want to be a wet blanket, but that might be afternoon, or later, depending on how much wind there is today."

"Be that as it may, I'll be home by dark."

"What do you plan to do in the meantime?"

"Bowl. What else?" She hung up.

Then I heard a vehicle pull up out front and beep its horn. I didn't recognize the silver four-wheel-drive Toyota pickup, but I did the young state cop driving it. In October, he and I had made a late-night visit to a former orphanage northeast of town. Clear-eyed and clean shaven, with a relaxed, yet commanding presence, he was my idea of what a state cop ought to be.

"Morning," he said with a smile, as I climbed up into the Toyota, which had been jacked up to clear everything but a redwood log. "It looks like we're working together again."

"It looks like it," I said, returning his smile.

"I ought to tell you up front. The captain's not too excited about this arrest." He drove to the intersection just north of my house where he made a U-turn. "We all stand to take a bath on this one."

"And we will," I said with certainty.

"You couldn't talk Sheriff Jacoby out of it?"

"No. I tried."

"So did the captain. He didn't get anywhere either."

"It's your call," I said. "We can always forget the whole thing."

"What if we're wrong and the sheriff's right? That's what the captain said. We're going to come off looking like fools, or worse."

"In either case," I said.

Jonathan Springer himself opened the front door to let us in. I wasn't encouraged when the first thing that I noticed was a pair of insulated rubber boots standing on a wet newspaper just inside the door.

"These yours?" I asked Jonathan Springer about the boots, as I compared my own boots to them and found mine an inch longer.

"As a matter of fact, they are."

"How are they in wet weather?"

"Better than yours, I would imagine," he said without even looking down.

"You don't seem surprised to see us, Senator," the young cop observed.

"You forget," Jonathan Springer said casually, as if this were an everyday occurrence. "I have friends in high places."

He stood there in his jeans and red-and-black plaid flannel shirt, looking as calm as someone could look under fire. Either he was a born leader or a great actor, or knew something that we didn't, because the fact that he was going to jail didn't seem to faze him at all.

Meanwhile I looked around for Allison Springer and was disappointed when I didn't see her. For a man that she loved more than life itself, she wasn't putting up much of a fight. Then again, maybe this was Jonathan Springer's show all the way down the line.

"So are you ready to go?" the young cop said.

"Whenever you are."

The cop looked at me. A shrug was the best I could do.

We drove in silence to the jail where Jonathan Springer waived his rights and let us put him in a cell two down from the one where I had spent most of Friday. Then the young cop handed the keys to me, and with great relief it seemed, left.

"So here we are," Jonathan Springer said, as he sat on one end of his cot, leaving the other open for me. "You might as well sit down if you plan on being here a while."

"You would have made a great governor," I said as I joined him on the cot.

His look said he wasn't so sure. "That remains to be seen . . ." He lost his composure for the first time, but just as quickly had it back again. "Will always remain to be seen."

"You're not going to try to clear your name?"

"It won't do any good. The damage has already been done. Besides, I'm not sure how much of my name there is left to clear."

"Then you're admitting that you killed Stevey La Fountaine?"

He turned to look at me. As he did, I could feel his humanity fill the cell. No one, not even he, would ever convince me that he was a cold-blooded killer.

"Is this off the record?" he said.

"Yes. If you want it to be."

"Then yes, I killed Stevey La Fountaine."

"I don't believe you."

"Believe what you will. It's true."

"Why? Over some incident that happened over thirty years ago in Mississippi?"

"It wasn't an incident, Garth," he said gravely, reproach-fully. "An innocent man was lynched."

"Well, an innocent man's about to be lynched here, too, so what's the difference?"

His smile at once forgave and embraced me. "You'd make one hell of a friend. I'm sorry to miss that chance. But the facts of the case are clear. I was arrested for murder. The only reason that I was never brought to trial was that none of us cracked under pressure, so all of their evidence against us was circumstantial."

"Your fraternity brothers, you mean? The Knights Exemplar?"

"That was just a front. There were no Knights Exemplar."

"So I've been told."

"What have you been told?"

"That it was a secret arm of the KKK."

He laughed so hard that he had to wipe the tears from his eyes. "It was a secret drinking fraternity," he said, when he could talk again. "We got together and drank. That was its sole intent and purpose."

"With the administration's blessing?"

"Hell no, though I'm not saying that they didn't look the other way on occasion. Boys will be boys, you know." His mood went from light to dark. "Until they lynch an old black man on his way home from church."

"You were there when it happened?" I had to hear it from him and no one else. Then I might believe it.

"No. But what does that matter? I know who was there."

"Why weren't you there?"

"It wasn't a matter of principle that saved me, if that's what you're thinking. I was still hung over from a party the night before. That was my only reason for not being there."

"Did they set out to lynch someone?"

"No. They set out to see how stinking drunk they could get."

"Did they ever say what happened, why they did what they did?"

"I don't think they even know. It started out as a joke. They had this ski rope in the car . . ." He looked helplessly down at his hands, as if he could feel the rope burning them as it slipped on through. "Then something happened . . . Who knows what?"

"Jesus," I said.

"Yeah. That's what I said, too. For the good it did."

"How did Stevey find out about it?"

"Who?" He was still in Mississippi.

"Stevey La Fountaine, the man you supposedly killed."

"I don't know," he said with sudden rancor. "But he was good at finding out things."

I studied him. The hatred in his voice seemed real. "Then he *was* blackmailing you?"

"Absolutely."

"And that part about your liking his work was only so much BS?"

"I liked his work. I despised him as a man. He used the money from Allison's farm, where she and I had planned to retire, to go on what amounted to a drunken spree. Then when the money ran out, he had the nerve to follow me here and ask for more."

"So you killed him."

"Yes." He looked me right in the eye as he spoke, daring me to call his bluff.

"How did you set it up?"

"I knew by the hour that he would be at the Corner Bar and Grill. So I called him from my car phone and told him to meet me at his house where I would give him the money he wanted. When he went there, I was waiting for him."

"So there will be a record of that call?"

"If it's needed, yes."

"And if it isn't?"

"Then it isn't."

I studied him again, trying to find out what his game was. But to paraphrase a line from one of my favorite protest songs, he had cards he wasn't showing.

"Okay, Stevey La Fountaine, maybe I can understand. But why did you take a shot at me and why did you put a slug in Wayne Jacoby tonight?"

"Wayne Jacoby deserved a slug on general principles," he said. "But the simple fact is that he got in my way."

"Your way of what?"

"As for you," he continued, without answering my question. "Everybody has his regrets. That's one of mine."

"Which is why you fired twice at me?"

He gave me a puzzled look, then smiled. "Nice try, Garth. But we both know that I fired only once."

"And the gun? I suppose you'd like to hand it over to me now?"

"I'm sorry, but I seem to have misplaced it."

I rose from the bunk. There was nothing more I would learn here. "You never did say why you went out into the storm after Wayne Jacoby last night."

He wore his brilliant politician smile—all teeth and no warmth. "You're right, I didn't. And Garth," he said as the smile began to wane, "it appears that I'm not going to be able to help you put in that window today after all. I'm sorry."

"Yeah. Me too."

As I walked out of his cell, it was with the greatest of reluctance that I closed the door behind me.

CHAPTER 26

I should have gone straight home from the jail and gone to bed. I was dead tired, defeated, and discouraged, and looking at more snow on the ground than I'd seen at any time in my memory. Nothing was moving that Sunday morning in Oakalla. No drunks were on their way home. No wayfarers were on their way out. Nobody was digging out or carrying in wood or zooming about on his snowmobile. Even the church bells were still.

The pity and the perverse beauty of it was that I loved days like this, when I had the whole town to myself, and mine were the only footprints that I met going and coming. There was a peace in the aftermath of winter's fury that I found nowhere else, not even the lazy river quiet of a summer afternoon, and even as I railed against it, the tug

on my legs and the wind at my throat, I smiled a secret
smile.

Danny Palmer looked as surprised at my appearance
as if the abominable snowman had just popped in his door.
Supposedly the Marathon was closed, as it always was on
Sunday, but all that meant was that if you wanted gas, you
had to pump your own.

"You have a sledgehammer handy?" I asked Danny.

"In the back. Why?" He was busy putting the blade on
his wrecker, knowing that the phone would start ringing
any second.

"I have a feeling I might need it."

"I thought you and Dudley Do-Right patched things up."

"We did. Sort of."

"Then what's the sledgehammer for?"

"I'm playing a hunch, that's all. And if I'm right, I don't
want to have to walk all the way back here after it."

"You know your way around here," he said, not wanting to be bothered.

"I should by now."

Leonard Frye seemed as surprised to see me as Danny
had been. Still in his robe, pajamas, and slippers, he was
sitting in his front office, wrapped in a comforter, smoking
a pipe with the door to the house closed. But it wasn't too
bad in there, with a kerosene heater going. And whatever
the tobacco that Leonard was smoking, I liked the smell.

"Morning, Garth," he said, kicking his footstool my
way. "What brings you around so early in the day?"

I sat down and took off my cap and gloves. I could
have used a cup of whatever Leonard was drinking, but I
hated to ask.

"I was wondering if you wanted to go on a walk with
me?" I said.

"Where?" Leonard's eyes were bright with suspicion

as he eyed my sledgehammer.

"La Fountaine's body shop. I hear there might be some money buried there."

"Not from me, you didn't."

"The game's on, Leonard," I said as I started to rise. "You can either be a player, or you can be a sitter, I don't care which."

Leonard waved me back down. He wasn't going to let me go without a fight.

"Who told you about the money?" he said.

"Hubert La Fountaine, among others."

"I doubt that. Hubert's about as closed-mouth as they come, especially where money's concerned."

"True. But he also believes—at least as late as Friday— that there's a sizable chunk of it hidden in there. So do you. But I'm betting that you know something he doesn't."

"Such as?"

"Exactly where it's hidden."

When his eyes grew ever brighter, I knew I had him. "How do you know that?"

"You figure it out, Leonard. Three people were dead set on buying that body shop—Stevey and Hubert La Fountaine, and you. I don't know Stevey's motives, but I can guess. He might have wanted it for the money, but I think his real reason was power—to keep everybody else from having it and at the same time make them dance to his tune. As for Hubert's motives, we already know his, or think we do anyway. That leaves you, Gilbert La Fountaine's former neighbor and friend. You wouldn't buy the place on speculation. You're not the kind of man to take that big of chance this late in life. So you must have inside knowledge of the situation. Translated, that means you know where the money is because you saw Gilbert put it there."

"What if I did? Why should I tell you where it is?"

"Because, with or without your help, I plan to take that place apart until I find it."

"You can't do that," he said. "It's not your property."

I rose and put my cap and gloves back on. "Try to stop me."

"If I don't, Hubert or Ellen La Fountaine will."

"Not if I tell them what I'm looking for and why. They think that money's forever lost."

"Stay right where you are," he said, as he laid down his pipe and scrambled to get out of the chair. "I'm going to put some clothes on."

Fifteen minutes later, Leonard Frye and I stood inside Gilbert La Fountaine's body shop. In his brown leather cap and tie-under-the-chin earmuffs, his scarf, coveralls, and five-buckle overshoes, he looked like a rural Eddie Rickenbacker about to take off on another flight. He, too, carried a sledgehammer that he'd brought from home. He wasn't going to be denied his swings either.

"Would you look at this place," he said. "Gil would roll over in his grave if he saw it now."

Since my Friday visit there, someone—more than one, it looked like—had torn the place apart. Everything that could be overturned had been overturned, including cans, buckets, tools, boards, car parts, a stack of sheet metal, welding tank and welder, and every other piece of equipment under two hundred pounds. The white cabinet had been pried from the shelves and the shelves themselves had been emptied of everything except dust.

"Hubert and Ellen La Fountaine would be my guess," I said.

"You think they've paired up?"

"Now that they're desperate."

"What's to stop them from coming after us?" Leonard was worried.

"Nothing. I hope they do."

"They'll play hell getting my share of the money," he said with force.

"I'm sure, for your guaranteed silence, they'll be willing to negotiate. Now, where is it?"

Despite what I'd told Leonard, I felt that we'd be lucky to get in and out of there with our hides, let alone with any of the money. For me, the joy would be in finding it to prove that it really did exist after all. Let the surviving La Fountaines fight over the spoils, which would shrink considerably once the tax man came—to nothing perhaps, if he could prove fraud.

"Over in the corner," Leonard said, as he led me to the northeast corner of the body shop. "That's where it'll be . . . if anywhere."

I didn't like the "if anywhere" that he'd tacked on. "For God's sake, Leonard," I said. "Don't be having doubts now."

"Well, I never did see the money," he admitted. "Only where he'd torn the floor up and patched it over again."

"How long ago was that?"

"Twenty-five, thirty years ago, somewhere in there. I saw him outside mixing concrete one day and couldn't figure out why. So when he took a wheelbarrow load inside, I followed him as far as the door to see what he was up to."

"You already knew he was hoarding money?"

"I'd heard rumors, that's all."

Leonard continued, "Then the next day, I walked in on him while he was at work on a car on the pretense that I needed to borrow his wheelbarrow. That's when I saw the fresh concrete over here in this corner. It hadn't set up all the way yet, so he hadn't had the chance to scuff it up and make it look like the rest of the floor."

"Which he did later?"

"That very day, in fact."

I stepped back out of Leonard's way. "Then be my guest."

Fortunately, Gilbert La Fountaine wasn't nearly the mason that he was body man, or we would have been lucky to dent the concrete with our sledgehammers. The way it was, the concrete began to crack and crumble with Leonard's first blow, and by the time that Hubert and Ellen La Fountaine arrived on the scene, we were nearly through it.

"What the hell do you think you're doing?" Hubert said.

"Saving you the trouble." Then I said to Leonard whose eyes were fixed on Ellen's shotgun. "Keep pounding."

"I think not," Ellen said, as she pulled back the hammer. When I heard it click, I knew that it was time to put our sledgehammers down.

Lightly dressed in jeans, cowboy boots, cowboy hat, and leather jacket and gloves, Hubert looked travel weary, as if he'd just dismounted after a long day on the trail. Wearing denim coveralls, leather work boots, a Cossack hat, and black knit gloves, Ellen had a glazed, slightly mad look, like someone with a bad case of cabin fever.

"Ellen, there's no need for that," Hubert said, now that all three of us men were eyeing her shotgun.

When she paid no attention to him, I thought that I might be in trouble. After all, here was a woman who had let her brother bleed to death while she went through his pockets.

"*You!*" Ellen hissed, while levelling her shotgun on me. "You've ruined everything!"

"Ellen, damn it, give me the gun," an alarmed Hubert said.

Meanwhile, out of the corner of my eye, I saw Leonard Frye begin to edge away from me and out of her line of fire.

"I don't think she's listening, Hubert," I said.

"Shut up, Garth," Hubert said. "She's been up all night. We both have. She's just tired, that's all."

"Tired of him," Ellen said. Meaning me.

"I have a deal for you," I said.

"We're not making any deals," Hubert said.

"I'm listening" was Ellen's answer.

"You and Hubert get whatever I find."

"We'll get it anyway" was her reasoning. "Whether I shoot you or not."

"Yes. But you'll never get a chance to spend it."

"I don't want to spend it. I just want to have it."

"In either case, you shoot me and it'll never be yours."

"Hubert?" she asked, never taking her eyes off of me.

"He's right, Ellen. I could never let you get away with murder."

"Of course not," she said, lowering the shotgun. "Because then all of the money would be yours."

Leonard Frye, who had been edging toward the door, picked that moment to break and run. Whether he distracted her or whether Ellen's finger just squeezed the trigger, I didn't know, but the shotgun went off at her feet, as all of us, except for Leonard who had set sail, stood in shocked disbelief.

"Give me that," Hubert said, taking the shotgun away from Ellen, who offered no resistance. "We'll be in the house if you find anything."

"You don't want to be here when it happens?"

Hubert's face showed the strain of the past few days. "To be honest, Garth, I'm sick of the whole mess by now, including any part I had in it."

Ellen let him lead her out the door. I found a shovel and started to dig.

"No. I don't know who it is," Hubert said an hour later when I brought him back out to the body shop to show him the human skull and bones I'd found.

In a state reminiscent of a few nights earlier, Ellen had been lying on the couch, staring off into space, when

I had entered the house to get Hubert. He was sitting on the floor with his back to the wall, trying (it seemed) not to think too hard about his life up to this point. I was trying to catch my breath. I had waded through chest-high snowdrifts all the way to the house.

"Would Ellen?" I asked, looking down at the skull and bones.

"I hardly think so."

This seemed the last straw for Hubert, who sat on an overturned bucket with both hands to his face. As if to add insult to injury, on his last possible breakeven hand, life had dealt him a pair of deuces.

Who did it leave, then? No one that I could think of—except for Merle La Fountaine, wherever she was . . . And maybe, just maybe, someone else.

"What is it, Garth?" Hubert said, noting my smile.

"I'm not positive, Hubert, but I think that these bones might just tell me what's been going on. Not all of it. But enough for me to start to make some sense of it."

"So where does that leave me?" He was talking about the money, I assumed.

"I thought you were sick of the whole thing by now?" I said.

I heard a noise behind me and turned to see Ellen La Fountaine there at the door. Apparently she'd caught her second wind, because she'd put her hat and boots back on and looked ready for another round.

"He's not sick of the whole thing yet," she said. "Not until we get our hands on that money."

As I glanced from one to the other, I thought about the Klondike and the gold fever that had driven some to fame and fortune and others to their deaths. Both had caught the same fever, though Hubert's seemed the milder case. It was a madness, really, if madness could be said to consume your every waking thought.

"How do you know there is any money?" I said. "Have you ever seen it?"

I was looking at Ellen, who after what was for her a painful pause, had to shake her head no.

"I have," Hubert said quietly, as if that admission might bring the walls down on top of us. "I hid in here once when I was in high school and watched him take it out of that white cabinet over there."

The cabinet that he was talking about was now on the floor with its back ripped out.

"He kept the money in an old leather suitcase about the color of Leonard Frye's cap," Hubert continued. "And he kept the suitcase in that cabinet, and he always kept the cabinet padlocked, along with the door to the shop whenever he wasn't inside.

"Where did he keep the keys?" I said.

"On him, I guess. He never let them out of his sight. I can tell you that."

"What about the day he died? Where did the keys go then?" I said.

Ellen and Hubert exchanged accusatory glances. Neither had the slightest idea. I had an idea, though they would be the last to know.

"You're sure about that suitcase?" I said.

"I'm sure. I've even dreamed about it . . . I can't tell you how many times. But even in my dreams, I can never seem to get my hands on it."

I didn't know how to tell him that, barring a miracle, he never would.

CHAPTER 27

I stopped by home to warm up and to make a couple phone calls, one to Ben Bryan, the other to Clarkie, before I went out again. I hoped then that today would be the end of it. I was ready for life to get back to normal, such as "normal" was in Oakalla.

I was ready for January to end and February to start, for "manure time" to come and go, followed by spring. Tired of snow, wind, cold, and deception, I would greet April, "the cruellest month," with eager open arms and try to hold it a while, even as I complained that it wasn't enough like May. But as I grumbled along through the snow, stopping every few yards to catch my breath, the sun, which had been teasing me all morning, broke through the clouds at last and showered me with light. Dazzled but not daunted, I gave it a cursory glance and told it that if it decided to hang around for a while, say a month or so, I might change my mind.

Allison Springer opened her front door before I ever knocked. She might have been looking out her bay window and seen me coming, as she had the night that the cross burned in her yard—when she saw Stevey La Fountaine and me carry it away and decided to follow us. That was only because she'd earlier seen Stevey sitting on the curb beside the Five and Dime, after he'd first called her, then called the fire in.

Allison Springer wore grey stonewashed jeans, brown hiking boots similar to mine, a checkered grey-blue flannel shirt, and no jewelry or makeup, except for her wedding ring. Even without makeup, she was still a beautiful woman. Like Abby, whose beauty flowed inside out, she needed little adornment because the package was so much better than the wrapping. Unlike Abby, she had killed at least one person in cold blood.

"I wish I could say that I'm surprised to see you," she said. "But that would make me a liar."

"Why should that bother you?"

"We all have our standards, Garth, even the worst of us."

She led me into the dining room, where we again sat at opposite ends of the table. I noticed that the rose was gone with no other to take its place—another casualty of the week gone by.

"Can we make this brief?" she said. "I was on my way to see Jonathan."

"You'll need a key to get in there."

"Mr. Johnstone said that he would let me in."

"How did you swing that?"

"Lawyer-client privilege."

I nodded. Of course. "Okay, I'll be brief," I said. "You killed Stevey La Fountaine because he was blackmailing you for killing your first husband, and had been for years."

"You have proof of this?"

"I have your husband's remains, along with a couple of slugs I found there. They seem to match the ones that were taken from Stevey La Fountaine, but I won't know for certain until this afternoon."

"And of course you have the murder weapon?"

"I'm working on that," I lied.

"Well, until you do, I doubt that you have a case."

"I bet I have a better case against you than Wayne Jacoby does against the senator. But that was the plan all along, wasn't it? He'd take the fall for you because he knew he could prove his innocence. All he'd lose in the process was his career."

"Don't remind me," she said. "And don't ask me how could I, because it was his idea."

"You could have talked him out of it," I said.

That brought out her first smile of the day—one born of love and sadness, it seemed like. "You don't know the Senator, once he makes his mind up about something. Besides, why should I? All I ever wanted was a little peace in my life. Is that too much to ask?"

"It is if you have to murder someone to get it."

"Stevey La Fountaine, you mean?"

"I was thinking of Neal Taylor, your first husband."

"Come again," she said. "Why would I bother when he was going to leave me anyway?"

"Because you were pregnant with Gil Fountaine's child and he found out about it. My guess is that he then went after Gil at the body shop, and you followed him there and shot him."

"You can't prove that. Not even if you can prove that it's Neal's body you found. Gil just as easily could have killed Neal himself."

"Not and then kill his own son with the same gun. That would make headlines around the world. So why don't you save us both time and tell me what really happened. Without the gun, it's all off the record anyway."

"And when you find it . . . if you find it?"

"I won't sit on it, if that's what you're asking. Not even to save the Senator."

"You drive a hard bargain."

"When I have no other choice."

She thought it over, then said, "You're right. I was pregnant with Gil's child, and I knew that once Neal found out about it, he'd kill me, or worse. I already had the gun. I swore that if he ever started up on me again, for whatever the reason, I'd use it." Her look seemed one of regret. "My chance came a lot sooner than I expected. I went to see Gil one night when Neal was supposed to be out of town on business. Don't ask me why. Gil was three inches shorter than I was and covered with paint most of the time that I knew him. But I couldn't seem to get enough of him . . ." She paused, as she played it all back to herself, as if still looking for a way out. "When I came back to the house, Neal was there waiting for me. He knew where I'd been, or had an idea, so there was no use lying to him. He went after Gil and told me that I'd better be there when he got back."

"So you followed him there and shot him?"

"I didn't think I had a choice."

As I watched the sun pour in through the bay window, I thought about all of the happy hours that I once had spent in that house with Diana. Too bad it hadn't known many since. Too bad about a lot of things.

"What did Gil have to say about that?"

"He was angry at me once he got over the shock. He'd been holding his own with Neal, in spite of giving away almost a hundred pounds to him. But he wasn't the one that Neal was coming back to that night. Neal's last words to me were 'I'll get that nigger bastard if it's the last thing

I do. Then I'm coming after you.'"

"It appears he did," I said. "Get Gil, I mean."

"I don't understand."

"Gil La Fountaine's life was never the same after that. From all reports, neither was he. And he died a bitter old man."

The news hit her harder than I expected. "Well, what did he want from me? I was broke, pregnant, and had just killed my husband. I couldn't very well hang around Oakalla, and have his child, could I?"

I watched the sun a while longer. Allison Springer seemed not to notice.

"How did Stevey La Fountaine figure into the equation?" I said. "Did he see you there with Gil?"

"Yes. It was a warm spring night, I remember that. Just that afternoon Gil had finished restoring a red Mustang convertible that he was so proud of . . ." Her eyes glistened with the memory. "He said he couldn't wait to show it to me."

"A 1967," I said, remembering Stevey's painting.

"What's that?"

"Never mind. I'm sorry I interrupted."

"Anyway, the door to the shop was open, Neal lay dead on the floor, and in ran Stevey, waving a piece of paper that he wanted to show Gil. Gil shooed him out of there, but it was already too late. He'd seen me with the gun in my hand, he'd seen Neal's body, he could figure out the rest himself."

"What did you do with Neal's car?"

"Gil drove it into his shop, then cut it up, and got rid of the parts. He gave me some money to have an abortion, along with a little extra to hold me over until I could find work again. But I used it to enroll at the University of Wisconsin, where, as you know, I later got my law degree."

"Did you have an abortion?"

"No. I couldn't do it. I went full term and put the baby up for adoption."

"Boy or girl?"

"I don't know. I never wanted to know."

I waited while she composed herself.

Then she said, "All those years without a peep from anyone here in Oakalla, and who does Jonathan bring home for supper one night, claiming he's the next Wyeth?"

"Stevey La Fountaine."

She was embittered by the irony of it. "I knew the instant our eyes met that he recognized me from somewhere. It was only a matter of time before he put all of the pieces together and started asking me for favors, which, of course, Jonathan was only too happy to grant. I knew it would never end once we started and told Jonathan so, but he said not to worry about it."

"He didn't know Stevey was blackmailing you?"

"I think he chose not to know."

"Do you resent that?"

"Why should I? I might as well resent the wind for blowing; or you, for seeing more than you should."

"I thought you did resent me," I said. "Otherwise, why take a shot at me?"

"Next question, please."

When I saw that she wasn't going to answer me, I said, "Why did you decide to sell your farm and give Stevey the money? Was that an attempt to get rid of him once and for all?"

"Yes. But he was the one who offered the deal. So I made him promise that if I came up with the money, this would be the last time. He agreed."

"So when he came here and hit you up for more, you decided to kill him?"

"I hadn't decided anything, really. I was too numb from it all to think straight. Then all those phone calls.

'Nigger lover,' I'll never forget that as long as I live. Such venom in that voice. It could only have been Stevey because he was the only one who knew about Gil and me. Then he burned that cross in our yard and then came after it to make sure I saw him."

"Are you sure it was Stevey who burned the cross?" I said.

"Who else could it have been? I know he was the one who called us right before it happened."

"What exactly did he say?"

"He said, . . ." As she thought it over, her certainty began to ebb. "He said, 'When do I get my money?' Then there was a pause, and the line went dead."

"Nothing after the pause?" I only asked because all the color seemed to have drained from her face.

"Oh, my God. It sounded something like, 'Oh, my God!'"

"It wasn't Stevey who burned the cross," I said. "At least I'm 99% sure of that."

"Then who was it?"

"I'm working on that."

"I have a right to know."

"You'll be among the first."

The sun disappeared behind a cloud for a moment, then found its way out again. It was strange how sunlight could make even the drabbest of rooms seem grand, and the grandest of rooms seem drab.

"*Why* did you take a shot at me?" I said. "I thought we were friends?"

"We are. But that first day when you left here, I felt undressed, that you had seen me in ways not even Jonathan had. And I wanted to kill you for it."

"To protect yourself?"

"Yes. To protect myself."

"I don't understand."

A rose had bloomed in each cheek. "That's because

you're not a woman."

"What about Wayne Jacoby? Did you feel the need to protect yourself from him?"

"No. Wayne Jacoby was never a threat."

I waited for an explanation.

"I had my scanner on when I caught the squeal about Merle La Fountaine. What a perfect opportunity, I thought, if I could find her first. She would be found with Stevey's murder weapon on her, and no one would be the wiser."

"You planned to shoot her first?"

"No. I didn't think I'd have to. I knew she couldn't last long in that storm. And you already had your doubts about her, so if I could somehow get the gun in her hands, you'd have no other choice but to blame her for Stevey's death. Neither would Wayne Jacoby, unless he perjured himself."

"Which he's perfectly capable of doing."

"I know," she said. "Since he claims that Jonathan shot him."

"Which he didn't?"

"No. I shot him when he wouldn't let me pass. I tried to go around him, but he kept blocking my way, so I shot him."

"To your everlasting regret?"

"What do you think?"

"I think you've shot too many people for me to overlook it."

"We've already established that."

The silence that followed only confirmed our positions.

"Did you ever find Merle La Fountaine?" I said.

"Obviously not, since I still had the gun. But I found evidence of where she'd been, if that was her I was following."

"You think it might not have been?"

"I don't know. At times I thought it was you."

I didn't doubt her. The way it was snowing and blowing, it was hard to know who was following whom.

"Why did you decide to wear Jonathan's boots?" I said.

She shrugged. "They were warm, dry, and handy. And not all that too big for me."

"And because he told you to?"

"He wasn't here at the time to say."

I wanted to believe her, but wasn't sure that I did. How much did Jonathan Springer know, and had known all along? He knew enough to put himself in harm's way in order to save his wife, so he wasn't a complete innocent. Neither was he a fool. You didn't sell your retirement home and then tell your mate, "Oh, by the way . . ."

"I'm telling you, he wasn't here," she insisted.

"It doesn't matter," I said. "It still won't change how I feel about him, or you."

"How do you feel about me really?"

I stood and took a long look around the place, doubting that I'd be back soon. "You really don't want to know."

"Is it that bad?" She seemed surprised.

"You tried to kill me, Allison. How am I supposed to feel about you?"

"I thought I explained that." And to herself, she had.

"And if your bullet had found its mark?"

"No explanation would have been necessary."

I forced a smile. "Case closed."

CHAPTER 28

I sat at one end of the couch, waiting for a call from Clarkie. Ruth sat at the other end, wearing her coat and boots, and her scarf tied around her face. She'd had to park her Volkswagen out front because the alley was still drifted shut. I'd offered her coffee, but five minutes later she had yet to say yes or no.

"I take it, it's been a long day?" I said. All I could see of her were her eyes, boring a hole in me.

"I'm waiting" was what she said.

"For what?"

"You know what. Let's get it over with."

Just what did I know? Then I smiled and said, "I told you so."

"Thank you." She got up, ripping the scarf from her face as she did. "I was about to smother in this thing."

The phone rang. It was Clarkie. "Second Janesville exit. Quality Inn, room 128," he said.

"Thanks, Clarkie. You do good work."

"I'll catch you later."

"Where are you headed?"

"Wherever my snowmobile will take me."

"Jump a couple curbs for me."

"Where I'm going, Garth, there's not a curb in sight."

Lucky him, I thought as I hung up and made another phone call. "Okay, Danny, we're ready to roll."

"You realize that this is above and beyond the call of duty?"

"You owe me."

"Yes, but when do I get to stop?"

"We'll talk about it on the way."

"Make sure we do."

"What was that all about?" Ruth said, as she poured herself a cup of coffee, then added a generous portion of my Old Crow. "Why are you putting Danny Palmer through his paces?"

"Because he's the one who put that gas can in our garage."

"Why would he do that?"

"Two words. Wendy Bodine."

She smiled one of her rare smiles. She knew, had known all along. "Electric, I believe, is the word you used," she said.

"That's when you knew for sure, wasn't it?" I said.

"Knew what?" she said, playing the innocent.

"That Wendy Bodine is Gil La Fountaine's daughter."

"I thought she might be. But when you couldn't find a record of her birth, I had to wonder."

"There's a reason for that," I said.

"Which is?"

I told her.

After she thought a moment, she said, "You know what that means, don't you, Garth?"

"It means we've all been taken in. It also means they're going to get away with it."

"How so?" She didn't much like the pronouncement.

"Because of Danny Palmer's involvement."

"He knew?"

"He knew enough to put that gasoline can in our garage, where he hoped I'd find it, or at least where it would be off his conscience."

"I guess love can do strange things to you," she said.

"Speaking of which, if Abby calls while I'm gone, tell her I'll call her back later tonight."

"Has she a reason to call?"

"I left her a message. Several of them, in fact."

"What changed your mind about doing that?"

"Good love, bad love—I know which I have."

"It's about time," she said, as Danny's wrecker pulled up out front.

"Where to?" he said as I climbed inside.

"Janesville, second exit off I-90."

"You realize that we're under a snow emergency. Nobody, and I mean *nobody*, is supposed to be out on the road."

"Except us." And Ruth in a Volkswagen bug with three other septuagenarians.

"We get a ticket, I'm not paying for it," he said.

"We're in a wrecker, Danny, with a snow blade on the front. Who's to say we're not official?"

"I still don't like the idea."

"You should have thought of that . . . earlier."

"Easy for you to say."

I gave him what I hoped was a fatherly look. "Do you want to make penance or not? If so, drive. If not, let me."

He put the wrecker in gear and made a spinning U-turn that nearly landed us in the neighbor's yard. "Not on your life."

The Quality Inn at Janesville looked a lot like the Comfort Inn, which looked a lot like the Holiday Inn, which is to say a lot like interstate motels everywhere—two long L-shaped floors, one on top of the other, an airport-size parking lot, three locks on the door, and a continental breakfast, if you liked hard rolls and cold coffee, and were in line by midnight.

"You want to come with me?" I said to Danny when we came to a stop.

"No. I'll wait here."

"It might be a while."

He laid his head back on the seat and closed his eyes. "I've got a heater."

Room 128 was on the first floor about halfway down the inside corridor that led from the lobby.

"Who is it?" Wendy Bodine asked after I'd knocked on her door.

"Garth Ryland."

She opened the door with the chain lock still attached. "I'm afraid you misunderstood me the other night," she said. "I wasn't issuing an open invitation."

"I'm afraid you misunderstand my being here," I said. Then I showed her my special deputy badge.

"We're not in Adams County any longer," she said.

"Would you rather I call the State Police?"

She opened the door.

"You might as well tell Merle to come out of the bathroom, or wherever it is she's hiding," I said once I was inside. "I need to talk to her, too."

Dressed in a heavy cotton bathrobe with her hair wet and a sweat bead on her nose, Wendy Bodine looked and smelled like she'd just come out of the shower. There were a lot of words that could be used to describe her. But electric would always be the first word that came to mind. She didn't have to do or say anything. She put a charge in me just by being there.

"I don't know what you're talking about," she said.

"I'm talking about a whole lot of money that's going back to Oakalla with me, if you don't cooperate."

The bathroom door swung open. Merle La Fountaine came out dressed in a long bright green velveteen nightgown. Her hair down and brushed, her eyes alert, but no longer wary, her face relaxed now that she no longer had to play her part, she looked, if not pretty, at least demure, with none of the harshness that I attributed to her. It seemed that, by fleeing Oakalla, she had left all of her acid behind. Either that, or she was putting on another terrific act.

Wendy chose the bed nearest to me and sat down. Merle chose the far bed, and she, too, sat down. I pulled a chair away from the small table where they had been smoking Marlboros and playing cards, and sat down to face them.

"Why?" was my first question.

"Why not?" Wendy was quick to answer. "What did we have to lose?"

"It all started some time ago when you contacted Merle, thinking that she was your mother?" I said.

"She *is* my mother," Wendy insisted.

"As she is my daughter," Merle said with pride.

"I know. You told me that." And I supposed there was a spiritual bond between them—a combination of toughness and steely resolve that come what may would not be denied. More than survivors, they were winners in the coldest, purest sense of the word.

Wendy went on to explain, "I had a friend in the Board of Health, who, even though my birth record was supposed to remain sealed, gave me Merle's name as the one on my birth certificate. Both of my adoptive parents were dead, so I didn't see the harm in looking her up. You can imagine her surprise when she found out she had a daughter."

But if I were to judge by the hard glint in Merle's eyes, it was not a surprise that she would want repeated."I knew immediately that she was Gil's daughter," Merle said. "After that, it didn't take me long to figure out who her birth mother was."

"So what were we to do?" Wendy said. "I had a mother, who obviously didn't want any part of me, and Merle had a family who didn't want any part of her, only to get her out of the way so that they could get at what they thought was my father's money. Wasn't it only right to give everybody what they wanted?"

"Did you already have the money?" I asked Merle.

"What money? There was no money. Gil spent everything he ever made."

I nodded in the direction of a worn brown leather suitcase that sat on the floor between the two beds. The one whose leather peelings littered the carpet. "Then you won't mind if I look in that suitcase over there."

All eyes were now on the suitcase. Merle's and Wendy's had dollar signs in them.

"Over my dead body," Merle said.

"Then answer my question. Did you already have the money when Wendy contacted you?"

With reluctance, Merle took her eyes from the suitcase, as if afraid it might somehow disappear after all her hard work to secure it. "From the moment Gil died. I pried the keys from his dead hand and got the money and hid it before I ever called someone to come after him. When awake, he always kept the keys on him. When asleep, he kept them in a sock tied to his side of the bed. Once I had the money, though, I didn't see how I could escape with it without letting my so-called children get their hands on any of it, or the government, or the lawyers. I wanted all

of it, you understand. I'd earned it. All those years of waiting, living like a pauper on what I made at the Five and
Dime, paying every bill, buying every loaf of bread, every
jug of milk out of my wages . . . I'd earned it." Her hands
were bent into talons, ready to clutch and hold all she per-
ceived as rightfully hers.

"Until Wendy came along," I said.

"Yes. Until Wendy came along. She told me how I could
pull it off and no one would be the wiser. It wasn't hard to
do. Any of it."

"I'm not sure Ellen was fooled," I said.

"*Her*," she said, with such hatred that it seemed to
poison the room. "Do you know that green dress I wore to
rags? Five years I saved for that dress, pennies at a time,
and the very next day she had Gil buy her one just like it.
To spite me. She hardly ever wore it after that."

"Why would Gil give her money and not you?" I said.

"Because he blamed me for wrecking his life. If I hadn't
gotten pregnant in the first place, he wouldn't have had to
spend the rest of his life in Oakalla, working like a 'nigger,'
as he put it."

"I thought he liked body work?"

"Not as well as he liked the good life. But over time,
we might have made it, if Allison Taylor hadn't come along
and ruined him for me."

"How so?" I said.

"By taking away his joy—what there was left in him
after the war. Gil was always tight with a dollar, but not a
miser, and not a mean man, which was what he became
over the years. And he used to love to dance, and we
danced . . . often. At home usually, but sometimes we went
out." Her eyes danced at the thought. "And he used to
laugh and cut up and bring me windflowers that he'd find
growing in the back lot. And he used to care about me a
little, what I thought of things, what I thought of him. And

in spite of our differences, we had a life together—an okay life, I used to think. It all changed, though, that night in May. I lost my husband and son both that night."

"Your son?" I said.

"Stevey. I sent him out to the shop to have him show Gil the picture he'd drawn of him. I'd given up long ago on the other two, who worshipped Gil, but would barely give me the time of day. But Stevey was still mine. He used to spend his every waking hour at my feet, it seemed. Not after that night, though. Not once he learned that he didn't need me anymore to get his way."

"Did you ever know what really happened there?" I said.

"No. And I don't want to know. The damage is already done."

"Why burn the cross?" I said. "Why not just take the money and run?"

Merle and Wendy exchanged glances. If I were to guess, neither wanted to explain her part in that.

"We couldn't let Allison Springer off that easily, we didn't think," Wendy said. "So we made a few phone calls to her, then burned a cross in her yard. Just to thank her for all she'd done."

"It got Stevey killed. Or didn't you know that?"

"She killed Stevey a long time ago," Merle said. "As far as I'm concerned. And before you ask who called her a nigger lover, I did. Having worn it for most of my life, I wanted her to try it on for size to see how she liked it." Merle's face was unnaturally serene. "Not much, I bet."

"And the green dress? Who wore it last night, and left a houseslipper for me to find?"

"No one wore it. I carried it," Wendy said. "Merle was safely in my truck by then."

"You took quite a chance going out in that storm."

When she smiled, Wendy Bodine was absolutely dazzling. "Yes, I did, didn't I?"

"And Wayne Jacoby? Was he a pawn in all of this?"

"I prefer to think of him as a casualty of war."

"You never had any real feeling for him?"

"No. Unless you count disgust."

"And Danny Palmer?"

"Don't ask."

"For his sake, I have to know."

She wiped angrily at a tear that had escaped her eye and started a slow slide down her cheek. "For his sake, you'll never know."

I rose and put my chair back in place. Whatever card game they were playing, it was being played with a pinochle deck.

"So what now?" Merle said, uneasy for the first time.

"Nothing. You get to keep the money. As you said, you earned it."

"Why? There's nearly a half-million dollars there."

I thought it over. A half-million dollars for Danny Palmer? It seemed like a fair trade to me.

"My own reasons," I said. My hand was already on the door. But I had one last question. "All those years, what was Gil saving the money for, if he never intended to spend it?"

A grin took over Merle's face, until she seemed to have no face at all. "That should be obvious. He was saving it for the day when Allison Springer would come back to him, and they would run away together. But she never did come back to him. And he was left holding the bag."

Danny was nearly asleep when I climbed back into the wrecker. "Home, James," I said.

We were thirty miles up I-90 before he said, "I have a

confession to make."

"I know. You knew about the cross. At least after you found the gas can in the bed of Wendy's pickup, you did."

"So why let me suffer so long?"

"To keep you in practice."

We were another ten miles up the road before he said, "Did she mention me at all?"

I said nothing. He interpreted my silence to mean that she hadn't.

"Damn," he said with tears in his eyes. "I really did think she loved me."

Again I said nothing for fear of giving myself away.

"So what do I do to make things right with my family again?" he said.

"Don't try. If they're going to, they'll come around on their own."

"And if they don't?"

"I happen to believe that they will."

It was at sunset. Nearly all the snow was shadowed, the sky orange and blue. We seemed to be the only people on the road. At dusk, the only people on earth.

"So what do you do now?" Danny said.

"After I call Abby, I'm going looking for a gun. You want to come along?"

He thought it over, then said, "No. I think I'll go home."

"Good choice."

I leaned back in the seat and closed my eyes. With any luck, I might sleep tonight.